UNCHARTED

BLAKE BRIER BOOK THREE

L.T. RYAN
GREGORY SCOTT

LIQUID MIND MEDIA

For information contact:

Contact@ltryan.com

https://LTRyan.com

https://www.facebook.com/JackNobleBooks

THE BLAKE BRIER SERIES

Blake Brier Series

Unmasked
Unleashed
Uncharted
Drawpoint (Coming July, 2021)

1

SATURDAY, MAY 29TH. AFTERNOON

Jason wiped the sunscreen-laced bead of sweat from the corner of his eye before it infiltrated his eyelid. He opened his eyes as much as the beating afternoon sun would allow. Satisfied that he thwarted the eyeball-stinging scourge of the SPF 15, he closed his eyes and sunk back into his thoughts.

Stretched out across the V-shaped cushions of his parents' twenty-two-foot bowrider, Jason had but one concern. Properly maintaining his tan.

"That's a hot look." Brian cracked another can of Miller Lite.

"Shush. You're interrupting my work." Jason formed the words by utilizing as few facial muscles as possible. He knew what his best friend was referring to and had expected the ridicule. The legs of his palm tree patterned swim trunks were hiked up to his groin and looked like a Hawaiian Sumo diaper. *Better than pasty white thighs*, he thought.

"Your girlfriend's getting jealous over here," Brian joked. "She won't say it, but she's worried you're gonna be prettier than her."

Shelly giggled. It was a running joke that her boyfriend was obsessed with himself. It wasn't entirely untrue, but she had to admit that he doted on her more than himself, which was all she cared about.

"Aren't you gonna have a beer, Jason?" Emma asked.

Jason sat up with a groan and adjusted his trunks. The answer was no. "Jay doesn't drink when he's driving the boat," Shelly said.

ALTHOUGH HE HAD EXPERIENCE OPERATING THE BOAT, IT STILL MADE HIM uneasy to be wholly responsible for it. If he had learned anything about boating, it was that whatever could go wrong *would* go wrong. Even in the tame waters of the Narragansett Bay.

"Ironic, right?" Jason pointed out as he moved aft to join his friends. "Since I'm the only one who's legal."

"Oh yeah, you're way cooler than any of us 'cause you turned twenty-one first. Even though I'm like three months behind you," Brian said.

"Still, I have to look out for you young kids." Jason plopped down next to Shelly, put his arm around her shoulder, and kissed her on the side of the head.

"Okay, Boomer." Brian shot a proud smirk.

Jason clasped his hands behind his head and kicked his leg out, crossing his ankles on top of his best friend's knee. "Tell me this isn't the life."

Brian shoved Jason's feet to the side, causing them to flop to the fiberglass floor.

"Let's get a group shot," Emma suggested. "I've gotta post this on Insta."

The group sputtered half-hearted protests while obediently squeezing together. Emma crouched on the floor in between the bench seats and extended her arm as far as she could.

"Jason, you're blocking the bridge," Emma said.

Using the preview on the screen of Emma's outstretched smartphone as a guide, Jason repositioned so that the Jamestown Verrazano bridge, some two miles in the distance, was in the frame. He tightened his abs, chest, and biceps, and pasted on his prepackaged social media smile.

The screen flashed. Emma slid onto her seat and began pawing at the screen.

"Ya get it? How do I look?" Jason asked.

Emma shrugged and handed him the phone.

"Oh, yeah. Post that," Jason said. "I look fine as hell."

Emma snatched the phone. "I don't. I look like a hot mess." She stood up and gazed to the west. "Anyways, I wanted to get more of the background. Like, look at this place."

Jason glanced over his shoulder to take in the view. The scene had been the backdrop of his whole life. So common that he rarely noticed it.

Anchored only a hundred feet offshore in a protected corner of the bay at the mouth of Zeek's Creek, the ripples of the calm shallow water smoothed out to a glassy sheen in the distance. Beyond the bobbing sailboats anchored in the harbor was Dutch Island, an uninhabited mound of dense foliage rising from the center of the West Passage. Along the shore, to their south, stood a row of quiet houses. Each of them a better example of old Rhode Island architecture than the next. In a way, Emma's enthusiasm had breathed new life into all of it.

"I can't believe y'all grew up here," Emma said. "It's awesome. God, I would never want to leave if I lived here."

Originally from Fort Worth, Texas, Emma and Brian met at the University of Notre Dame. They had been dating for the past two years, but this was the first time she had visited Rhode Island. Not to mention the first time Jason and Shelly had the chance to set eyes on her.

Since their early teens, Brian and Jason had rated the girls they met on a number scale. One being the most undesirable and ten being, well, impossible. Jason had to admit, Emma far exceeded his expectations. In his estimation, she was a solid eight and Brian should have felt lucky to land a five.

"Don't you think so?" Emma asked.

"Yeah, I mean, I do," Shelly said. "I never really thought so when I was growing up. Just took it for granted I guess."

"Well, I think this is paradise." Emma sprawled out across the cushions of the port side bench seat. She rested her head on Brian's lap.

"If you're visiting, maybe." Brian brushed a loose strand of hair from Emma's cheek. "Me, I couldn't wait to go to school. Trust me when I tell you nothing interesting ever happens here."

"Oh, come on," Shelly said. "We had fun growing up. Remember? We'd ride our bikes everywhere as kids. Body surf at Mackerel Cove. Play hide and seek in the tunnels at Fort Wetherill. Before they buried most of it."

"You mean that time you kissed me?" Brian asked. "She left out that part, Em. We were hiding in the fort and it was dark and, all of a sudden, Shelly plants one on me. Tongue and everything."

"We were twelve." Shelly shook her head as if to force the blood away from her reddening cheeks. "Don't let them fool you Emma, there are so many great memories. Just take this one spot. See that opening to the marsh right there? When the tide goes out, that whole marsh drains back into the bay through that spot. Before low tide, it's like a moving river. We used to hang out on that beach for hours, waiting for the perfect conditions. Then, we'd walk up a ways, float on our backs and ride the current back into the bay. Over and over."

"I wanna do that." Emma said.

"Too late," Jason said, "the tide's almost out."

"There were tons of other things going on. The Fool's Regatta. The Tall Ships. There were even movies being filmed. Look, ya see that house there?" Shelly pointed out a large rustic cottage clad in weathered cedar clapboards, a stone's throw from where they floated. "It's called Riven Rock. Steve Carell filmed a movie in that house."

"Really," Emma said, "what movie?"

"I don't remember the name. We were like, I don't know, seven. I didn't know who Steve Carell was at the time, but I thought it was cool that there was a real movie star here."

"Jim Carrey made a movie here too," Brian said.

"Yeah, before you were born," Jason said.

Emma sat up, pulled her hair into a ponytail, and secured it with an elastic band. "What's that over there?"

Jason followed Emma's pointed finger. "In the water? Those are oyster beds."

"Oh my god, I've never had oysters. Can we try 'em?" Emma asked.

"Sure. We'll grab some at dinner. Every restaurant has a raw bar around here."

"No, I mean like right here." Emma said. "Can't we just go over there and grab a bunch?"

"Girl, are you crazy?" Shelly said.

Jason chuckled. "What Shelly means is that's like a cardinal sin around here. Worse than murder. Oyster beds and lobster pots. Don't even think about it."

"The last person who got caught trying to poach oysters got put in the stockade in the center of the village and the townsfolk stoned them to death with live steamers," Brian said.

Jason tried to hold in the laughter, but the frightened look on Emma's face made it a futile effort.

"That's not true," Shelly said. "Stop messing with her. We'll find you some oysters. I was thinking we should go over to Newport tonight, anyway. We can eat there and then do a little bar hopping."

"I'm into that," Jason said.

"Definitely," Brian said. "We can hit the Landing. That was the first place I ever used my fake ID. It'd be funny if it were the last, too."

"Cool, it's settled then. You're gonna love Newport, Emma." Shelly finished the last swig of her beer, opened the cooler and tossed the empty can inside.

"Well, if we're going out, we should probably head back and get cleaned up," Jason suggested. He picked up a couple of cans Brian had left rolling around the floor of the cockpit and added them to the cooler. "You ready?"

"I'm good." Shelly maneuvered her way into her tank top.

"Brian, help me pull the anchor," Jason said.

Brian moved through the gap in the center of the windshield and took his position on the bow.

Jason spun the wheel, straightening the big outboard, and turned the ignition key. The motor fired up with a plume of white smoke.

"Let me get you some slack," Jason said. He pushed the throttle forward slightly. The motor clicked as the prop engaged, then shuddered and let out a squeal before stalling.

"Damn it. Do you have tension on that line, Brian?"

Jason was pretty sure he knew what happened. The anchor had likely dislodged, and the line had drifted near the back of the boat. If the anchor rode had fouled the propeller, he hoped it hadn't caused any permanent damage.

"I've got tension, Jay. The anchor's seated."

Shelly moved to the stern, rested her hands on the cowling and strained to get a look at the propeller. "I think there might be something wrapped around it, like a piece of clothing. Raise it up a bit."

Jason pressed the trim button on the throttle and the motor began to tilt with a mechanical whine.

The ear-splitting scream that erupted from Shelly's lungs sent Jason's heart rate skyrocketing. "What happened?" he yelped.

The response came as a duet of ear-piercing screams, followed by a splash as Emma dove into the water and began swimming toward shore.

Jason leapt up and bound to the stern, almost crashing into Brian who was also barreling toward the back of the boat.

"Are you ok?" Jason grabbed Shelly and hugged her tight. As she buried her face into his shoulder, her screams morphed into muffled ramblings. Jason leaned over and immediately saw the source of her terror.

"Holy shit, holy shit."

"No way, dude, I think it's a girl," Brian said. "Is she dead?"

"What do you mean, 'is she dead?'" Jason's body trembled. "She's got no face!"

Brian's eyes twitched, as if catching quick glimpses of the body without committing to facing it. "She must've swum into the prop. Oh god, this can't be happening."

The blood curdling shriek resumed as Shelly pushed off Jason and, without warning, launched herself into the water.

"Shelly, wait..."

But she was off.

"What are we going to do?" Jason asked himself as much as Brain.

"Dude," Brian said, "this is messed up. I can't. I just can't. Let's get out of here."

Before Jason could respond, Brian was in the water, his arms flailing in an overhand stroke. Within a few seconds he caught up to Shelly, who, herself, was halfway to shore.

On the beach in front of Riven Rock, Emma stood with her back to the cove and her head in her hands.

Alone, Jason remained frozen, shivering under the oppressive afternoon sun. His neck tensed as he forced himself to look at the sickening scene once more. He struggled to make sense of any of it. *Who was she? Where did she come from? What was going to happen to him now?* He couldn't begin to answer most of the infinite number of questions that swirled in his overloaded brain.

But there were two things that had solidified themselves as facts. This girl— if it was, in fact, a girl— was dead. And he had most definitely killed her.

2

SATURDAY, MAY 29TH. AFTERNOON

BLAKE STARED AT THE RED AND YELLOW SPLOTCHES OF ACRYLIC PAINT THAT coated the stretched canvas, fully expecting to find order in the seemingly haphazard pattern.

A fat fish. No. A slice of bread.

The inner door of the waiting room swung open and Dr. Maritza Perez appeared, accompanied by an attenuated but welcoming smile.

"Ready, Mr. Brier?"

Her voice was melodic, which served to soften her sharp appearance. Dressed in a gray business suit and high heels, the ensemble would have predicted corporate attorney more than therapist.

Perez was attractive and, Blake guessed, older than she appeared. The clues were subtle but conclusive. Plump lips that moved in a slightly unnatural way. Eyelids pinned at the outer corners. The work was good. Almost imperceptible, if not for the discrepancy between her face and neck. The neck always gave it away.

Blake stood up and took a step toward Perez. He paused in front of the mounted artwork and squinted at it. "A horse, right?" Blake's hand hovered an inch from the surface. "The eyes. Here and here. The nose. And this is the mane."

Perez's smile grew less subdued. "If you say so."

"Am I at least close?"

"It can be whatever you want it to be. But it's not a Rorschach test, Mr. Brier."

Blake shrugged it off as Perez led him to her office, and he took a seat on the couch. Perez closed the door before taking her own seat in the opposite high-backed leather chair.

The room was sparsely decorated but achieved a sense of warmth, nonetheless. There were two doors. The one he entered through, and the one he was to exit by. The purpose of the forced traffic pattern was obvious. He appreciated Perez's respect for her patients' privacy.

"If you want to know the truth, a couple of months ago I went to a winery with a few girlfriends. They happened to be putting on a painting event. The theme was *Abstract* something or other. Basically, there was an actual painter demonstrating, and the rest of us were supposed to copy what she did. Turns out, I wasn't very good at it. But it was fun. Plus, the colors worked nicely in the waiting room, so I hung it up. I never thought it would end up being so thought-provoking."

"Maybe you have more talent than you think."

Blake may have been a perpetual schmoozer, but in this instance, it was part of the game. During his first visit, Blake was struck by how similar a therapy session was to an interrogation. While he had no experience with the former, he was an expert at the latter.

The first step in any interrogation is the rapport building phase. In it, the interrogator shares an innocuous story, usually fabricated, with the purpose of establishing a conversational tone. An interpersonal connection. Dr. Perez's use of similar tactics was not lost on him.

"I must tell you, knowing your reluctance to all of this during our first session, I wasn't sure if you'd show up today," Perez started.

"Like I said before, I made a promise to Haeli. I'm not in the habit of breaking promises."

"That's admirable. But could it also be that you found some value in our previous conversation, apart from appeasing Haeli?"

He considered it. While he couldn't say he had been counting the days until his next visit, he found himself looking forward to it.

Blake had never been under any delusions that he was a well-adjusted individual. Even beyond his idiosyncrasies, he carried a hefty share of baggage. But so did everyone else he knew. The solution, for all of them, had always been one of compartmentalization. As far as he was aware, he was the first of them to find himself in these circumstances.

"Look, Doc. I hope I didn't come across as rude when we last met. I'm fully aware that I've got my issues. As much as Haeli does. Probably more so. But I have a hard time buying into the huggy-feely stuff."

"Is that what you think this is all about? Some kind of love fest, where we cry it out?" Perez laughed. "Well, I hate to disappoint you, but you're way off. I'm going to ask you hard questions and you're going to be expected to provide even harder answers. It'll be contentious, at times. But my job is to hold your feet to the fire. So, to answer your question, no, you were not rude. You were honest. And if you can be that, I believe this can be of some benefit to you. Whether *you* believe it or not."

At some point, the soothing timbre of Perez's voice evaporated, leaving only its raw mechanics. Blake figured she had hoped to hit a nerve and, he had to admit, she had. Blake could subscribe to this version of psychotherapy. No indulgence. No excuses. She had pivoted in her approach. Parried his attack. He would have done the same.

"Honesty I can do," Blake said. "What do you want to know?"

"Why don't we pick up where we left off." Perez flipped to the previous page of her notepad. After a quick glance, she flipped the page back and looked him in the eyes. "Last we spoke, Haeli had brought up the idea of the two of you moving in together. You believed your hesitancy was causing a strain on the relationship. Have you spoken to her about your concerns, as we discussed?"

"No. She hasn't brought it up again, so I left it alone."

"Then things have improved?"

"Things are fine. I mean, they were never bad. But..."

"But?"

"Ever since she brought it up, she seems off. We still spend a lot of time together and we have a good time, but I can tell she's not right."

"Do you think it could be that she feels hurt? Hurt that you're not willing to take the next step. Can you understand why she might feel that way?"

"Of course I can. The thing is, I don't know what's wrong with me. It's not that I don't love her. And it's not that I'm not committed to her. I really am, even if it doesn't seem that way. The weird thing is that she stays at my place almost every night and it's great. But when I think about her moving in, I have a physical reaction. It's like I'm in fight-or-flight mode. It's ridiculous."

"Good. You recognize the trigger and the response. That shows an adequate level of self-awareness. It seems you have an aversion to the idea of cohabitation that may even be unrelated to Haeli. The type of reaction you are describing is often indicative of past trauma. Can you identify a past traumatic experience?"

Blake laughed.

Perez's neutral expression remained unchanged.

"We're going to need a lot more than an hour and a half," Blake said.

"I see." Perez scratched at the notepad, then paused. Her brow tensed as if saddened or, more likely, concerned. "Did you serve?"

"I did."

"Tell me about that."

"I won't lie to you," Blake said, "there's a lot I can't tell you. But I can say that I've seen many terrible things. And I'll admit that I've had to do terrible things."

"That must have been difficult for you."

"That's part of the problem, I think. Being in the thick of it, life or death situations, dangerous situations, is when I feel most at peace. The hard part is fitting into regular life, as crazy as that sounds. When I'm set into action, I'm a totally different person. A better person. It's like I have a split personality."

"Well, you don't," Perez assured. "That's called Dissociative Identity Disorder, and it's very rare. It's characterized by completely separate personality states, almost as if more than one person is inhabiting one body. What you're describing is something that is much more common, even expected for a man with your experience."

Blake knew what she was alluding to. He had known for many years. "Post-Traumatic Stress Disorder," he said.

"Yes. Exactly. PTSD manifests itself in a number of ways, at different levels of intensity."

"I know. Too well, unfortunately. I've known more than a few good men who have lost their battle with it. It's the reason I'm here in the first place. Or it's the reason Haeli felt the need to seek professional help. Then convinced me to do it with her."

"Here's where I ask a tough question, Mr. Brier."

"Please, call me Blake."

"Thank you, Blake. What I want to ask is if you have experienced extreme depression. Suicidal thoughts, suicide attempts, self-mutilation?"

"No, never. Just the opposite. I want to live *more*. Bigger. With a purpose. I'm going stir crazy right now. That's the real diagnosis."

"Many in your position, typically task-oriented individuals, struggle with feelings that they are no longer useful. You mentioned you are retired. Have you considered part-time work? Maybe join an organization or get involved in community service. Something to focus your energy on."

"Yes. In fact, it's in the works. A few old friends and I have been considering starting a new venture."

"That sounds excellent, Blake." The injection of enthusiasm was jarring. Almost patronizing, however unintentional. "What type of venture?"

Blake weighed his words. "The details are being finalized, but its mission will be to help those in need."

"That sounds worthy, indeed."

A loud electronic chirping cut through the relative quiet. Blake admonished himself for forgetting to shut his ringer off as he reached in his pocket to retrieve the device. "Sorry about that."

"No worries."

Blake pressed the button on the side to silence the sound and, before stowing the phone in his pocket, glanced at the screen.

Andrew Harrison.

It was the last name he'd expected to see. Especially after so much time had passed. The last time he had spoken to Anja's partner was around the time of her death.

"What I would like to do," Perez continued, "is dig into some of these events. You may leave out whatever details you feel necessary. The important thing is the impact they may have had on you. Now, I want you to recall an event that affected you. The first thing that pops into your mind, okay?"

Blake was aware that a question had been posed to him, but his mind was preoccupied with questions of his own. *Why would Harrison be calling him? Had there been new information? Something to do with Anja? What could possibly cause him to reach out after all this time?*

He touched his phone through the coarse fabric of his jeans. The mystery of what words would have been spoken from the other end of the call tugged at him.

Even though Blake hardly knew the man, he felt they shared a bond. A bond forged by mutual suffering. He recalled the pain on Harrison's face when they'd met at the cemetery, as clearly as if the man were standing in front of him.

A surge of grief overwhelmed him. Anja's delicate face permeated his thoughts. A mixture of deep longing and outrage hijacked his rational brain. Tears welled in his eyes.

"Blake?"

He swallowed hard, then cleared his throat.

"Anja," he said.

"Okay, good. Who's Anja?"

Who's Anja? Blake was struck by the absurdity of the question. Not on Perez's part, but his own. The death of his beloved Anja defined him. Near crippling flashbacks snuck up on him on a regular basis, becoming more frequent as more time passed. Yet, he had not mentioned her to Perez.

"Someone I loved very much," Blake said. "She was murdered."

"I'm sorry to hear that."

Blake took a breath and tried to slow his pulse. He reached into his pocket and brought his phone to his lap. He stared at the missed call notification for a moment, then thrust himself to his feet.

"I'm sorry, Doc," he said, "something has come up. We're going to have to cut this session short."

"Blake, we've touched on something that I think is extremely important we talk about."

"You're right. And I promise we will. Next time."

Perez stood as Blake made his way to the exit.

"I wish you'd stay," Perez said.

"If it's any consolation, you were right. It never had anything to do with Haeli."

Blake tapped the notification, causing the phone to redial Harrison's number, and held the phone to his ear.

"Next time," he said and disappeared through the door.

3

SATURDAY, MAY 29TH. EVENING

THE TIRES OF TOM HOPKINS' CHEVY IMPALA CRUNCHED ALONG THE substrate of crushed seashells as it approached the end of the pier. He scanned the landing for an open parking spot.

With boating season in full swing, parking at the West Ferry was notoriously hard to come by. And with the overflow of vehicles stretching several blocks up Narragansett Avenue, he hadn't been optimistic.

As Jamestown's Chief of Police, he would have had the latitude to wedge himself in somewhere. Possibly along the small area set aside for picnic tables or up against the small outbuilding that housed the bathroom. But it would have been obnoxious, and the last thing Hopkins needed was another complaint.

Instead, he lingered a minute while a stout man loaded three fishing poles into the back of a minivan. Inside, his two young boys bounced back and forth between the second-row seats.

After the man hopped into the driver's seat and presumably persuaded the children to buckle themselves in, the illumination of a single working reverse light signified that it was worth the wait. He slid into the vacant spot as the minivan pulled away.

Hopkins walked to the edge of the pier and down a metal gangway leading to the dingy dock. Despite posted signs that the dock was reserved for those utilizing the services of the Dutch Harbor marina, Hopkins found the dock occupied by two local teenage girls. Wearing what he considered age-inappropriate bikinis, they were performing a choreographed dance to a cell phone they had propped on the shorter of two adjacent pilings.

Upon noticing his presence, the startled girls grabbed their towels, scooped up the phone and scurried up the gangway. Having changed from his uniform into civilian clothing, Hopkins figured they probably didn't know who he was. They had hurried off, not because they thought they would be in trouble, but because they were embarrassed. Or, more likely, creeped out.

At least they have some common sense.

Hopkins held his bladed hand to his brow to block the glare from the low hanging sun. He quickly located what he was looking for.

About a quarter mile in the distance, the twenty-five-foot rigid inflatable boat, easily identifiable by the words *Jamestown Police* scrawled along the side in block letters, had already turned out of the channel and was moving through the mooring field toward his position.

As the boat drew closer, Hopkins could make out Lieutenant Charlie Fuller's enthusiastic wave. Although not close enough to see the details of his face, he imagined the exaggerated motion was being accompanied by an equally cheesy grin.

A lifelong Jamestown resident, Charlie Fuller was among the nicest people that Hopkins had ever met. So much so that when Hopkins retired from the Providence Police Department and took the job in Jamestown, he distrusted Fuller more than anyone else. In his experience, at a place where even the new recruits were jaded, anyone who was that friendly, that happy, or that helpful was full of crap and likely angling for something.

Eventually, Fuller's relentless positivity had won him over. Before long, Hopkins had taken the young officer under his wing, even helping him prepare for the Sergeant's exam and then the Lieutenant's exam a year later. Ultimately, Fuller was only competing with himself for the

Lieutenant position because the other Sergeants, mostly older retired guys, didn't want anything to do with the added responsibility. But he did well, nonetheless.

Unlike Providence, the fifteen-man police department had no need for a deep cadre of supervisors. There were no Deputy Chiefs or Captains, which made thirty-one-year-old Charlie Fuller second in command. Technically.

As Fuller approached the dock, he cut the wheel, allowing the starboard edge to kiss the dock. Hopkins stepped in with one foot while kicking off with the other in a single motion.

"Were you waiting long?" Fuller asked.

"Not at all. But we'd better get moving. We're losing daylight."

Fuller had made good time, thanks to favorable conditions. Jamestown's only police boat was docked at the Conanicut Marina, located at the East Ferry on the opposite side of the island. Connected by the one-mile-long Narragansett Avenue, traveling between the two points by vehicle took a few minutes. By boat, the journey was considerably less convenient. It required one to first travel south through the east passage into open water, then west around the southernmost point of the island, known as Beavertail, and, finally, north through the west passage toward Dutch Harbor.

It was for this reason that Hopkins had twice proposed funding for a second police boat and dockage at Dutch Harbor. Unfortunately, the line item was shot down by the council on both occasions.

Fuller steered the boat north through the moorings, taking care not to kick up too much of a wake. Many of the boaters were on deck, enjoying a cocktail or a meal. As was the custom, they returned each friendly wave in a repetitious pattern.

"I called everyone like you asked," Fuller said. "Mostly everyone's already here except for Bobby and Allison. Both said they were out of town."

"I'm aware," Hopkins said.

Robert "Bobby" Berret was the department's only detective. It was ironic that Berret was absent from the first investigation in two years that involved more than petty theft or mischief, but there was little Hopkins could say about it. After all, it was a Saturday and Berret's regular day off. On top of that, Berret had put in for a few vacation days to extend the weekend. He said he was visiting family in Maine, but Hopkins knew it was a lie. He and Officer Allison Konesky had been carrying on for some time and, although they went to great lengths to keep it a secret, Hopkins was aware. In fact, after approving Berret's leave, he penciled in Konesky's coinciding vacation before she submitted the request.

"Did you read the statements from the kids that were on the boat?" Fuller asked.

"I did."

"The way they'd described it sounds like this is gonna be gnarly."

"Most boating accidents are," Hopkins said.

"Do you think they're telling the truth? I mean, all of their stories match and everything, but it seems like they gotta be leaving something out, right?"

"It's possible," Hopkins said. "They did have time to agree on a story before we separated them. But even the smallest details matched. That's the stuff you've got to focus on, Charlie. The things that otherwise seem insignificant. I've never seen a group of career criminals that could put together a story that tight, let alone a bunch of scared college kids. As it is right now, I think we have to assume they're telling the truth."

Through the swaying masts of the last few sailboats, the flickering strobes of two identical Coast Guard RBS-II response boats marked the outer perimeter of the scene. Positioned at the mouth of what was essentially a cove formed by a V-shaped recess in the coastline, the two crews could easily cordon off the area by intercepting any approaching vessels.

"Hook up with them for a minute," Hopkins directed.

Fuller nodded. Having cleared the harbor, Fuller jammed the throttle forward. The bow of the small RIB lifted and planed over the rollers, slapping the crest of each tiny wave in a hypnotic rhythm.

As they closed in on the nearest of the two Coast Guard vessels, Fuller cut back on the throttle. Hopkins grabbed hold of one of the canopy stanchions to steady himself as Fuller swerved hard to the left, then again to the right. The wide S-turn maneuver brought them parallel and about four feet off the port side of the orange and white craft.

A young man with jet black hair and a broad, hairless chest was step-ping into the second leg of a wetsuit. His name was Paul Russo. Both Hopkins and Fuller had crossed paths with the guardsman many times, but neither could say they liked him much.

"Feeling better, Tom?" Russo asked. "'Cause you look like hell."

Hopkins never ceased to be amazed at how fast gossip travelled. It was bad enough he had to deal with the residents. But if Paul knew about his recent issues, that meant half of Newport knew, or would soon enough.

Hopkins had a few words he wanted to throw back at Paul Russo, but decided not to give him the satisfaction. He tried to force a smile but couldn't quite pull it off.

"Come on, Tom. Just foolin' with ya. We ready or what?"

"Give me a few minutes," Hopkins said. "We've gotta take some shots. Charlie, grab the camera. I'll take the helm."

Fuller stepped away and Hopkins grabbed the wheel. "Hang here, Paul, I'll flag you down when we're ready."

Hopkins didn't wait for a response before he goosed the throttle, leaving Russo in his literal wake.

Ahead, the small abandoned bowrider bobbed and tugged at its anchor. Beyond it was Zeek's Creek. Hopkins noticed that several cars had stopped on the edge of the roadway that crossed over the marsh. Motorists gathered outside of their vehicles, no doubt drawn by the Coast Guard's display of flashing blue and red lights. That kind of attention is exactly what he was trying to avoid.

Hopkins keyed his handheld radio. "Alpha Two."

"Alpha Two," came the reply.

"Swing over to North Road. I've got a bunch of onlookers impeding traffic. Standby and make sure no one else congregates."

"Roger. En route."

Hopkins tossed the radio onto the seat and slowed the boat to a comfortable speed.

"Charlie," Hopkins said.

Fuller, with the strap of the bulky DSLR camera slung over his neck, came closer.

"I'm going to make the largest circle I can around the scene," Hopkins explained. "Think of it like a clock. I want you to take a shot at every hour mark. Center the boat in the frame on each shot. Then we'll get in closer and I'll do another circle. We'll do that three or four times, okay?"

"Got it," Fuller said.

As patronizing as the basic instructions would have sounded to a third party, Hopkins knew Fuller needed clear and thorough instructions. It put Fuller at ease to know exactly what was expected of him, and it was a time-saver for Hopkins, avoiding the barrage of questions that would inevitably follow a vague direction.

Hopkins started his circuitous route. Face pressed against the camera, Fuller snapped away. Hopkins struck up a one-sided conversation.

"One of the things I learned early on—" Hopkins projected over the wind and churning motor. "—is to document the crap out of the crime scene. Even in the case of an accident. You never know where it'll go. When I was new to the Detective Bureau, we had a suicide. My partner and I went out to the scene. Just like patrol reported, the guy had offed himself with a forty-five. Gun was still in his hand with an empty magazine and there was one spent cartridge on the floor a few feet away. Cut and dry. We decided not to call in the Crime Scene Unit. We did take a couple of pictures, but not before we manhandled the body. Then we left it to patrol to release the body to the medical examiner, in time to make it to lunch. See where this is going?"

Fuller continued squinting into the viewfinder. "It wasn't a suicide?"

"Nope. The gun and the shell were sent to the State Lab for ballistics as a matter of policy. Turns out, the spent cartridge wasn't from the gun that was on scene. And, to make matters worse, the old forty-five wasn't even capable of firing a shot."

Fuller dropped the camera a few inches and turned to face Hopkins. "What happened?"

"We botched a murder scene is what happened. No search, no fingerprints, no anything. My partner got the brunt of it because he was the veteran guy."

"But did you end up catching the killer?" Fuller stared like a child waiting for the dramatic conclusion to a bed-time story.

"No. Never did. Now, pay attention to what you're doing."

Fuller jerked the camera to eye level.

"The point is, you can never go back once you've disturbed the scene. If a case ends up going to the jury, all they have to work with is what you documented. The goal of these photographs is to let them see what you saw."

Of course, Fuller knew all of this. It had been in every book he was required to read for his promotional exams. But Hopkins couldn't help but use the real-world scenario as a teaching aid. Things like this didn't happen often and, accident or not, it would likely be the most useful experience Fuller would have had to date.

Hopkins completed several circles with the final lap being only fifteen feet from the bowrider. He slowed the boat to a crawl. As they passed the back, they got their first close-up look at the deceased.

"Aw, that's sick," Fuller said. "What a horrible way to die."

Hopkins couldn't think of a truer statement. The damage to the poor girl's face was catastrophic. A blade of the propeller was buried deep into her skull where her nose and eyes would have been. The motor, when tilted, had lifted her body halfway out of the water and her thin, delicate arms dangled as if she were pushing herself up by an imaginary ledge, hidden below the waterline.

Hopkins completed the circle, then came around to the port side. He tossed a line to Fuller, who lashed the police boat to the side of the bowrider, such that the back of the RIB jutted out ten feet past the transom of its counterpart.

"Take some pictures of the interior from here," Hopkins instructed. "Then jump on and take more. Be careful not to disturb anything. And get a picture of the inside of that cooler. I'll raise Paul and let him know we're ready for him."

Fuller set out to complete his task as Hopkins retrieved his radio. Before he could call, he noticed Russo was already motoring toward him. He crouched down and leaned over, getting as close as he could to the victim without falling in.

"What were you doing here?" Hopkins whispered.

Based on her petite frame, long hair, and feminine clothing, it was clear the victim was a female. How old she was, that was another story. The natural postmortem processes had mottled her skin, and she had already begun to bloat. More so than he would have expected. Hopkins wondered if being half submerged in water had somehow accelerated decomposition.

The Coast Guard vessel arrived and set up in the opposite configuration. The three boats tied together created an open-ended box around the victim. Hopkins was satisfied that the configuration provided some shielding from the nosy residents who had come out of their homes along the shore to gawk.

Russo zipped up his wetsuit and slid into the water. He was able to stand on the bottom with his head and a sliver of his shoulders above the water.

"Ready for me to pull her loose?" Russo asked.

"Yeah, go ahead. Charlie and I will help you pull her up here." Hopkins waved to Fuller. "Charlie, get some shots while he frees her from the prop."

Russo moved in close, with a pair of neoprene diving gloves, he grasped the girl's head on either side and pulled.

"She's stuck," Russo said. "Her hair is all wrapped around the prop. I'm going to have to cut it free. Frank, grab me a pair of scissors."

One of the other two guardsmen handed Russo the scissors. He cut away a clump and held it out toward Hopkins.

"Charlie," Hopkins said, "grab a bunch of paper bags from under the seat. And a sharpie if we have one. I want to bag each one of these clumps individually. Number the bags sequentially and put the time on them."

"On it," Fuller said.

Hopkins pulled two pairs of rubber gloves from one of his pants' cargo pockets. He put on a pair and tossed the other to Fuller.

Fuller put on the gloves, then took the first clump of hair from Russo, whose slack facial expression gave away his impatience.

Russo continued cutting. On the fourth cut, before anyone was prepared for it, the weight of the body pulled itself free with a grotesque suction sound and a splash.

"Okay, see if you can lift her up a bit. Charlie, give me a hand."

Russo reached under the girl and lifted her as if performing a military press. Hopkins and Fuller guided her into the boat and laid her on her back.

"Oh my god." Fuller blurted.

"This was no accident," Hopkins said.

The thin fabric of the girl's shirt was torn and tattered, exposing most of her chest, including one of her breasts. A dozen half-inch long stab wounds dotted her torso. Stranger still, the fingers of her right hand appeared to be missing, and the portion of her hand that remained was tightly bandaged.

"Looks like you got yourself a murder," Paul said. "You up for this?"

Hopkins was in no mood, especially not now. "Thanks for your help Paul, we've got it from here."

"Always glad to help," Russo hoisted himself out of the water and unzipped his suit.

"If you guys don't mind holding the perimeter until we can collect the evidence off of the boat and get Sea Tow out here, I'd appreciate it," Hopkins said.

"Sure thing." Russo untied, and the crew set off to join their colleagues.

"I had a feeling this girl was in the water for more than just a couple of hours," Hopkins said. "She didn't swim into the prop, she was dumped somewhere else and washed up here. Those kids will be relieved. As much as you can be about someone being stabbed to death."

Fuller grabbed the camera and snapped a few shots of the body. Hopkins lifted the seat and pulled out a small, flexible ruler. "When you take closeups of the wounds, make sure you put the scale in the picture. Closeups can be deceiving without a reference." He laid the piece of plastic on the victim's chest, next to the top-most wound.

"What do you think she was stabbed with? It looks like something real thin. Almost like a screwdriver, or something like that," Fuller said.

"Not necessarily. When someone's stabbed, the skin stretches and then closes back up. The wound always looks smaller than the instrument that caused it," Hopkins said.

"Ah, ya learn something new every day. So, what do we do now? If this girl has been dead for a little while, someone would have reported her missing. And we did get that missing—"

"I know, Charlie. I was thinking the same thing."

4

SATURDAY, MAY 29TH. EVENING

BLAKE PRESSED THE BUTTON ON HIS KEY FOB AS HE WALKED ALONG KING Street. His Dodge Challenger let out an abbreviated honk from behind him.

The call to Harrison had set his mind at ease. He didn't call about the Evangelists, or even Anja. Harrison simply asked for a favor.

Blake noticed a loosening of the tension that had been taking up residence in his shoulders, back and jaw. He felt good. Better than he had in a while. Could there have been something to this therapy stuff? Or was his newfound optimism rooted in having been given a task to focus on? Whatever the reason, it seemed to increase his appetite. He looked forward to what promised to be an enjoyable meal.

Old Town Alexandria was bustling, as it always was on a Saturday night. But the warm air and cloudless skies seemed to have drawn people from their homes more than usual. Ahead, seated on the sidewalk in front of a bookstore, was a disheveled man playing a violin. A smartly dressed couple had stopped to listen. Blake could see the man toss a bill into the open violin case before the pair moved on.

As he approached the violinist, he noticed a beautiful young woman with flowing black hair standing in front of Brabo across the street. She wore a sheer top that sat off her shoulders, accentuating her delicate neck. She was something to behold, and Blake reminded himself to never take it for granted.

"Mick!" Haeli waved.

Blake waited for a break in the traffic and jogged across the street to meet her. They exchanged a kiss.

"How did it go?" Blake asked.

"Great, how did yours go?"

"Better than expected. We'll talk about it once we sit."

Blake pulled open one of the double doors and waited for Haeli to enter. She put her hand on his hip, letting it slide off as she passed.

"Hey!" A labored cry came from across the street.

Blake turned to find the violinist standing at the edge of the roadway, his violin clutched at his side.

"Come back!"

A streak of movement caught Blake's eye as an emaciated man slipped into an alley that ran along the side of the restaurant, pressing a violin case to his chest.

Blake let go of the door and took off running. He cut into the alley and sprinted through the overgrown weeds and saplings filling the narrow passageway.

As he emerged into a parking lot, he could see the man's pace had slowed. Blake called out to him as he closed the distance.

"Drop the case," Blake demanded.

The skinny man stopped and turned. He was breathing heavily, and his expression bore the hallmarks of a trapped animal — fear and desperation.

Blake dialed back his gait to a series of slow, methodical steps. "Just give me the case and I won't hurt you."

The man dropped his arms to his sides. The unlatched case fell to the ground, landing on its end and spilling its contents onto the ground. The man fumbled in the pockets of his baggy jeans until his left hand emerged, holding a rusty steak knife. "Get back!"

"Now, that was a bad idea," Blake said, his voice soft and measured. "Trust me, you don't want to do this."

"I'll kill you man. Leave me alone. This is my money."

Blake wasn't sure if the man would have the stomach to attack him. His wavering speech said no. But desperate people do stupid things. Either way, Blake didn't intend to give him the chance.

"Listen, here's what's gonna happen. You're gonna try to stick me with that thing, and when you do, I'm going to break your arm in three places, take that sorry-ass kitchen knife, and jam it in your eye. Just so you can't say I didn't warn you."

Blake had no intention of following through with the last part, but it sounded good in the moment. The man's arm, however, would not be of use to him for a long while.

"Make your choice," Blake said.

The man's eyes squinted. Blake readied himself.

With a blur, a black object careened from over Blake's head and crashed into the junkie's face, opening his nose like a faucet. The man staggered backward.

Blake rushed in, grabbed the man's arm, shook the knife free and levered him to the ground. A foot away laid a single high heel shoe.

Blake pressed his knee into the man's lower back and torqued his arm, pinning his bloody face to the asphalt.

"Get off me!"

Blake ignored the muffled pleas. "Thanks for the help." He turned toward Haeli.

She walked closer, the click of her remaining heel sounding off in half time. "Sorry to interrupt, just wanted to let you know our table's ready." She bent down, scooped up a handful of bills and dropped them into the case. "It's a shame though, now that he's seen our faces, we're going to have to kill him."

Blake smiled. The statement was cold and extremely convincing. If he hadn't seen the wink, even he might have thought she had gone Natural Born Killers on him. The junkie, on the other hand, wasn't amused.

"Okay. Okay. I'm sorry. I'll go. I didn't see anything. You can have the money."

Haeli stood up, planted her bare foot beside the man's face and, with her other foot, pressed the point of her stiletto heel into the back of his neck. The man groaned and his body wiggled. Blake held him tight.

"How much money do you have on you?" Haeli asked.

"You can have all of that. Take it," he said.

"Not this money," Haeli said. "This money doesn't belong to you. How much do *you* have?"

"I don't know, like five dollars."

"Where is it?" Haeli asked.

"In my pocket."

"Which pocket?" She shifted her weight to apply more pressure.

"Right pocket!"

"Good." Haeli removed her heel from the man's neck and used it to kick the violin case closer to him. It skidded into his forehead. "I'm sure that poor man will appreciate your donation."

Without hesitation, the man reached into his pocket with his free hand, retrieved a bunch of crumpled dollar bills, and brought them over his head. Haeli kicked the case over a few more inches and the man dropped the bills in. She closed the case and latched it. With her bare foot, she tilted her shoe upright and slipped her foot into it.

Blake stood up, letting go of the man's arm. He picked up the knife and slid it into his back pocket. "Well? You gonna hang around?"

The man hopped to his feet and bolted, never looking back. Blake and Haeli watched until they lost sight of him.

"I can't leave you alone for a second." Haeli said. "Look at you, you're a mess."

"That's nothing new." Blake brushed at his knees and then jammed the tails of his white button-down shirt back into his waistline. He reached into his pocket, pulled out a hundred-dollar bill and held it out toward Haeli.

Haeli unlatched the case and cracked it open. Blake tossed the bill inside. "Let's get this back to where it belongs."

As the two walked toward the alley, Blake tossed the knife into a dumpster next to the building.

"Just like old times," Haeli said. "Kinda nice to have a little excitement, right?"

"You'd better get used to it, once Fezz and Khat wrap things up with the Agency, you'll have more excitement than you know what to do with."

At the end of the alleyway, the violinist stood waiting. As they got closer, Blake noticed that the man was crying.

"Thank you," he said.

Haeli handed him the case. "Our pleasure."

"Take care of yourself." Blake patted him on the shoulder, then took Haeli's hand and headed for the restaurant.

"Bless you," Blake heard the man say as the door closed behind them.

"Sir. Madam," the host acknowledged, "your table is waiting."

Blake and Haeli were seated as a runner delivered a basket of warm bread.

"So?" Haeli said, "Tell me about it. Was it helpful this time?"

"Ya know what? It actually was," Blake admitted. "It shed some light on a few things. Just how messed up I really am, I guess."

"You're not messed up. You know what you are? You're real. That's what I love about you. You have a big heart, Blake Brier. I mean, how many people would help a perfect stranger like that? That's why I suggested the therapy. All I want is for you to be happy."

"You make me happy," Blake said.

"Do I? Because..."

Haeli shifted her gaze downward as if the words she was looking for were in the linen-lined gap between the array of forks and knives.

"It's all right," Blake assured her, "go on."

"We haven't even ordered the wine yet," Haeli said. "Let's not get into it right now."

"No. You were right before. Part of this therapy thing is about getting into it. So, say what you want to say."

Haeli paused. Long enough for the waiter to seize the opportunity to interrupt. He introduced himself, provided them with the menu and wine list, and promised to be back in a few minutes.

Alone again, Blake waited for Haeli to speak. After a moment of awkward silence, she did.

"I'm not Anja, Mick. I'm never going to be Anja." Her eyes watered and flittered up and down as if gauging his reaction.

Blake reached out and took both of her hands in his. "That's what you're worried about? I know you're not Anja, and I don't want you to be. You're perfect the way you are."

"That's not what I mean. You know how sorry I am about what happened. I know you loved her. I know you still do. And even though she's not here, most of you is still with her. But if you and I are going to have a chance, I need you here with me. Can't you see that?"

"I can." He squeezed her hands. "And I'm trying."

"I know. Maybe I'm just being selfish and needy, but it's been on my mind. I'm sorry."

"No. Don't apologize. I understand how you feel, but I need you to know that I'm one hundred percent in this. I'm committed to you and I love you. Okay?"

Haeli nodded.

"Now let's enjoy the evening. We've both had a long day of head-shrinking."

A chuckle and an accompanying eye-roll assured Blake that she would come around.

The waiter returned. Blake admitted they had gotten distracted and had not had a chance to peruse the menu. He quickly looked over the wine list and settled on a bottle of 2015 Château Margaux Pavillon Rouge. The waiter validated the selection with a canned compliment, then moved on to another table.

"Not to stay on the subject of Anja," Blake said, "but do you remember me telling you about her partner, Harrison?"

"Of course."

"I got a call from him today. Out of the blue."

"What did he want?"

"He asked if I would help out a friend of his. Apparently, his friend's daughter ran away with her boyfriend. It seems the boyfriend is somewhat of an unsavory character. That's how he put it, anyway. He said the family forbade the girl from seeing the kid, but she snuck off with him anyway. They think she might be in over her head. She's only fifteen."

"But why call you?" Haeli asked.

"The family has the girl's phone, but they don't have the password. Harrison said the police couldn't rip the phone, and he wasn't able to allocate federal resources for a local runaway case, so he reached out to me. He figured I could get the info off the phone and possibly track her down."

"That'll be nice of you," Haeli said.

"Thing is, Harrison isn't in D.C. anymore. He transferred up to Providence, Rhode Island. He wants me to fly out there. Says he's arranged a room for me for a few days. The truth is, I owe the guy big time. During the Evangelists thing, he didn't go digging. If it were anyone else investigating the case, I'd probably be in prison."

Blake heard the words come out of his mouth. He knew what it must have sounded like to Haeli. *Anja this and Evangelists that.* But he didn't know how else to broach the subject. At least he had tried to play it off as casually as possible.

"So, what do you think?" he asked.

"I think you should go," Haeli said.

"You do?"

"Sure. I think it'll be good for you to have something to do. You said you missed having a mission. Think of it as a mini mission. Plus, a change of scenery might do you good for a day or two."

"I'm so glad you feel that way," Blake said.

"Of course. You should book it tonight. As soon as you get home."

Blake could have left it at that. He could have said, "Okay, I will." But he felt guilty, and he was sure that guilt was written all over his face.

"I already booked it," he admitted. "I leave tomorrow morning. Early."

Haeli tilted her head to the ceiling and let out a flustered laugh.

"I would have cancelled it if you didn't approve."

"You don't need my approval, Mick. Don't make me out like I'm some nagging housewife."

Blake laughed. "You, my darling, are about the farthest thing from it."

Even with limited exposure to the workings of the average American family, Blake was confident there weren't many housewives who could kill a trained assassin with their bare hands.

"There's one other thing," Blake said. "I wonder if you would stay at my place while I'm gone. You know, look after it. Water the plants. Take in the mail."

"You'll only be gone a couple days, right? I could just stop in a few times," Haeli said.

"You could, but you might as well get settled in if you're going to be living there permanently."

"Are you serious?" She clenched her fists and tapped her feet in a kind of ritualistic dance of excitement, then threw her arms around his neck and kissed him.

Blake took a deep breath. It was done. And there was no turning back now.

5

SUNDAY, MAY 30TH. MORNING

YOUR DESTINATION IS ON THE RIGHT, THE GPS ANNOUNCED.

Blake slowed the rented Nissan Sentra to a crawl. There was a small parking lot on the right, but it was nearly empty and much smaller than he expected. Enclosed by a white picket fence, the whole lot looked like someone had plucked it from a farm stand and dropped in the middle of the city.

He checked his rearview mirror. No cars behind him. In fact, the multilane US-44 appeared devoid of traffic all together. Before turning into the lot, he paused to read the message that swung from the arm of a folksy wooden signpost.

10 Weybosset. Private Assigned Parking.

Pulling in, he chose a spot opposite the other two cars that occupied the lot.

Blake stepped out. He took a moment to stretch his legs and survey his surroundings.

Based on what he could see from his unremarkable vantage point, he suspected there was quite a bit of history to behold. A stately looking building rising from the far bank of the river. An impressive five-story mural of a Native American woman painted on the side of an old brick building.

But it was the people who stood out the most. Or, rather, the fact that he didn't see any. Having never been to Providence, he envisioned it being busier. Even on a Sunday.

It was decided. He liked it. Despite the pothole riddled roads and clusters of loose trash that had taken up residence in every corner and recess, the place had a gritty charm.

Blake walked around the adjacent building in search of the main entrance. Along the north side, he found a tinted glass vestibule. There were no markings or any other indication that the building housed the Federal Bureau of Investigation. Nor did it appear to be open.

He considered calling Harrison but, before he could give it another thought, one of the dark glass doors rattled and then sprung open. Harrison took a step out and leaned back against the door to hold it open.

"Come on in," he said.

Blake hurried over to greet his old acquaintance with a spirited handshake.

"Wasn't sure I had the right place," Blake said.

"Yeah, we like to keep a low profile. Follow me." Harrison led the way through the empty lobby and toward the elevators. "Was your trip okay?"

"Fine," Blake said. "That's a nice little airport, T.F. Green. Twenty minutes after landing, I had my rental and was on the road."

Harrison laughed. "Yeah, try doing that in D.C."

"It's good seeing you." Blake said. "How have you been?"

"Great. The promotion's keeping me busy. But it's been pretty smooth. We've got a good team here."

"How did you end up in Providence? Did you request it, or was it a '*you take what we give you*' kind of thing?"

"I actually put in for Boston so I could see my kids. For reasons I won't get into, Boston was out of the question. Providence was the next best thing. It wouldn't have been my first choice, but it's been working out great. Takes me about an hour to run up there. I pick them up every other weekend and I can catch my son's games or my daughter's dance recitals. Plus, I really needed a clean slate after, ya know, everything."

Blake did know. More than he was willing to discuss.

36

The elevator arrived, and the two stepped in. Harrison pressed the button for the fourth floor.

"How about you?" Harrison asked. "Keeping busy?"

"Not really. Mostly enjoying retirement," Blake lied.

The elevator lurched to a stop. Blake stepped out and looked around. Typical to a government agency, the rows of messy cubicles, cheap commercial carpeting, and outdated decor brought a sense of nostalgia.

"We'll be in the conference room." Harrison motioned to a corner room partitioned off from the rest of the space by two walls made of floor-to-ceiling windows, covered with an opaque, mint green film.

"Why don't you fill me in on the details before they get here?" Blake suggested.

"She's already here," Harrison said. "She's waiting for us inside."

"Oh. What are we waiting for then?"

Blake moved toward the conference room and reached for the chrome handle.

"Wait!" Harrison rushed past Blake and put his hand on the door. "Before you go in, I want you to take a breath."

"Take a breath? What for? I thought we're supposed to be meeting your friend about her missing kid."

"We are. I just want you to prepare yourself. I'll explain afterward."

Blake couldn't begin to decode what Harrison was getting at. But it was clear there was more to his visit than he had been led to believe.

"Open the door, Harrison." The pitch of Blake's voice dropped as drastically as his patience.

Harrison stepped back.

Blake pulled at the door and froze. His stomach sank and tears welled in his eyes.

Anja!

For a fleeting moment, she was there. Alive and well.

Blake caught his breath.

"Christa?"

In the many years that had passed since he last saw Christa Kohler, he had forgotten how much she looked like her sister. The dizzying effect of the initial shock had worn off, but he still could not take his eyes off her.

"Hi Blake," she said. "I hope you're not upset."

"I'll be in my office if you need anything," Harrison said.

Blake waved him off without looking back. "Upset? Why would I be upset? It's great to see you." He moved around the table. Christa stood, and the two shared a brief hug.

"I thought...," she hesitated. "...because of the way we left it...."

During the time he and Anja lived together, and Christa lived in Virginia, the three of them would get together often. So much so that he considered Christa a good friend of his own. That is, until he and Anja split.

A few hours after Blake had watched Anja leave in that taxi, there was a knock at the door. It was Christa. And she was angry. She cursed him out, called him selfish, spit on him, and told him never to contact any of Anja's friends or family ever again. Blake did as she asked, out of respect. But he never held a grudge. She was understandably angry at the time and only trying to stick up for her baby sister. In fact, he remembered thinking it rather noble.

"Why didn't you just call me directly?" Blake asked.

"I was afraid you wouldn't want to help if you knew it was me. I asked Andy not to tell you until I could talk to you, face to face. Until I could apologize."

"I absolutely would have come if I knew it was you that needed help. Even more so. And really, you don't have anything to apologize for."

"But I do," Christa said. "Anja called me after you reconnected. She was so happy. Giddy, like when we were kids. I know she wasn't supposed to say, but she told me what you used to do. And the real reason you pushed her away. I was wrong about you and I was wrong to act that way. It wasn't my finest moment. I'm sorry. Truly, I am."

Blake sensed that this had been weighing on her. Her need to apologize wasn't for his sake, but for her own. If it was peace she was after, he was happy to give it to her.

"I appreciate that and I accept your apology. And I'm glad I'm here, however it happened. I only hope I can be useful."

Christa exhaled. The small lines at the edges of her eyes softened until they were barely visible.

So much like Anja.

"Harrison tells me your daughter ran away. Why don't you fill me in on exactly what happened? To be honest, I didn't even know you had a daughter."

Blake felt a twinge of shame in the realization that in the few days he had spent with Anja before her death, he had never asked about Christa. What she was up to. How she was. But it was a chaotic time, and there were many things they never got the chance to talk about.

"Yes. Her name is Lucy," Christa said. "My wife Gwyn and I adopted her about seven years ago."

Blake was surprised to hear that Christa was married. Although, less surprised to learn that she had married a woman. For as long as he had known her, she had never had a boyfriend. He had even tried to set her up with a couple of his friends, but she didn't have interest in either of them. He was happy to see she had figured herself out. That was more than anyone could say about him.

"Lucy came from a really bad home environment," Christa continued, "but she was a sweet girl and never gave us any problems. Until, about two years ago when we left Virginia and moved to Rhode Island. That's when things started to change."

"How so?"

"She started disobeying our rules. Acting out. Normal teenage stuff, I guess. But then we found out she was involved with an older boy. A local kid named Owen, who everyone says is trouble."

"And you think she ran off with him?"

"It's the only explanation. Two days ago, she went missing. I went to the Jamestown Police and filed a missing person report, but I don't think they'll be much help. There're only a few cops there and the Police Chief is a drunken idiot, judging by what everyone says. I actually tracked down the kid's grandmother myself and she said that Owen hadn't been home in two days either."

"She didn't know where he was?"

"No. And she didn't seem worried about it. She said that sometimes he doesn't come home for a week at a time." Christa paused. The deep lines returned to her temples. "I'm worried about her, Blake."

"Don't worry, we'll find her if she doesn't show up first. You have her phone?"

"It's at my house. I thought we'd head there from here."

"That's fine. How far is it?"

"Forty minutes," Christa said.

"Okay, I'll let Harrison know I'm going to take a ride. And I need to find out from him where I'm supposed to be staying."

"Actually, I was hoping you'd want to stay with us. I've made up the guest room for you."

"The room he arranged," Blake said. "It was with you."

Christa smiled and nodded.

Blake laughed to himself. Seeing Christa, talking with her. It was the next best thing to seeing Anja again. The question wasn't whether he wanted to stay, but whether he'd ever want to leave.

"I'd love to," he said. "Come on, let's go find your girl."

6

SUNDAY, MAY 30TH. MORNING

HOPKINS LEANED BACK IN HIS CHAIR. THE CHATTER, COMING FROM somewhere outside his office, faded into the background. His eyelids drooped.

"Knock, knock." The cheerful voice of Charlie Fuller burrowed into Hopkins' ears and traveled down his jaw. His eyes snapped open. A surge of misplaced anger waxed and waned.

It was customary that one waited for permission before entering the office of a superior. Fuller was diligent in observing the custom, but over time had devised certain workarounds. On this occasion, he had employed the famous *Insert Head Through Eight Inch Gap Between Door and Frame* method. Fuller's theory, Hopkins assumed, was that if he kept his feet in the hallway, it wasn't an invasion of privacy.

"What is it?" Hopkins asked.

Fuller smiled. A cardboard coffee tray containing a single paper cup with a plastic lid appeared below Fuller's floating head and left shoulder. "I picked you up a coffee if you want it."

"Just come in, Charlie," Hopkins said.

Hopkins ran his hands over his face and through his hair. Fuller hustled over and placed the coffee on the desk in front of him.

"Is there anything you need?" Fuller said.

"Whatever you're on," Hopkins said. "Bring me some of that."

"Sir?"

"It's a joke, Charlie. Jesus. How the hell are you so chipper?"

Fuller had been up all night, just as Hopkins had. The only difference between them was that Fuller didn't look like he'd been run over by a Buick. Then again, Hopkins had been the same way in his younger years. During intense homicide investigations, he would work for two or three days straight without sleep. And he had loved every minute of it.

"Never mind," Hopkins said, "What'd we find out with the missing persons reports?"

"Middletown was able to run down the one they had. Turns out the girl returned home yesterday, but her parents never called to report that she was found. Narragansett was a misunderstanding. The roommate reported her missing but didn't realize that she had gone to visit family in upstate New York."

"And the Jamestown girl?" Hopkins said.

"Lucy. No, nothing yet. We haven't been able to get in touch with anyone. Alvarez swung by the house an hour ago. No one was home. Unfortunately, we don't have cell phone numbers on file. It seems he neglected to document a phone number on the initial missing person report and we have no other contacts with them. I did an Internet search and found a cell number, but it looks like it's old. The number's disconnected."

"Keep trying," Hopkins said. "That's our number one priority. If we can rule her out, then it's just a matter of passing this off to the right juris-diction. Are we waiting on any others?"

"Jones is working on it. I believe he's heard back from Portsmouth, Bristol, Warwick, and one other. North Kingston, maybe? No matching cases yet."

"What about Providence?" Hopkins asked.

"I don't know if he's gotten to Providence yet. I'll check with him."

"That's okay, tell him I'll take care of it."

If Hopkins had to wager, he'd put his money on Providence. While it wasn't Chicago, there were about thirteen murders a year in the city, on average. By Hopkins' math, that made his old stomping ground about thirteen hundred percent more likely than any place else in the vicinity. And while he was no expert in tides and currents, it made sense that if the girl was dumped in the Providence River, she could have easily washed up in Jamestown a couple days later.

"I'll let him know," Fuller said. "Anything else?"

"Not now. Just keep me updated. And thanks for the coffee."

"You're welcome." Fuller walked into the hallway.

"Charlie," Hopkins hollered.

Hopkins heard the squeak of Fuller's shoes before he reappeared.

"Have someone else take over for Jones. I need him to go up to the medical examiner's office for the autopsy. Have him call to find out what time. Should be soon. And make sure he takes a camera."

"Roger," Fuller said.

"And tell Alvarez I want to see him. I want to know everything he's done in the past two days on the Lucy case. Tell him it better have been something. And while you're at it, tell him I want an answer as to why he failed to fill out the police report properly."

Fuller smiled. "Sure thing."

"Go."

Fuller turned and squeaked down the hall.

Hopkins opened his desk drawer and looked at the half-full bottle of Bullet bourbon.

A small taste. That's all.

Hopkins eyed the wide-open door. He stood up and walked over to shut it. Before he could, another face appeared. The last face he needed to see at that moment.

"Good morning, Madam President."

"Don't Madam President me, Tom," she said. "Tell me you're fixing this."

Arlene Whitman, President of the Town Council, wielded most of the power when it came to local matters. An old friend from high school in East Greenwich, Whitman had been instrumental in convincing the council to hire him as Chief, and she wasn't keen on letting him forget it.

"Which thing?" Hopkins asked.

"Start with the girl."

"We're making progress. Still working on identifying her."

"How did this happen, Tom? Things like this don't happen here. Do you realize how bad this looks? People come here because it's a safe little community. They trust that the police are preventing things like this. I'm up for reelection in a few months. And I backed you, for God's sake."

"First of all, how in the world can anyone prevent someone from killing another person? Are you listening to yourself? On top of that, you're jumping to conclusions. We don't know that the murder even happened here. Likely, it didn't. And when we piece it together, the story will be *Providence Victim Washes Up in Jamestown*, or something like that."

"You want to talk about stories?" Whitman pulled a thin newspaper from her handbag. "Do you want to know what the Jamestown Press has to say about you?"

Hopkins walked around to the back of his desk, closed the drawer with his thigh, and sat. "No, but I'm sure you're going to tell me."

Whitman skimmed halfway down the front page. "Here. According to the official police report," she read, "Evans found Hopkins' slumped over the wheel of his town vehicle at the four-way stop in the center of the village. Unable to revive him, Evans called 911. Officer K. Jones responded to the scene and paramedics were dispatched. Upon arriving, Officer Jones determined that medical intervention was not necessary and cancelled the Fire Department. The Police Department released an official statement which attributed the incident to the fact that Hopkins had been ill with a virus for several days, which prevented him from getting an adequate amount of sleep." Whitman looked up from the paper. "A virus? Really?"

Hopkins shrugged. "What? That's what happened."

"Hold on, that's not all of it." Whitman resumed reading. "In an interview with the Jamestown Press, Mr. Evans provided a contradictory account of the incident, wherein Mr. Evans stated, 'He [Hopkins] woke up before the officer got there. I could tell he was intoxicated because he smelled like booze and he was slurring. There was an empty bottle of something on the front seat. I told the officer that, but he just took my information and told me to leave. It's a cover up, that's what it is.'"

"Cover up? Please. They're just trying to create trouble. No one reads that thing, anyway."

"Everyone reads this thing. Have you been outside this morning? Have you not seen your fan club gathered in the parking lot?"

Hopkins tried to appear cavalier about the situation. To act as though it would all blow over. But inside, he knew it wouldn't. It would mean the end of his career. Soon, but not today. Today was one of the rare occasions when he legitimately had more important things to worry about.

"I know it looks bad, Arlene. I'll handle it, I promise."

"You know that I've always been on your side. But I'm not going to be able to sway the council on this one. A hearing has been scheduled for Thursday, Tom. There will be a vote."

"Dismissal hearing?" He phrased it as a question, but it wasn't.

"They'll hear the evidence, but I'm telling you, their minds are already made up."

"Let me guess, you'll be voting in favor of dismissal because it would be political suicide if you didn't."

Whitman avoided eye contact, busying herself instead with the task of folding the paper and shoving it back into her bag.

"Look. I know it's been hard after everything that's happened to you. And I'm sorry about that. Right now, you're in a bad place and I get it. That's why I've called the State Police and asked them to take over this investigation."

"You did what?" Hopkins stood up. He could feel his face reddening.

Whitman had been well within her rights to admonish him for his conduct. But with this, she had crossed the line.

"You don't have the right or the authority to call anyone," Hopkins said. "Last I checked, I am the Chief. I run this Police Department. Until Thursday, at least. And I will not have the State come in here and muck it up."

"Come on, Tom. This department isn't prepared to handle something like this. And you're in no condition."

Hopkins gritted his teeth. "I told you before. We don't even know if this is our case. And let me remind you I've worked dozens of homicides.

Not to mention the assaults, rapes, robberies. You think some traffic cop is going to come in here and show me how it's done?"

"The residents don't have confidence. It would set everyone's mind at ease."

"Call them back and tell them they are not needed. Or I will. Either way, I'd better not see one single trooper show up on my doorstep or so help me, Arlene."

"Fine," Whitman said. "Have it your way. You have until Thursday. But, for that poor girl's sake, I hope you know what you're doing."

Whitman stormed out of the room in a huff. Hopkins responded by making a show of slamming the door behind her.

Teeth still clenched, he took a deep breath through his nose. He walked behind the desk and dropped into his chair with a groan.

Maybe he had overreacted. She wasn't wrong. His life was a mess. Hell, he'd be in jail if it weren't for Jones. But the one thing he had left, the source of his last remaining shred of pride, was that he knew the job. He was good at it. Or, at least, he used to be.

He slid the drawer open. The amber liquid sloshed against the sides of the bottle, pulling at him as if he were a flimsy piece of steel caught in the field of a powerful magnet. He paused a moment to gather himself. Then he slapped the drawer shut.

7

SUNDAY, MAY 30TH. LATE MORNING

BLAKE ROLLED HIS WINDOWS DOWN. THE AIR WAS THICK AND SALTY. HE looked at his speedometer. Twenty-Four.

On the trip in, Christa drove like a bat out of hell. Blake had to devote more attention than he intended to keeping the grey Lincoln MKZ in his sights as it swerved through traffic. After crossing the bridge and landing on the island, however, Christa hadn't broken the modest speed limit once. He attributed her vigilance to the likelihood that the small-town police department occupied much of their time by handing out speeding tickets.

The Lincoln came to a stop at a four-way intersection. Blake rolled to a stop behind it. He took a quick three sixty. The town was quaint and very much like Christa had described it. There was a small post office on one corner, a church on another, and on the left, an old iron gate guarding what appeared to be a miniature cemetery. A handful of severely worn headstones protruded from the ground like a row of rotten teeth. Either the cemetery was ancient, or the weather conditions on the island were often brutal. Blake figured both.

Christa turned right. Blake caught the street sign affixed to a telephone pole.

Narragansett Ave.

Lined with homes, the road was straight and strangely dark, thanks to a thick canopy of overhanging trees. Blake was surprised at how lush the landscape was. Despite the small houses being set close together, it had a wild, overgrown quality.

Within a quarter mile, the canopy parted, and the sunshine returned. The Lincoln slowed, its left blinker announcing they had reached their destination. A small bright yellow Cape Cod style house with a picturesque front porch.

Blake waited as Christa pulled into the short gravel driveway. Ahead, the shimmering water of the bay was visible. Once the oncoming pickup truck passed, Blake made the turn.

Along the right side of the driveway was a scraggly hedgerow meant to mark the property line between the Cape and the small, rustic Georgian style home that sat next to it. Just behind the hedges, a man stood waving. Blake figured him to be about thirty years old, but he had the bearing of a child.

It was clear to Blake, based on his exuberance and giant, happy-go-lucky smile, that the man had a mental handicap. At least, Blake hoped so. Because, if not, he had just stepped into the Twilight Zone.

Blake inched the Nissan as close to Christa's back bumper as he could to avoid sticking out into the road. He popped the trunk and stepped out.

"Hi." The man's arm still furiously waved back and forth.

"Hi," Blake responded, "what's your name?"

"Lucas," he said.

"I'm Blake. Nice to meet you, Lucas."

"Yeah. Nice to meet you, Lucas," he said.

Blake smiled. He was struck by the young man's sheer, unadulterated joy. He guessed that many people would feel sorry for him. But not Blake. What he felt was something akin to envy.

"Lucas is our welcoming committee." Christa walked up beside Blake.

"Well," Blake said, "he's doing an excellent job at it."

Lucas laughed.

"Mr. Brier is going to be staying with us for a day or two," Christa explained, "so he has to go and get settled in. Okay? We'll see you later?"

"Yeah, we'll see you later," Lucas repeated.

Christa walked toward the front porch. Blake grabbed his bag and closed the trunk. Movement in the second-floor window of Lucas' two-story house caught his eye. It was a woman. Lucas's mother, no doubt. Blake gave a wave. The old woman stared back at him with a scowl. It was clear that Lucas didn't get his happy disposition from her.

Blake followed Christa inside. She gave him the quick tour.

Just inside the front door and straight ahead was a steep staircase leading to the second floor. To the left, Christa pointed out, was the door to the guest room, blocked by the open front door.

To the right was a little living room that continued into a dining area with a rectangular table and six chairs. Behind the table was a sliding door that led outside, toward the back. Blake slid the screen and stepped onto the deck while Christa waited just inside the door.

The backyard was heavily wooded on three sides. In the middle was a patch of yard, half-occupied by a meticulous flower garden.

Rejoining Christa, Blake moved into the kitchen, segmented from the dining room by a half-wall. Still carrying his bag, Blake snuck around a two-by-three wooden table that sat in the middle of the kitchen floor and served as an island.

Midway through the cramped kitchen was a door that, he was told, led down to the basement. At the far end, just behind the fridge, was the bathroom. Christa lamented the fact that it was the only bathroom in the house.

Blake thought it strange that Christa asked him to follow her into the tiny bathroom. It made more sense once he realized that there was a second door leading from the bathroom into the guest room. Blake cut through behind her.

Christa made a show of presenting his temporary space. She had already made up the pullout couch, which took up most of the available floor space. There were three windows. One of which looked out to the front porch.

Blake dropped his bag onto the bed before visiting the upstairs. Christa pushed the front door closed so that they could pass out of the guest room and into the stairwell.

Upstairs in what was essentially a finished attic, there were two bedrooms. Each situated on either side of the top stairway landing. The outside walls of both rooms followed the contour of the roof. It was easy to pick out which room belonged to whom. One was decorated by teenage sensibility. Or a bomb had gone off. One of the two.

All in all, the hundred-year-old house was in great shape. The common living space was decorated in a tasteful nautical theme. Lighthouses, boat anchors, and rope seemed to be the main ingredients in the art and decor. As far as Blake was concerned, it was perfect.

The tour culminated where it began. On the front porch. Much like the rest of the house, the nautical theme pervaded. Cushions and throw pillows, all in rich navy blues and grays, adorned white wicker furniture.

"This is our favorite room of the house." Christa laughed. "We spend most of our time out here when we're home. Not in the winter, of course."

"I don't blame you."

There was a quietness to the place. Not just the house, but all of it. A sense that there was nowhere else to be.

A group of people passed by, spreading into the middle of the road. They waved and said a friendly hello. Blake waved back.

"Boaters headed into town," Christa said. "There's a marina right at the bottom of the street. Come here."

Christa walked off the porch, across the small patch of grass and into the road. She pointed down the hill, toward the water.

"That's the West Ferry." She turned around the other way. "If you follow this road to the other end, you'll be at the East Ferry. That's basically the downtown area. A few restaurants and shops. The hardware store is down there, the fire department, let's see, what else? There's a dive bar, the 'Gansett. And McQuades, the grocery store, is about half-way down, just around the corner from that four-way intersection you saw on the way in."

"I'll have to take a drive down at some point and look around," Blake said.

"No. You don't drive. You walk. That's the best part. Drive? You sound like Gwyn."

"Where is Gwyn?" Blake said.

50

"She's on her way back from the restaurant now. I told her to bring lunch for you."

"You didn't have to do that. I don't want you going to any trouble. I can fend for myself. I'll take a dr—, a walk, after I take a look at that phone."

"Don't be silly," Christa said, "she already has the food. Plus, what's the point of owning a restaurant if you can't enjoy the perks?"

"You own a restaurant?"

"Not me. Gwyn. 'Ohana, it's called. It's on the wharf in Newport. That's actually why we decided to move out here. But I'm sure Gwyn will tell you all about it, ad nauseam."

"Well, I look forward to it," Blake said.

"I should warn you. She and I have been at each other's throats for the past two days. This has put a lot of stress on both of us. I haven't been sleeping. I have no appetite. I don't know what to do with myself. I feel so helpless, you know? Every minute of the day, I feel like I should be doing something to find her. But I don't know what to do. I took time off from work and all I ended up doing was driving around in circles, trying to see if I could spot her. Gwyn is so busy with the restaurant, it's like I'm alone in this."

Christa wiped a single tear from her cheek.

"I'm sorry, I don't know why I'm telling you. You're not interested in my marital problems. What I meant to say was, I'm just glad you're willing to help."

"Tell you what," Blake said. "It's gonna take a while to break the passcode and dump the info, why don't I go in and get that started before Gwyn arrives. This way we don't waste any time."

Christa nodded.

Before the two could step out of the road, Blake noticed an elderly man hobbling up the hill toward them. He had an intent look and was motioning as if he was trying to get their attention.

"Who's this?" Blake asked.

"That's just Chief."

"Chief? As in Police Chief?"

Christa laughed. "He was. About forty years ago. His name's John. But everyone around here just calls him Chief." She dropped her voice as the man got closer to earshot. "Chief knows everything about everyone around here."

Blake whispered, "Looks like he's gonna hurt himself."

"This damn knee." Chief had a noticeable accent.

Many years prior, Blake had attended a five-week long sniper school in Georgia. The participants were paired up, one spotted while the other shot. Blake was with a kid named Collin, from South Boston. The way Chief spoke was not exactly the same as Collin, but it was similar. Only more subtle. Blake considered that it may have been the first time he had ever heard a Rhode Island accent.

"I'm sure it's not her," he said.

Whoever *wasn't her*, Chief's expression did not emote the same certainty as his words suggested.

"You didn't hear?" he said. "Last night. They found a girl in the water over by Zeek's. Awful thing. Probably one of these party boats. Girl probably got too drunk and fell off or somethin'. I'll tell you what, nothing like that woulda happened on my watch."

Blake could see that Christa had checked out. She stood motionless. The dread that must have been clamping down on her was almost palpable.

"Watch behind you," Chief said.

Blake had been so caught up with Christa and with trying to process this new information himself, he had forgotten that they were standing in the middle of the road. The Range Rover that had approached from behind them had stopped only a few feet away.

"Gwyn." Christa began bawling at the sight of her wife, who sat dumbfounded at the wheel of the SUV.

"What happened?" Gwyn said. "Is it Lucy?" The words came out more as if she were barking an order than expressing concern.

Blake was surprised at her physical appearance. Not because there was anything wrong with her, she was beautiful. But because the image he had in his head was so far off. He had pictured her more like Christa. Tall, blonde, sharp German features. In reality, Gwyn was tiny. He guessed she would be no more than five foot one or two if she were standing. And her jet-black hair and Asian features were about as opposite to Christa as could be.

"We have to go to the police station," Christa managed to say. "Now."

Christa ran around to the passenger side and jumped in.

"You must be Blake," Gwyn said.

Blake nodded.

Gwyn jerked her head toward the rear. "Get in."

8

SUNDAY, MAY 30TH. EARLY AFTERNOON

THE JAMESTOWN POLICE DEPARTMENT CAME UP ON THE RIGHT. CLAD IN the same weathered cedar as everything else in town, the only distinction of the building from its residential neighbors was a large antenna mast towering above the roofline. That, and a sign along the roadway, marking the entrance to the lot.

As they made the turn, they were immediately met by a congregation of people waving handmade signs. Gwyn slowed. With little urgency, the group began to part for the Range Rover.

"Watch the people," Christa said.

"Thanks. I know how to drive," Gwyn snipped. "You think I don't see them?"

"What is all this?" Blake asked from the back seat.

"It's about the Police Chief," Gwyn explained. "There's a big scandal in town right now because someone found him passed out drunk in his police car a couple of nights ago."

"Can we just get in there?" Christa's impatience worsened by the second.

"I'm trying," Gwyn crept through the hole the group had offered and snuck into an open parking spot. The moment the car stopped, Christa jumped out and headed for the entrance. Blake hurried to try to catch up to her.

As Blake entered the lobby, Christa was already at the desk, speaking to an officer.

"Sure thing," the cop said. "I know Officer Alvarez was looking to speak with you, but he's on the road right now. Let me call the Lieutenant. You can have a seat."

Looking at Christa, he thought it would be safe to say that no sitting would be happening. Pacing in a tight circle, she pursed her lips as she exhaled and shook her hands at her sides as if they had fallen asleep and she was trying to bring the blood back to them.

Gwyn stood beside Blake. Unlike Christa's outward display of nervous energy, Gwyn remained still and contemplative. Her gaze locked on Christa. Blake wondered what she was thinking. The answer came in a gesture.

Gwyn reached out, offering her hand. Christa took it, then wrapped her arms around her wife and began sobbing.

A gruff voice came from behind them. "Christa. Gwyn."

Christa let go of Gwyn and hotfooted to the door where the man stood waiting. "Yes, that's us."

"I'm Chief Hopkins," he said. "If you'll follow me, I'd like to speak with you both."

Christa looked back at Gwyn and then at Blake. "This is Blake. He's a family friend. We'd like him to come too, if that's okay."

"That's fine. Let's find a place to sit."

Hopkins led them further into the building.

The unfortunate target of the hate that gathered outside, Hopkins was not what Blake expected. Although, he wasn't sure what to expect, exactly. A weaker, more pathetic character? A dumpy old man? Hopkins did not appear to be any of these things. Maybe he was a lush, but he had a commanding presence and a confident bearing. While first impressions weren't everything, Blake tended to trust his instincts. And his instincts told him that this guy had been around the block.

At the end of the hall, they entered a cramped conference room. Aside from several framed pictures hanging on the wall, there was nothing in the room but a long table and eight chairs, which almost hit the walls when pulled out far enough to be able to sit. On the otherwise bare table sat one item. A Manila folder positioned square at the far end.

Not good.

Hopkins wasn't looking to "find a place to sit," as he said. This was prepared. He was planning to tell them something. Show them something. Blake was afraid it could only be one thing.

"Please, take a seat." Hopkins stood at the head of the table and waited for them to sit before doing so himself. He placed both of his hands on the folder. "I'm glad you came in. We've been trying to get in contact with you."

"Is it her?" Christa said. "The girl in the water. Please, just tell me if it's her."

"Honestly," Hopkins said, "we don't know. That's why we needed to see you."

"I want to see her. Is she here? Where is she?" Christa said.

"The body is at the medical examiner's office. But I have something here I want you to look at. In this folder, I have pictures of the clothing that the deceased was wearing. I'd like you all to look at them to see if you recognize it. Would you do that?"

"Yes. Of course," Gwyn said.

Christa nodded in agreement.

Blake watched and waited.

"This is the shirt she was wearing," He removed a letter sized printout and held it up so all three of them could see it.

The torn garment appeared to be unique. Dyed with a gradient, it was black at the top and transitioned to a teal color at the bottom. The teal section was printed with a series of black swirls. The wispy design was reminiscent of peacock feathers.

"That's not Lucy's," Christa said. She turned to Gwyn. "Have you ever seen that?"

"I never bought her anything like that," Gwyn said.

Hopkins exchanged the picture with another. "These were her shorts."

"Maybe," Christa said.

"Lucy has a bunch of pairs of khaki shorts. There's no way to tell," Gwyn added.

Hopkins held up the picture of the shirt a second time. "You're sure she didn't own this?"

"I'm definitely sure," Christa said.

"Okay." Hopkins tucked the pictures into the folder. "Did Lucy have any surgeries recently?"

"No," Christa answered. "Why?"

"I'm just trying to piece a few things together. Bear with me. Was there anything wrong with her hands?"

"Don't you have pictures of the body?" Gwyn interrupted. Blake could hear the agitation building in her voice. "Instead of ridiculous questions, if we could just look at her, we'd know for sure."

"I'm afraid that won't help. The girl we found, her face was... damaged."

Blake had made it a point to stay quiet. His primary goal was to provide moral support and observe. But as was often the case, he couldn't help himself.

"I know you're trying to spare us the shock of seeing her like that," Blake said. "But these two women need to know if their daughter is alive or dead. You need to show them the pictures."

"I agree with you," Hopkins said. "The trouble is, the girl's face was severely damaged by a boat propeller. And when I say damaged, I mean completely gone. Beyond any recognition. On top of that, most of her hair had to be cut off because it had gotten wrapped around the propeller shaft. That's why I—"

"Wait," Christa said. "Wrapped around? How long was her hair?"

"I'd say about shoulder length, maybe longer," Hopkins said.

Christa burst into something of a cross between sobbing and giggling.

Gwyn took Christa's hand and held it to her lips. She closed her eyes, squeezing tears past her lashes and down her cheeks.

"Lucy cut her hair off a few weeks ago. Not herself, the salon did it. Even though we told her not to. She came home looking like an elf. It was no more than two inches long on top. Shorter in the back." Christa sniffled. Two strands of saliva spanned her top and bottom lip as she smiled. "I was so mad at her. I've never been so happy that she didn't listen to us."

"Another detail Alvarez neglected to report," Hopkins said to no one in particular. He stood. "Thank you for coming in. I'm glad we were able to clear that up. Let me assure you that my officers are doing everything they can to find Lucy. She's been entered into the national database as a missing person, so if any law enforcement agency has contact with her, we'll know about it.

Hopkins walked to the door, signaling that it was time for them to leave.

Christa and Gwyn stood. They shared an embrace.

Blake felt the surge of relief himself. He could only imagine how the two women were feeling.

Hopkins opened the door. A younger man, wearing the Jamestown black and red uniform, stood patiently in the hallway. Blake noticed the lieutenant's bars on his shoulders.

"I need a moment, sir," Fuller said.

"Sure, we're all set here." As an afterthought, Hopkins made the obligatory introduction. "Lieutenant Fuller, this is Lucy's family. I'm sure you'll be relieved to know that we were able to rule her out."

"Very good news," Fuller said.

"Thank you so much, Chief Hopkins." Christa walked by Hopkins and into the hallway. Gwyn and Blake followed suit. As soon as they cleared the threshold, Fuller moved into the room.

"You know where you're going, right?" Hopkins said. "Straight down the hall, left at the end."

"Got it," Blake said.

Hopkins swung the door to the conference room. It creaked to a stop, three-quarters closed.

"You go ahead," Blake said, "I'll meet you at the car."

They did so without question.

Blake moved to the conference room door and rested his back against the door jamb. He listened closely.

"Another one?" Hopkins said.

"Her name is Zoe Morris. Her parents are in the interview room now.

The mother said she thought Zoe was sleeping in. Mom went to check on her and found her missing. The bed was made like she never slept in it. They think maybe she snuck out last night and never came home."

"I don't like this, Charlie. It doesn't smell like a coincidence."

With that, the door flung open, taking Blake by surprise. He spun around, coming face to face with Hopkins.

"Sorry to bother you," Blake said. "I was coming back to see if you needed help with anything. Maybe I can be of assistance."

Hopkins chuckled. "How about you leave the police work to the police, Mr.... "

"Brier."

"Right." Hopkins turned and walked away. "Charlie, see Mr. Brier out, please."

Blake made his way to the exit with Fuller in tow. As he stepped outside and worked his way through the protesters, he had an idea. If there was a connection between Lucy and Zoe Morris, he needed to know. If he couldn't get the information from Hopkins, he'd go right to the source. Zoe's parents. All he would have to do is blend into the group for a bit and wait for a man and a woman to come out of the building together. It was possible they could help each other get to the bottom of this.

Blake knocked on the window of the Range Rover. Christa pressed the button to roll it down.

"You two head back. I'm going to stay here for a bit. Check out the area."

Christa's face scrunched. "There's nothing over here but the golf course across the street and the toll plaza for the Newport bridge. Get in, we'll take you wherever you want."

Blake didn't want to tell them that another girl had gone missing. It would only serve to worry them. As it stood, Lucy had merely run off with her boyfriend. But, then again, what if there was an obvious connection between the girls? What if they were friends? That would be significant. He decided he would have to fill them in.

"Does the name Zoe Morris ring a bell?" he asked.

It didn't.

"Her parents are inside now, reporting her missing. I wanted to wait and see if they'd speak with me."

"Why, do you think it's related?" Christa asked.

"I don't know. But it's worth asking."

"Then we wait," Gwyn said. "We all speak with them, together."

Blake smiled. "Deal."

9

SUNDAY, MAY 30TH. EARLY EVENING

GWYN JERKED THE WHEEL AND CROSSED THE DOUBLE YELLOW LINE. FACING oncoming traffic, if there ever happened to be any, she stopped halfway into the patch of grass in front of the yellow cottage.

The mood had been deflated since the two-minute conversation with Zoe's parents. While they were able to get some information, it hadn't been anything useful. Perhaps the couple was skeptical about giving too much detail to a group of strangers. Perhaps there was nothing to tell.

Either way, they had been standoffish. The man in particular. But Blake couldn't blame him. Fathers should be protective of their daughters.

Still, he couldn't help but wonder if they would have been more helpful if it were only the two women who were asking. Blake's outward appearance tended to put people on alert.

His whole purpose of being there was to help find Lucy and, so far, he was not proving to be much help at all.

"I'll leave you two here." Gwyn grasped the shifter. "I'm needed at the restaurant."

Christa rubbed the back of Gwyn's hand. "Can't Rupert handle it? What's the point of having a manager if he can't manage?"

"Don't start," Gwyn said. "I'll be back in a little while. You know I—"

Blake saw himself out of the conversation by climbing out and closing the door. The airtight seal of the Range Rover was effective in keeping whatever else was being said private.

A few feet away, behind his parked car and across the knee-high hedgerow, stood Lucas. Waving with all his might.

Blake gave a quick circular wave to relieve him from his duty. "Hi, Lucas."

"Hi, Mr. Blake."

"You remembered," Blake said as he walked closer.

"Yeah." Lucas said. "I remembered."

Every syllable Lucas spoke was elongated, as if he were intentionally building suspense. With the addition of a slight lisp and a tendency to use the same rising inflection for every sentence, it sounded as though he was perpetually facetious.

Blake leaned on the hood of the Nissan. It felt awkward speaking with someone over a couple of obstacles. But it was as close as he could get without walking around and either shimmying between the cars and the bushes or going into Lucas's yard. He wanted to be friendly, not invade the guy's space.

"You keeping an eye on the neighborhood?" Blake asked.

"Yeah," Lucas responded.

Blake got the sense that Lucas would have responded in the affirmative to pretty much any question he posed. He wondered if Lucas understood anything he said. There were two viable scenarios. Either Lucas was extremely low functioning or just not very talkative. He had yet to figure out which.

Behind Blake, the SUV's engine whined as it made the U-turn and headed back the way they came. Christa hurried toward the house. Her head was low and she wiped her cheek. She didn't give him or Lucas a second look.

Blake's first instinct was to check on her, but decided it would be better to give her some space. He didn't want to give the impression he was meddling.

Instead, he'd shoot the shit with Lucas for a few more minutes. After all, he didn't see anyone else lining up to keep the poor guy company.

"How old are you, Lucas?"

Lucas paused as if lost in thought, then shifted his attention to the oversized plastic watch on his wrist. The neon digital readout was so large that Blake could almost read it from where he stood.

Blake smiled. "Okay, or you can tell me the time," he muttered to himself.

"Thirty-five years, two months, fourteen days, five hours, and sixteen minutes."

Mouth agape, Blake stood speechless. He had known he liked Lucas. His cheerful energy, his endearing manner of speech. But now Blake was downright captivated by him.

"Jeez," Blake chuckled, "couldn't you be a little more precise?"

Lucas burst out with a barking laugh, which stopped as abruptly as it started.

Yep, they were going to be fast friends.

A faint knocking sound caught Blake's attention. It was tinny, as if someone were tapping on a window. He looked back at the storm door, expecting to see Christa trying to flag him down. The inner door was open, but she wasn't there. He scanned the other windows. Nothing.

It wasn't until he glanced at the side of Lucas's house that he noticed the old woman's face hovering in the second-floor window. It looked as though she was saying something, although he couldn't hear a word through the thick panes. By the dirty looks she was throwing at him, he guessed whatever it was, it wasn't anything nice.

"I don't think your Mom likes me talking to you," Blake said.

"Yeah. Mommy lives in heaven with the angels," Lucas said.

"Oh, I'm sorry. I assumed.... Who's that in the window?" Blake motioned to the second floor.

"Auntie," Lucas said. "Yeah. I take good care of Auntie."

"I'm sure you do," Blake said.

"I go get the groceries. Monday and Wednesday and Friday. At the market. But not if it's a holiday. They said you can't go inside 'cause it's a holiday. Even on Monday or Wednesday or Friday."

"Wow," Blake encouraged. "I'm sure that's very helpful. You walk all that way by yourself?"

Blake could see that Lucas was coming out of his shell. He seemed more relaxed. And a whole lot more talkative.

"Yeah. I walk to see Doctor John. He's in Newport. Tuesday and Thursday. Don't be late he said."

"How do you walk to Newport?" Blake was trying to keep him engaged, but it was also a legitimate question. Did he walk over the bridge? He couldn't imagine that was even possible.

Lucas let out another abrupt laugh. "Eight twenty-six, A.M. I show Captain Bill my ticket. Then I can go on."

Using his right hand to pull open the edge of his pants pocket, Lucas reached in with his left and retrieved a laminated card. He held it out toward Blake.

"I see. Very nice," Blake said.

Lucas reversed the process, returning what Blake assumed was his ferry pass to his pocket. "He leaves at eight thirty. Then he says 'Ann Street' at eight forty-six or at eight forty-seven. Once at eight forty-eight. Then I walk to see Doctor John. He helps me because I have some conditions, he says."

Blake was amazed, both at Lucas's independence and at how easy it was for him to assume that Lucas wasn't capable of holding a conversation, let alone taking the ferry in order to get himself to a doctor appointment. Blake had always respected those who had the grit to persevere. In battle and in life.

He had originally set out to befriend Lucas because he felt bad that he was standing by himself with no one to talk to. Now, Blake felt lucky to know him.

Lucas checked his watch. His eyes widened. "Four minutes. Then I go on my walk."

"That sounds fun. You like to walk, huh?"

"Yeah. I walk to Sheffield's Cove. Monday and Tuesday and Wednesday and Thursday and Friday and Saturday and Sunday."

"Every day. Impressive." Blake said.

Even if Blake was only trying to be supportive, he was rather impressed. It was clear that Lucas's schedule was highly regimented. Blake figured it was a kind of coping mechanism. It was like what they always say about toddlers. They need structure. A routine. Otherwise, they feel uneasy. Hell, the same could be said about most of the military men he knew.

Lucas stared at his watch. "Yeah. Every day. Sheffield's Cove. Sometimes I see nice people. Ms. Mary is nice. She says don't listen to the mean kids. Even when they laugh at me and call me bad names."

"Well, you tell me if someone's being mean to you and I'll have a talk with them. Okay? Will you do that?"

"Yeah."

Lucas pinched either side of the watch with his free hand and stood as anxiously poised as a sprinter waiting for the report of the starter pistol. Although, with a considerably less athletic posture.

Fifty feet beyond Lucas, Chief limped up the pitched roadway toward them.

As the enormous LCD display flipped to the anticipated digits, so did Lucas's internal switch. He dropped his arm, turned, and walked away without another word. He shuffled past Chief, giving him a silent but vigorous wave, then set off down the side street that ran along the west side of his house.

"Strange kid," Chief said as he rounded the Nissan. "Seems to like you, though. Never says two words to me. What happened at the police station?"

"You were right, it wasn't Lucy," Blake said.

"I told ya. To fall off a yacht and drown, you gotta actually have a yacht. That kid she's runnin' around with doesn't even have two cents to rub together." Chief walked as he spoke. Blake kept pace until the two of them stood on Christa's front porch. Chief took the liberty of sitting in one of the wicker chairs. "I knew his father when he was a young boy. Dickey, they called him. He was a loser too, even back then. Always in trouble. What did Hopkins say about Lucy?"

"Not much of anything," Blake said.

"I'm not surprised. That guy Hopkins is useless. If you ask me, I don't think he could solve a littering complaint. I wouldn't've hired him. But I'm not in charge."

"You say you know this kid Owen's family. Do you know where he might be? Christa said she spoke with the grandmother. Where's the father, then? Could they be with him?"

"That'd be a trick," Chief said. "He died about ten years ago. Drank himself to death. I don't know what the kid is up to. Probably off somewheres, knockin' up Lucy."

"Jesus, let's hope not." Blake blocked out the mental image. "What about the Mom?"

"She was never in the picture. Don't even know what her name was. Dickey moved away for a little while, then showed back up with a baby. I guess the mother didn't want it, so he ended up with it. Dickey moved back in with his mother, Betsy, and she took care of the kid."

"I see."

"Lucy'll turn up. She's a good kid. Just being stupid. Right now she's thinkin' with her hormones, but it won't take long for her to figure out her boyfriend's a loser." Favoring one leg, Chief used his arms to push himself out of the chair. "I'd better get back, my wife's gonna send a search party. Tell Christa I stopped by. And tell her not to worry."

Blake couldn't tell Christa not to worry. Not anymore. Christa may not have been exaggerating when she said that Chief knew everything that was happening in town, but even he didn't seem to know about the murder. Or that another girl had gone missing.

From what little they could gather from Zoe's parents, her disappearance couldn't be rationalized by raging teenage hormones. There didn't seem to be a boyfriend, defiant behavior, or a history of running away. She had simply vanished.

Blake could have filled Chief in, but the information hadn't been officially released yet and he didn't want to step on Hopkins's toes. Not if he was ever going to get Hopkins to trust him.

Chief hobbled down the single step and onto the grass.

"Quick question before you go," Blake said.

"What's that?"

"What's the deal with the old woman next door? She seemed angry that I was talking to Lucas."

"Cathy?" Chief said. "She's angry at the world. Hasn't been out of that house in years."

"You mean at all?"

"Cathy's lived there for forty years, if not longer. She used to be out in the neighborhood when we were younger. She had these big flower beds in the front yard, and she was always planting and watering. I'd stop and talk with her quite a bit. The woman's loaded. I mean, loaded. But she was a hoarder. And a bad addict. It got to the point where she stayed in her house and would only come out to go buy her dope. I went inside to give her a hand with something, years and years ago. It was horrible. You could barely walk around, there was so much trash. Can't imagine what it's like in there now."

"That's a shame. Lucas has to live in those conditions."

"You're not kiddin'. But it was good he came. As soon as Lucas moved in with her, she stopped the dope. Just like that. Best thing that coulda happened, in my opinion. 'Cept for one thing. 'Cause she didn't have to get her fix and she could send the kid to run her errands, she shut herself in completely. I don't think she'll ever come out again. She'll die in that house. Alls I know is I wouldn't want to be the fire department when they've got to go in there and get her."

"Hell of a thing," Blake said.

There was no way for Blake to know whether Chief's stories were true. He figured they were probably based in truth if nothing else. But he was a natural storyteller and Blake could have listened to him all day.

Chief gave another, "See ya later," and sauntered off with his uneven gait. He almost made it to his own driveway before stopping to talk with a tall woman who was walking a large, puffy dog.

Blake rested his elbows on the half-wall that enclosed the porch on three sides. He wondered what sensational tale Chief had spun to draw the woman in and cause her head to bob in increasingly amplified nods. Even the dog seemed to be paying close attention.

Behind Blake, the rattle and squeak of the storm door announced Christa's return.

"You just missed Chief," Blake said.

"I know. I wasn't in the mood to talk."

"Funny guy." Blake turned toward her. "Gotta love the accent."

"We do have some colorful characters around here," Christa said.

Blake noticed the iPhone in Christa's hand. The sparkly purple case screamed teenage girl. "Is that Lucy's?"

"Yes," Christa handed Blake the device. "I tried guessing the passcode. Her birthday. Our birthdays. No luck."

"That's okay, it won't be an issue. I'll hook it up now." He started for the door, then paused. "Hey, did Chief tell you he knows Owen's family?"

"He did. That's how I found out where Owen lived. I only had to mention his name and Chief knew exactly who I was talking about. He told me he lived with his grandmother in the apartments on Pemberton. It was lucky I even found out that Lucy was hanging around with the kid. I happened to be downtown and saw them outside of Spinnakers."

"Spinnakers?"

"It's a little ice cream shop on the pier," Christa said. "I wouldn't have thought anything of it if he didn't have his arm around her and his hand on her ass. I was so pissed I marched right up to him and asked him who he was. Ya know what he says? 'Who the F are you?' Can you believe that? I say I'm Lucy's mom and tell him he's not to come around her anymore. Lucy says his name is Owen and that he's only a friend. I could see she was embarrassed, but I didn't care. The kid looked like he was twenty-five."

"How old is he?"

"He's nineteen. But a fifteen-year-old girl shouldn't be hanging out with a nineteen-year-old."

"No, you're absolutely right. But this Spinnakers, is that where Lucy normally hangs out?"

"I don't think so," Christa said. "There's a whole group of kids that she usually hangs out with. I really don't know any of them. There's a girl named Sam, I know that. From what Lucy's told me, they basically meet up and walk around. They go to the park up the street. Downtown. The beach. God knows where else. It's a small island, there isn't a whole lot to do."

"I'm guessing I'll be able to track down some of these friends by looking at her social media, her contacts, that kind of thing. Was it like her to leave her phone behind? You'd think, at her age, she'd be glued to the thing. Maybe she was worried you'd track her down if she took it with her."

"No." Christa's voice cracked and her top lip began to quiver. "I took it away. As a punishment." Her effort to maintain her composure failed. Tears flowed freely. "What if she needed help and she had no way to call me? If I had just let her keep it..."

Blake didn't know what to say. He had no condolences, no answers. Not yet. In a couple of minutes, he would go to work dissecting Lucy's digital life. But right now, he did what felt necessary. He wrapped his arms around the fragile woman before him and let her cry.

10

SUNDAY, MAY 30TH. NIGHT

Zoe snapped her head in the direction of every creak, clink, and clunk. But to no purpose. There was nothing but blackness and the burn of the abrasive burlap rubbing against her nose and forehead.

With every inhale of recycled air, the coarse fabric adhered to her lips and nostrils. Her bruised and broken ribs screamed in pain. Panic surged again. Zoe dug deep to fight it. Screaming was not an option. Giving him a reason was not an option. She couldn't have endured another crushing blow.

Unsure of how much time had passed, she estimated eternity. She imagined the faces of her mother. Her father. Her little brother. How disappointed they would have been. She caught a glimpse of the motion in the wooded lot as she passed. She felt the pit in her stomach before it all happened. She could have run. She wanted to run. But she hesitated. Debilitated by fear, instead of motivated by it. This was her fault, and now she would give anything to tell them she was sorry.

Beneath her, the hard, hollow floor rocked and swayed. Her body shifted back and forth, tugging on the rope that had been tightly wound around the outside of the sack. The pressure caused the burlap to bite into the bare skin of her neck, arms, and legs.

Outside, the dulled clanging of the buoys, squawking of the gulls, and slapping of the water left no doubt in her mind that she was in the belly of a boat. Where, exactly, she didn't know. But the rumble of the motor told her they were on the move.

Zoe tried to steady her mind. If she were to survive, she would need to think. She would need to be ready. As it was, she was just beginning to admit to herself this was really happening. Her father had been right all along. He told her there were bad guys out there. That she needed to protect herself. Since she was a little girl, she remembered thinking it was stupid. This was her town. Everyone was nice and friendly. No one was going to try to steal her or hurt her. She had never been more wrong about anything in her life.

She rolled herself to her back to take the pressure off her aching left shoulder. She panted. Pining for just one breath of crisp air.

The terrifying events replayed in her mind. Not in any coherent order, but in flashes. She strained to remember. To fill in the gaps.

She had been walking home after leaving Tyler. She remembered him offering to walk with her. It was sweet, but she didn't want to take the chance that her parents would see him. Anyway, it was a short walk. And she was perfectly capable, she told him.

She remembered walking along the edge of the roadway. The over-grown lot to her right, dark and quiet. Did she hear a rustling?

The next thing she could remember was the hands. Clamping around her chin and over her mouth. She was being dragged by her head. Had she seen a man? No matter how hard she tried, she couldn't visualize it happening. She could only feel it. The pain in her neck, as if her captor tried to rip her head from her body. Knocking the wind out of her as he thrust her to the hard ground. The scratchy twigs and leaves all over her body. And most of all, the incredible strength.

Zoe knew now that there had been a man. But at the time, it hadn't occurred to her. At first, her chaotic mind was convinced that she was being attacked by a bear. She felt a twinge of embarrassment at recalling the notion. There were no bears on the island. She had never even seen a bear in person. Yet, it was the first thing that came to her mind.

She remembered the hand leaving her face and retreating into the darkness. She had tried to call out. She had tried to push out the words,

"Help me, somebody." That was when it came. As if a boulder had fallen from the sky and landed on her chest. She heard the crack and felt him try to force her life out of her lungs. She waited for death. It didn't come. Instead, the foul-smelling bag slipped over her head. Hands ran along her sides and her feet were lifted high above her head.

Looking back, she had been aware she was being carried. The pressure of the man's shoulder pressing into her abdomen as she bounced with each step. His forearm along the back of her legs. But at the time she had been consumed with the pain, stabbing into her lungs and stealing her breath. Maybe if she had paid better attention. Listened more closely.

They had somehow gotten to the boat. Were there other people nearby? Could she have missed her opportunity to call out one last time?

The slapping of the water on the hull transitioned to more of a lapping. The motor fell silent. Panic rose again. Zoe knew there would be a destination, but she wasn't ready.

Heavy footsteps preceded the sound of wood grinding against wood. Then there were hands around her ankles. The edge of a wooden step scraping along her back. She was being hoisted again. The shoulder, the forearm. With each bounce, her chest caved. Then she was weightless.

For a split second, the pain released. Her stomach dropped. And then the concrete floor came up to meet her, bringing the pain back with it. Tenfold.

Light beamed through the mesh. A flash of brown burlap filled her view, then receded into darkness again. There was a tugging and then the pressure of the rope released. The bag slid along her body. She knew what it meant. She was about to come face to face with her captor. She would be ready. To study. To remember.

As the last bit of harsh fabric ran over her forehead, the bright beam of the flashlight blinded her. She bent her knees and used her arms to push herself into a half-seated position.

The outline of a man hovered behind the searing beam. Zoe blinked and blinked, hoping her eyes would adjust. The smell of mold, urine, and excrement accosted her.

The light bouncing off her illuminated her immediate surroundings. Bright colored graffiti covered the filthy concrete floor and low ceiling. A few feet away was the faint outline of what looked like a rusty metal gate. The silhouette of the man moved toward it.

What is this place?

Zoe squinted. She peered past the blinding light to get a look at the man's face. She couldn't quite make out his features with any detail. He was wearing a white hat. Though old and dirty, the hat's bright color reflected the light, making it stand out from everything else in view. Zoe had seen the same hat a million times in her life. It was part of a boat captain's uniform. She was sure of it.

With the clanking of metal and the squeal of the gate swinging open, Zoe heard the man's voice for the first time. "Get in," he said. It sent chills down her spine.

Despite her best effort to avoid it, the tears found their way down her cheeks. "Please," she whimpered. "I just want to go home."

"Get in," he repeated. There was no emotion. Not even anger.

She didn't want to get in. But what was she going to do? Fight? The man was stronger than she had even thought possible. She had no idea where she was. If she could get to her feet, she could run. But to where? Outside of the flashlight's beam, there was only pitch darkness. And she had no doubt that a refusal would only bring more pain.

Zoe crawled toward the gate. The man stepped back, keeping the beam fixed on her as she moved.

As she passed through the opening, the light reached the back of the small concrete cell. Her pulse quickened, and the hair stood up along her neck and arms.

I'm not alone!

In the shadows, Zoe saw two girls, each cowering in opposite corners. As quickly as they appeared, they faded back into the darkness.

Zoe's mind churned as iron bars clanged shut. The jingle of keys gave way to the sound of footsteps as the last bit of light disappeared around the corner.

He was gone.

"Are you okay?" Zoe called out, "Where are we?"

There was no response. Could she have imagined the two girls? Was this a waking nightmare?

Zoe slid herself on her back side, a few inches at a time, until she could reach out and feel the cool concrete wall. She pushed her back against it, drew up her knees, and wrapped her arms around her shins. The pitch darkness played tricks on her brain. Were there actually girls in there with her? Were they ghosts? Evil spirits? What else was in there with her? Her whole body was frozen with fear.

"Please," Zoe yelled. "If you're there, say something."

"Shhhhhhhh." The hushing came from her right. Zoe swung her hand but caught nothing but air. "Are you real?" she asked.

"Be quiet." The words came from her left. It was a whisper but still clearly a girl's voice. "The Captain doesn't like when we talk."

A strange sense of relief washed over Zoe. She had been attacked, beaten and imprisoned. But at least she wasn't crazy. She dropped her own voice to a whisper. "Who's the Captain? Where are we?"

"Go to sleep," the girl on the right said.

"We have to do something," Zoe said. "We have to get out of here."

There was no response. And after a few more attempts, Zoe got the hint that there wouldn't be.

Zoe closed her eyes and tried to rehash the events that brought her there. Maybe this time she could remember all of it. And maybe, if she were lucky, sleep would follow.

11

SUNDAY, MAY 30TH. NIGHT

BLAKE SNAPPED THE LAPTOP SHUT, UNPLUGGED THE PHONE, AND HURRIED off to find Christa. Out of pure conditioning, he tried the front porch first.

Before opening the glass storm door, he could see that Gwyn had returned. She sat with her elbows on her knees and her face was rimmed by flickering orange light. A candle inside a tin bucket sat on the ledge behind her. Black smoke poured from the wild flame.

Although he couldn't see Christa, he sensed she was there too. By the looks of it, the two were engaged in an intense conversation. While he didn't want to interrupt, he had important information to deliver. After all, his whole purpose of being in Rhode Island was to examine this phone, and it had been delayed long enough. He pressed the latch lever.

"Finished." The door squeaked against the hydraulic closer.

Gwyn straightened up and cleared her throat.

"Did you find anything?" Christa implored. Even by candlelight, Blake could see that her eyes were red and puffy. She looked as though she hadn't slept in a week. That morning, he couldn't look at her without seeing Anja. Now, he could hardly see a resemblance.

"I did." Blake took a seat next to Christa on the settee and placed Lucy's phone on the wicker coffee table. "And there's something you should know."

"Good or bad?" Gwyn asked. She sucked in air through her teeth and squeezed the arms of her chair as if physically bracing herself for the answer.

"A bit of both. I read the text threads between Lucy and Owen. It seems that the two had a falling out."

"A falling out?" Gwyn questioned. "What does that mean? Are you saying they broke up?"

"I don't know," Blake said. "Maybe. Temporarily? It was clear Lucy was upset with him."

"Over what?" Christa said.

"For one thing, Owen tried to get Lucy to try heroin."

"Heroin?" Gwyn blurted. "Oh, my god. She's run away with a goddamn drug dealer."

"Shhhh." Christa took a paranoid glance to her left, as if the darkness harbored a crowd of eavesdroppers with delicate sensibilities. Even if it had, she couldn't have seen anyone from inside their candlelit cocoon anyway. "Why don't you tell the whole neighborhood?"

Gwyn lowered her voice. "I can't believe it. A drug dealer."

"Now you're surprised?" Christa snipped. "I told you he was trouble. I knew it, I just knew it."

"Hold on, we don't know that he's a dealer," Blake said. "But he's definitely a user. He mentions it several times. In one text, he says something like 'scored some H, wanna party?' He uses the word *smack*, as well. But the good news is, Lucy isn't using."

"How do you know?" Gwyn asked.

"In the last few texts—I assume right before the phone was taken away—Owen was asking her to come see him. She wrote something along the lines of 'leave me alone.' Owen calls her a prude and says he doesn't want to be with anyone who's afraid to get high."

"Thank God," Christa said. "I knew she would be smarter than that."

"There's more." Blake paused. "It seems that Lucy was angry at him because she believed he cheated on her with another girl. She was upset because..."

Blake considered how he would phrase it. He wished he had printed out the conversation so that Gwyn and Christa could read it verbatim. Somehow, paraphrasing made him feel complicit.

"Because?" Gwyn prodded.

"Because he took her virginity," Blake said.

"No, he didn't." Gwyn said, more in disapproval than denial.

"Aw. Poor baby," Christa said. "I wish I could give her a big hug. I don't understand why she'd go back to him after he treated her like that."

"Because she's fifteen and she thinks she's in love." Gwyn said.

Blake was surprised at how well they were taking the revelation. He figured it must have been a woman thing. If Lucy were his daughter, he'd be looking to crack some skulls.

What worried him more was their reluctance to see the whole picture. If he were thinking out loud, he'd have asked the obvious questions. What if she hadn't gone back to him? What if he took her against her will? Or worse, what if he had nothing to do with it? How much time would they have wasted, looking in the wrong direction? It was going to be on him to find out. And fast.

"I compiled a list of phone numbers and social media accounts," Blake said. "People that Lucy has talked to in the last month. I promise, I will find someone who knows something." Blake stood up. "Right now, I have to go for a ride to do some digging."

"Now?" Gwyn said. "It's late."

"That's exactly why I need to go now. I don't know if you're aware, but iPhones, like Lucy's, have a feature called Significant Locations. Basically, the phone keeps track of the locations you visit most often and, if you drill down into the data, the times at which you visit them. Have either of you ever gotten a notification in the morning telling you that there's a traffic delay and that you should leave for work earlier than normal?"

"Yes. I have. And it's creepy," Christa said.

"No. But I assume my phone tracks everything I do, all the time." Gwyn said.

Blake chuckled.

If you only knew.

"Lucy's most frequent location, aside from this house, appears to be at the end of a pier. And it's usually at night." Blake pulled his own phone from his pocket and navigated to a screenshot of Google Maps. A teardrop shaped icon marked the point in question. He dropped the device onto the coffee table between Christa and Gwyn. "There."

Christa picked it up and examined it. "The public pier at the East Ferry? I know a lot of people fish off it, but Lucy doesn't fish. What else could she be doing down there?"

"Sometimes the big yachts that come in will dock there," Gwyn said. "Christa and I will take a stroll down there once in a while to check them out, maybe that's what she's doing?"

"That often?" Christa wondered.

"I'm guessing it's where she and her friends hang out," Blake said. "They get together somewhere, right? I figure it's a good place to start."

"What can we do?" Gwyn asked.

"The most important thing both of you can do is get some rest. It's been a long day. I'll let you know what I find out first thing in the morning."

Blake pressed his key fob. The Nissan's headlights illuminated, cutting through the darkness beyond the candles and lighting Blake's way off the porch.

"Thank you for doing this," Christa said.

Blake nodded and headed to the car.

Gwyn stood up but didn't go inside like Blake had tried to suggest. Instead, she moved over and sat on Christa's lap, nuzzling her nose into Christa's shoulder and neck. As Blake backed out, his headlights overpowered the orange glow, putting the couple on display like the featured act in a cabaret. Shifting into drive, he left them to it.

* * *

BLAKE SCANNED EITHER SIDE OF THE ROADWAY AS HE PASSED THROUGH THE tunnel of trees. There were no streetlights here, and the canopy effectively blocked out the moonlight. In the day, Blake had noticed a heaved sidewalk running along the north side of the street. Even in broad daylight, the asphalt path blended with the trees and overgrown bushes. At night, it had disappeared completely.

Ahead, his headlights reflected off the light blue tank top of a man, walking in the opposite lane. As he passed, the man staggered toward the shoulder.

Past the four-way stop and over the hill, streetlights cast an ominous shimmer over the sleeping village. Empty streets and dark windows welcomed him.

Halfway down the hill, there were two people standing together on the sidewalk, smoking cigarettes. In the windows behind them, colorful neon signs advertising Budweiser and Corona made it clear that not every place was closed for business.

At the bottom, Blake could see the marina. Fog swirled in the radiance of the decorative lamp posts. To the left, the looming expanse of the Newport Bridge in the distance cut through the inky soup, its massive cables lit up like a string of Christmas lights draped across the bay. To the right, a row of charming shops lined a small, empty parking lot. He pulled in.

There were several piers and docks branching out from the area of the lot and the adjacent patch of grass, which featured a stone monument. He pulled up the screenshot and compared the layout to the image. He was in the right place.

Blake turned off the car and stepped out. The breeze rustled through his hair.

It was amazing how still the air was at the house. Yet, at the water's edge, nothing was still. The waves lapped loudly against the walls, pilings, and hulls. The light escaping from skinny windows made the entire field of bobbing boats look like a miniature, undulating city. A warm, blustery breeze carried the scents of aquatic life—and death. It was peaceful. A strange contradiction to the turmoil existing within it.

Blake headed for the pier. At the end of the shops and just before the start of its wooden deck, a sign marked the entrance to a gangway leading to a floating dock.

Jamestown-Newport Ferry.

He thought of Lucas and his biweekly adventures, traveling across the bay. The actual boat was smaller than he'd imagined while talking with Lucas.

Ironically, the last time he was on a ferry boat was in Jamestown, Virginia, while visiting Williamsburg. Traversing the James River between Jamestown and Scotland, the large ship could carry dozens of cars along with passengers. Its Rhode Island counterpart was probably less than thirty feet long and didn't look like it could hold more than a dozen people. It made sense. With the bridge connecting the two islands, the ferry was hardly a necessity.

Blake stepped onto the narrow pier. In the distant shadows, he saw movement. For the sake of his purposes, he hoped he would find a bunch of dopey-looking kids rather than fishermen. As he approached the end, the strong odor of burning marijuana swayed the odds toward the former.

With their backs turned to him, four figures sat along the far edge of the pier with their legs hanging eight feet above the water. Two males and two females, he thought. One of the males leaned against one of the pilings supporting the wooden deck.

Blake realized he had been walking heel-to-toe. It was a habit he picked up long ago. By rolling the foot, each step was virtually silent. While useful when attempting to take an enemy by surprise, he had inadvertently startled more than a few people, including Haeli. One evening, Haeli was chopping lettuce in his kitchen. If Blake had gotten any closer before opening his mouth, he undoubtedly would have lost a lot of blood.

In this instance, he didn't want anyone going swimming on his behalf. He intentionally let each foot fall flat to sufficiently announce his presence.

The taller of the two males looked back with little affect. He had a baby face and jet-black hair, apart from the section hanging over his eyes which had been dyed bright green. He reminded Blake of a taller Billie Joe Armstrong, although the kid was probably too young to even know who that was.

Blake stopped a few feet away. "Hi there."

The three others looked back, then turned away again.

Blake had been wrong. He could see that they were all teenagers, but there were three males and one female. One of the males had long blonde hair that protruded from the back of his baseball cap and flowed halfway down his back. He didn't know what Owen looked like, but he was sure Goldilocks wasn't his guy. The other two were a possibility.

"Would one of you guys happen to be Owen?" Blake asked.

Billie Joe ignored Blake but spoke to the others. "Look at this creeper."

The group giggled.

"It's a simple question." Blake could already feel his temper heating.

Billie Joe swung his legs onto the deck and worked his way to his feet in a slow-motion display of apathy. "Whatta you want with Owen? He owe you money or something?"

"Nothing like that," Blake said. "I'm looking for Lucy. I was hoping you'd seen her."

"What are you, her father?" the kid said. "The way I heard it, her father's a child molester or somethin'. That you? How 'bouts you get lost."

Jackpot.

These kids knew Owen. They knew Lucy. And Blake had no intention of parting company until he got some answers.

Goldilocks and the third kid stood up and flanked Billie Joe. Blake assumed their intention was to look intimidating. The effect was the opposite.

Blake noticed the girl remained seated but had shifted to one side so she could see what was happening. Even though he had seen pictures of Lucy, it would have been difficult to recognize her in the low light. Luckily, this girl also had long hair, which immediately dispelled any suspicion.

"I'm a friend," Blake said. "I just need to talk to them."

"We ain't tellin' you shit," Goldilocks said.

"Come on guys, don't make this harder than it has to be." Blake raised his open hands. "I'm not here for any trouble. Just tell me where I can find them, and I'll be on my way."

Billie Joe turned to Goldilocks. "This guy's got some balls, don't he? I think you need to show him your thing." He bobbed his head in a slanted nod. Goldilocks didn't move. Billie Joe nodded again.

Based on the apprehensive look on Goldilocks's face, Blake was a little worried the whole interaction was about to take a weird and obscene left turn. Goldilocks finally reached into his pocket and withdrew a set of brass knuckles. He slid the metal device onto his fingers and dropped his fist to his side.

"I told you, guy, we ain't playin' around," Billie Joe's eyes were like slits. Blake had no doubt the weed was kicking in.

The third kid stayed silent. He was small. Much younger than the others. He avoided making eye contact with Blake. It was like a Penn and Teller act. Only it was Penn and Penn and Teller. And it was obvious Teller didn't want any part of it.

"Here's what's going to happen," Blake said. "You're going to take those knuckles and throw them in the ocean. Not just because they're illegal, but because they're going to cause you to write checks your fists can't cash, if you get my drift. Then you're going to tell me exactly where I can find Owen and Lucy, like I asked. So why don't we just cut to the chase? Save ourselves the extra steps. Whatta ya say?"

"Screw you, old man," Billie Joe said.

Blake tried to always give sound advice. He considered himself a straight shooter and strove to be sincere when interacting in less than amiable situations. So why did no one ever take his advice? Ever?

And these three knuckleheads were a different breed altogether. Blake chalked it up to lack of experience. They had probably grown up on the island, isolated from the larger world. Anyone else in their position, if they possessed a shred of sense, would have taken one look at Blake and been afraid. But not these jamokes. They wanted to fight. Or, rather, Billie Joe wanted Goldilocks to do it for him.

The truth was, under the bravado, these were teenage kids. The last thing Blake wanted to do was hurt them. But, he figured, a good life lesson couldn't hurt.

"Okay," Blake said. "Do what you've gotta do. But understand that none of us are leaving this pier until you tell me what I need to know. Or you knock me out. Whichever comes first."

Billie Joe stared at Goldilocks and reemployed the cockeyed nodding routine until Goldilocks stepped forward. Teller took a step backward.

Goldilocks shifted his weight and cocked back his fist. His lips scrunched together. Blake almost wanted to stop him and give him a few pointers about telegraphing. Instead, he let him roll with it.

The fist came in high, about eye level. With his right hand, Blake deflected it from coming anywhere near his face. The motion put the kid off balance, sending him toward the edge of the pier.

Blake reached out and grabbed a fist full of the kid's hair with his left hand. With his right, Blake grabbed hold of the piling to prevent himself from being pulled in by the kid's weight and inertia. Blake's muscles tensed and his arms stretched. Goldilocks dangled, headfirst, above the water. His knees against the edge of the dock. Blake rotated his wrist, twisting the hair around his hand for a more stable grip. It was, after all, the only thing stopping Goldilocks from taking a swan dive. Goldilocks screamed in pain.

"Get off him," Billie Joe yelled as he approached.

Blake swept his foot behind Billie Joe's heels, kicking his legs out from under him and sending him to the deck. He landed on his back side. If anything was injured, it was his pride. But it was enough to convince him not to get back up.

"Toss 'em, Goldilocks." Blake said.

For a moment, Goldilocks paused his moaning and begging. Long enough to shake the brass knuckles free from his fingers. They landed in the water with a plop.

"Where are they?" Blake said.

"I'll tell you! I'll tell you!" Goldilocks panted. "I know where he's at. Just help me, I'm gonna fall." His hands grasped at the air as if reaching for something to hold on to, then clasped onto Blake's wrist.

Blake pulled upward until Goldilocks's body was perpendicular to the deck. Blake slid him backward until he could support himself on his hands and knees. Goldilocks sat with his legs stretched out in front of him. His forehead was wet with tears.

Billie Joe remained seated but had scooched himself back several feet. The girl was standing with Teller, as far as they could get to the end of the pier without being in the water.

"Where?" Blake said.

"I don't know where Lucy is, I swear. She hasn't been around for a bit. Owen's in Cranston. He's got a side piece there."

"What's her name?"

"Lily." Goldilocks paused. "Shit, I don't know her last name. But I've been there. I can tell you where she lives. Owen will be there. Far as I know."

Blake patted Goldilocks on the side of the shin. The kid sucked in air as if he were expecting it to hurt.

"See," Blake said. "I knew we could work it out."

12

MONDAY, JUNE 1ST. EARLY MORNING

Zoe awoke in a panic. She sprung to her feet and tried to get her bearings.

The journey from the dream world to the stark reality had only taken a second. Just enough time for her brain to catch up.

Moments ago, she had been dreaming that she and her family had moved to a horse farm. It was her birthday and her father led her to the barn to surprise her with a horse of her own. A beautiful white stallion. She had never ridden a horse in her life but was somehow able to climb on and run the animal through the fields and over the creeks. But then the horse bucked, throwing her to the ground. An intense pain radiated from her neck. It was the pain that woke her.

Before she opened her eyes, she was in her bedroom. Surrounded by her posters, heaps of clothes, and the electric guitar she had begged her parents to buy her but never learned to play. She felt the warmth and security of the familiar four walls. But it was short lived.

The sensations of reality rushed back. The hard concrete beneath her and against the back of her head. The cramp in her neck, caused by the awkward position she had slumped into. The putrid odor.

Now, standing in the center of the small cell with her knees slightly bent and her fingers stretched out like a cat baring its claws, she was at a loss for what to do next. There was no one to fight. Nowhere to run. There was only her. And the other two lost souls with whom she would share the nightmare.

Zoe looked at the girl crumpled in the corner to her left. She was wide awake, looking back at her with a blank stare. Bruised. Badly beaten. Her lips were cracked, and her long blonde hair was filthy and matted. The light-yellow sundress she wore looked as though it had been used as a mechanic's rag.

To her right, it was much the same story. Bloodied and covered in dirt, the petite girl's wide eyes were blank. Her short hair stood out in all directions.

Sunlight streamed in from behind the rusted iron bars and around the corner. It wasn't bright, but there was enough light to see clearly.

Graffiti covered every inch of the room and the visible portion of the hallway.

A pile of human waste sat at the intersection of the iron gate and the wall. A puddle of liquid crept along the floor toward the center of the cell like tentacles. Zoe tried to put it out of her mind that, eventually, nature would call, and she would also be forced to contribute to the squalor.

As grim as the surroundings were, Zoe took some solace in the fact that they were familiar. Anyone who had grown up on the island had been in similar rooms. Tons of abandoned forts and bunkers, built during World War II, could be found around the island. Zoe wasn't sure if it was an urban myth, but she was told that the underground rooms and tunnels were infested with rats. Others swore that cults of devil worshipers lived deep within and were waiting to snatch unsuspecting children and use them as human sacrifices.

Despite the spooky stories, Zoe had visited Fort Wetherill often, and once even worked up the courage to enter one of the tunnels. She had only made it a few feet before succumbing to her fear that she would be attacked by a giant rodent. Satan worshipers were a little farfetched. Rats, on the other hand—well, it wasn't worth the risk.

Although Zoe assumed she was at Fort Wetherill State Park, other places had similar structures. She had seen them at Fort Getty Park and a few other locations around the island.

The common theme in these parks, other than the forts, was that they were heavily visited. In her experience, during the daytime there were always people walking, picnicking, taking pictures, and doing whatever else they do. Surely if she were to yell loud enough, someone would hear and come to investigate. She sucked in as much air as her lungs would hold.

"Help!" she screamed. "Hel—"

Zoe felt the clammy fingers press against her mouth.

"Be quiet," the short-haired girl whispered. "You're going to get us killed." The girl put her lips against Zoe's ear. Even at that distance, her voice was barely audible. "We've tried that. No one can hear us. But he can. If it's the Captain, he will hurt you. He will hurt all of us. Please sit down and stop talking. Please."

The short-haired girl let go and dropped back into her corner.

What had this man done to these girls? Why were they so terrified to make a sound? Was she the only one who was willing to put up a fight?

Zoe moved to the gate. A modern looking padlock ran through two rusted metal tabs. One attached to the gate and one to the stationary section of bars. She tugged at it. Secure. She looked around for a loose piece of concrete or a rock or anything that she could use to try to break the rusty tabs. There was nothing.

The other two girls remained still and quiet.

Zoe found the silence maddening. In retrospect, it was better than the sound that broke it. Heavy footsteps. The crinkling of plastic.

A ghostly shadow appeared in the opening to the hallway. A man appeared after it.

"I've brought you something to eat," he said. He carried a white plastic Cumberland Farms bag in one hand and what appeared to be a collapsible camp stool in the other.

Finally, Zoe had a clear view of her captor. She examined every detail of his face. She was struck by how normal he looked. No scars. No jagged teeth. No neck tattoos. Just a soft expression and a pleasant demeanor.

He had neatly parted hair, wire-rimmed glasses, and wore a short-sleeved button-down shirt. He looked like a typical dad. Was this the same man who'd assaulted and kidnapped her? It was too dark the night before to get a good look at the man. But this man had a different bearing. His voice was higher. No, this was someone entirely different.

Shit. There's more than one of them.

"What's your name?" His full attention was focused on Zoe.

Zoe shifted her eyes to the short-haired girl for some direction. Was she supposed to answer him? Wasn't she supposed to be silent? There was no help from the corner.

"Ah," the man said. "They've told you, have they? Not to speak?"

Zoe nodded.

"That's his rule, not mine. I apologize for his behavior. The Captain tends to lose his temper quickly. It's a terrible personality flaw, in my opinion. Anyway, he's not here so we can talk freely. Understand?"

"What do you want with us?" Zoe's voice quivered.

"*I* want to help you, of course."

The man leaned the folded stool against his leg, reached into the bag and withdrew a small clear plastic package.

Ho-Hos? He brought Ho-hos?

The man tossed the package through the bars. It landed on the ground in front of the short-haired girl. She tore into the package and shoved one of the two chocolate covered cakes into her mouth. She devoured the second before fully swallowing the first.

He threw another. The second girl pounced.

"Would you like one?" the man asked.

Zoe shook her head.

"They're delicious. You sure?"

Zoe didn't react. She didn't want anything from him. To be beholden to him in any way, despite her growling stomach.

The man opened the stool, placed it two feet away from the bars, and calmly sat. He crossed his legs. "Now, where were we? Ah, yes, you were about to tell me your name."

"It's Stacy," Zoe said.

"Your real name," the man snapped back.

"Zoe."

"Nice to meet you, Zoe."

The whole thing had become surreal. Nice to meet you? What kind of sick mind game was this guy playing?

"You can call me Doc, if you'd like," he said.

"Doc? Are you a Doctor?" Zoe asked.

"I am." He leaned in. "The very best."

"Why are you doing this?" Zoe fought back the urge to cry. "If you're a doctor, you're supposed to help people. What did I do to deserve being locked in a cage? What did any of us do?"

"It's for your own good, Zoe. I can treat you. I can cure you. I know I can."

"But I'm not sick."

The doctor laughed.

"What? I'm not." Zoe's tone became more defiant.

"All of my patients say that. It just goes to show how ill you really are. Trust me, you are in good hands. I told you, I'm the best in the world. My therapies are groundbreaking. They'll see, they'll all see. The Captain doesn't believe I can save you. That's fine. We're going to show him that he's wrong. The trick is to catch the disease before it takes over the entire girl. It's simple, really. When you think about it."

As he spoke, his gaze drifted away from Zoe and fixed on the ceiling. What started out as pleasant had become almost deranged. Zoe didn't understand what he was jabbering about, but there was one message she received loud and clear. This guy was screwed up in the head.

"Let me out. Please. I want to go home." Zoe pleaded.

"I'm sorry. I can't do that."

Zoe balled her fists. "I hate you!" She turned her back to hide the tears that had begun to flow.

"Why would you say that? I love you, Zoe. I love all of you. I would never hurt you like he does. It's him you hate, not me. And, believe me, I understand. The Captain is difficult to get along with." He looked over his shoulder. "Can I tell you a secret?" He took another glance behind him and lowered his voice. "He thinks he's in charge. But I just let him believe that. I'm not afraid of him."

Zoe wiped her cheeks and stole a glimpse of the other two girls. Both sat with their heads bowed, staring at the floor. This had to be a dream.

The Doctor. The Captain. What were they, characters from a comic book? If she ever got out of there, no one would ever believe the story. But she would get out of there, somehow. She just needed a plan.

As crazy as the Doctor sounded, he seemed less dangerous. Having been beaten and bound by the Captain, Zoe was aware of his capabilities. So far, the Doctor seemed only interested in administering psychotherapy. And, while she was no expert, there seemed to be a rift between him and his buddy. It was her only hope.

She steadied herself and turned to face him. "I can tell you're smarter. That's why you're really in charge. You could let us go if you wanted, and there's nothing he could say about it."

"You're exactly right, young lady. He can't tell me what to do. I could let you go if I wanted." He grinned. "But why would I ever want to do that?"

13

MONDAY, JUNE 1ST. MORNING

HOPKINS SNATCHED THE PHONE'S HANDSET ON THE FIRST RING. HAVING crashed hard the night before, the chunk of uninterrupted sleep made him feel like he had acquired superhuman reflexes. Compared to last night, his mind was firing on all cylinders.

"An investigator from the M.E.'s office is here for you," the front desk officer said.

"Great. Send him down." Hopkins hung up the phone and stepped out of his office to greet the visitor.

Emmanuel Lawson, a sleek and slender man with a shiny bald head and smooth, dark skin, floated down the hallway. As usual, a huge smile dominated his face. There were few people Hopkins knew that were as charismatic, even from a distance.

Originally from Togo, West Africa, Lawson had served twenty years with the Providence Police Department before retiring and taking a job with the Medical Examiner's office.

After leaving to take the position as Chief, Hopkins concluded Lawson had chosen the better path. Dead people would have been so much easier to manage than live ones.

"Manny," Hopkins said, "Good to see you. Come in."

"Look at you. Chief."

The two embraced and moved into the office. Hopkins sat behind his desk and Lawson took a seat in one of the two chairs positioned on the opposite side.

"How's Jess? The kids?" Hopkins asked.

"Everyone's great," Lawson said. "Justine just finished her first year at Brown."

"That's fantastic."

"How about you? How've you been?" Lawson asked.

"Livin' the dream," Hopkins said.

"Yeah, I bet. Heard you've been getting your share of press lately. No wonder so many people are lined up outside to get your autograph."

"Don't believe the hype." Hopkins laughed. "To what do I owe the visit?"

"I was going to give you a call," Lawson said, "but I figured I'd take the opportunity to stop in."

"Glad ya did, it's been too long. I assume this means you've got new info."

"I wouldn't say that. More questions than answers, really. You know we've identified her, right?"

"I do," Hopkins said. "Misty Brighton. I've got my guy sitting in with North Kingstown while they interview her parents. At this point, we're just trying to determine if she was in Jamestown at any time before she was killed. Those guys are already trying to run with it like it's their case."

"If I didn't know you, I'd say you were trying to find a reason to keep it." Lawson smiled. "If North Kingstown wants the case, let them have it. If you've learned anything from working in the ol' Renaissance City, it should've been that."

Hopkins chuckled. "You're right. It's just..." He lifted his hand to his face and rubbed his brow with his thumb and middle finger. "I've got two girls missing, and it doesn't add up. Something's not right, Manny. Do you remember in Providence when that nurse left on her lunch break and didn't come back? I think you were still there."

"Yeah, Roger Williams Hospital, right? What about it?" Lawson asked.

"At the same time the hospital reported her missing, someone found her boyfriend hanging from the second-floor porch at his apartment.

When we made the connection, we knew she was dead. We hadn't found her body yet, but I think we all had this awful feeling that there was a gruesome crime scene somewhere, just waiting for us to stumble on it. That's the feeling I have now."

"If I recall, we found the nurse a day later with a bag full of oxycodone that she stole from the hospital. She was high as a kite, but she was alive."

"Fine, maybe that's a bad example," Hopkins said. "The point is, I can't let this go. Not yet. I've got everyone I have on the missing person cases and still, nothing."

Lawson shook his head. "I will say that if these cases are related—and I'm not saying they are—but *if* they are, I wouldn't want to be one of these two missing girls. Whoever killed Misty Brighton was one sick bastard."

Lawson unzipped a black leather padfolio, removed a packet of paper, and slid it to Hopkins.

"Stabbed seventeen times," Lawson said. "Three-and-a-half-inch blade. Possibly a folding knife."

"Whoever did her was angry, that's for sure." Hopkins opened the packet and skimmed through the pages.

"That's not the half of it," Lawson said. "The presence of semen was discovered in her vagina and rectum. And there was heavy damage to the vaginal walls, caused by some foreign instrument. The poor girl was repeatedly and brutally raped before she was killed."

"Jesus."

"But that's not the sickest part. The fingers of her right hand were also severed."

"That was apparent," Hopkins said, "but that part probably isn't related. We're still waiting to hear from the parents about whether or not she had undergone surgery before her disappearance. Her hand was bandaged when we found her. I doubt the killer would have taken the time to patch her up before dumping her."

"No, you don't understand," Lawson said. "This was no surgery. The fingers were removed with a rusty hand saw. Like the kind you'd have hanging in your garage."

"How could you know that?" Hopkins asked.

"We recovered one of the teeth from the saw blade that broke off and embedded itself in the remaining bone at the base of the pinky finger. It was heavily oxidized and extremely dull. Based on the size and shape of the fragment, and the mangled condition of the surrounding flesh, we believe it to be consistent with a hand saw."

"But the bandage?" Hopkins visualized the tightly wrapped appendage. It had been bandaged so well that it remained in place even after being submerged in the water for hours, possibly even days. The thought reminded him he hadn't asked the obvious question. "Do you have a time of death?"

"Our best guess, about twelve hours before you found her."

"Twelve hours. That puts—"

"Knock, knock," Charlie Fuller said from just outside the office. "I'm sorry, don't mean to interrupt."

"It's fine, Charlie, come in," Hopkins said. "This is an old friend, Emmanuel Lawson. He's with the ME's office."

"Good to meet ya." Fuller took a seat in the empty chair next to Lawson.

"How did it go? How's the family doing?" Hopkins cringed at the absurdity of his own question. They had just learned that their daughter was sadistically tortured and murdered. It was safe to assume they'd been better.

"Not good." Fuller said. "Ended up having to call an ambulance for the mother. She vomited and passed out. Now she's on suicide watch at Newport Hospital."

"Were you able to get a statement?" Hopkins said.

"Yes. The husband was pretty helpful. He answered questions for a while. North Kingstown took the statement. A Detective Knapp. She said she'd email it to us when she got back to the office."

"Did he say anything about Misty being in Jamestown the day she disappeared?" Hopkins asked.

"No. Apparently, she went to the beach in Narragansett with a group of friends. Knapp said she already spoke to the friends after Misty went missing. It sounds like they went down in a few cars but didn't leave at the same time. When the friend who drove Misty couldn't find her, she assumed Misty jumped in with another friend. It wasn't until later they realized she hadn't come back with them. I'm guessing she was dumped right there in Narragansett."

"Maybe," Hopkins said, "but doesn't it seem unlikely that she'd end up in the bay?"

"I'd say that seals it, Tom," Lawson said. "If she was never in Jamestown, it's off your plate."

"I didn't say that," Fuller said. "I mean, I didn't say she was never in Jamestown. In fact, she came often. She was seeing a psychologist here. Walton is his name. He has an office on Southwest Ave and, according to the father, one in Newport as well. What are the chances, right? Can't be a coincidence."

"What?" Hopkins said. "That she was seeing a psychologist on the island? She clearly wasn't seeing him that day if she was going to the beach with her friends."

"No, not that." Fuller said. "Did you read Zoe's parents' statement? Zoe was seeing the same doctor. Doctor Walton. It's what we were looking for, right? A connection?"

It was exactly what they were looking for. Something. Anything to dig their teeth into. But this was more than a breadcrumb. This was big.

"I could kiss you right now," Hopkins said, prompting Fuller to flash a proud smile. "Tell me Lucy was seeing him too."

"That I don't know," Fuller said. "It didn't come up. But I can find out."

"Don't worry about it," Hopkins said. "I'll speak with Lucy's family. I want you to take a couple of guys and bring me Walton. You might have just broken this thing wide open."

Fuller stood up. "On it." He left the room.

"Good kid," Hopkins said.

"Seems like it," Lawson agreed. "Wanna grab some lunch before I head back? Catch up a bit?"

"Maybe next time." Hopkins gathered the paperwork and shoved it into a manila folder. He stood up and tapped the spine of the folder on the desk. "Right now, I've got a murder to solve."

14

MONDAY, JUNE 1ST. MORNING

Blake passed the Herbie's Window Tint shop and then turned right onto the next side street. It was a dead end, just as Goldilocks had described.

Tiny houses on postage stamp sized lots lined the street. On his left was a one-story home with a small side yard bordered by a chain link fence. Blake counted at least five doghouses in the yard but didn't see any dogs.

Chain link seemed the motif on this block. Almost every property had a stretch of it, although most of the fences had missing sections or were falling over in disrepair.

Just past a brown three-family unit, Blake found what he was searching for. An old three car garage, its flat roof only eight feet off the ground. The branches of the trees growing behind and beside it swallowed the stand-alone building, but the three doors, each a different color, were still visible. Goldilocks had said he couldn't miss it, and he was right.

It meant the house across the street, the little white Cape Cod with the peeling paint and crumbling driveway, was his ultimate destination. Inside, he'd find Lucy, or he'd find answers. Either way, if the look of the place was any indication, he was likely to find trouble.

Blake pulled over in front of the garages, shut the car off, and stepped out.

The neighborhood was quiet. Quieter than its appearance would suggest. Although, it was a Monday morning, so most of the residents had probably already left for work.

Blake crossed the street and passed through the open chain link gate. He climbed the single step to the concrete landing in front of the front door. The windows were dark, but the door was cracked a few inches. He knocked.

"Hello, anyone home?" he said.

There was no answer.

Blake pushed the door open.

In front of him was a dark hallway that led to a kitchen. Blake could see sunlight streaming through the kitchen windows at the back of the house. The linoleum floor of the hallway was filthy. Filthier still was a set of wooden steps to his right, leading to a second floor.

On the left was an arched doorway. There were no doors, but a blanket had been hung to block off the space behind it. Cockroaches scurried off the dark colored fabric and onto the cracking plaster wall.

"Hello?" Blake stepped inside.

Again, no response.

Blake took two more steps, slid his hand between the drywall and the blanket, and pushed the makeshift curtain to the side. He peeked in.

The room was dark, thanks to several more blankets nailed above the three windows. The smell was a combination of body odor and the liquid that collects at the bottom of a dumpster.

The odor was unpleasant, but it wasn't the pungent sulfur smell that comes along with decaying flesh. Blake was hopeful it meant that the four bodies, strewn about the floor, were merely sleeping.

Blake ducked by the curtain, taking care to not let it touch his head, walked to one of the windows and yanked on the blanket. It tore free, flooding the room with daylight. None of the occupants moved.

The floor was littered with empty bottles, fast food wrappers, and a myriad of other trash. Intermingled throughout were at least a dozen used syringes, although Blake suspected there were more buried under the sleeping bags and the rest of the rubbish.

It would require him to pay extra attention to his surroundings. Being stuck with a dirty needle was a sure-fire way to pick up any number of nasty pathogens, including Hepatitis and HIV.

About fifteen years prior, Blake had been involved in a raid on a residence in Kabul. While searching one of the detainees, he was pricked by an uncapped syringe. The detainee was tested for blood borne diseases. Even though the results of the tests were negative, Blake had to take a cocktail of prophylactic drugs that did a number on his digestive system. It was the last time he blindly stuck his hand into anyone's pocket.

There were two females and two males, sound asleep. Both females had long hair. By the looks of them, they had been living in squalor for some time.

Blake crouched next to one of the males. His buzzed brown hair was about an eighth of an inch long, except for a two-inch bald patch on the side of his head.

Christa had described Owen as having short hair and a bit of thin facial hair. Both males in the room could have fit that description.

Blake shook the first kid's shoulder. "Hey, wake up."

The kid stirred. His eyelids parted.

"Owen?" Blake said.

The kid lifted himself onto his elbow. "Over there." He dropped back to the floor and closed his eyes.

Blake moved to the second male and shook him.

"Owen?"

The kid's eyes snapped open wide. He scrambled to his feet and backed himself up against the wall. He was almost as tall as Blake, but probably weighed half as much.

"Who are you?" the kid said. His voice cracked and wavered as if there were a frog in his throat.

Blake spoke slowly and with a stern tone. "Are you Owen?"

"Yeah, man. I'm Owen. Who are you and whatta you want?"

"I'm a friend of Lucy's. I need to speak with her."

"That stupid bitch?" Owen said. "She ain't here, man. She's probably off readin' a book or some shit. I don't mess with her no more."

Blake stepped forward and grabbed Owen by the chin with his left hand. He squeezed his thumb into one side of his face and his fingers into the other. Blake could feel his teeth through his thin flesh. His lips were forced to purse.

"Tell me where I can find her."

"I don't know, man," Owen said. "I dumped her ass. She was a shitty lay, and she got all preachy and shit."

Blake cocked his right fist.

"I don't know what you want me to tell you. I haven't seen her in, like, a minute, man. Lily's my bitch now. She's right there. Wake her up and ask her."

Blake let go of Owen's face and took a step backward. He looked around. Despite the commotion, the other three junkies weren't even stirring. "If I find out you hurt her in any way—"

"I never touched her, I swear. I mean, I *touched* her, but I never hit her or nothin.'"

The sound of footsteps came first, then the excitable voice. Blake turned around just in time to watch the kid finish delivering his line.

"Don't move asshole," he said.

Wearing nothing but a pair of shorts and a bandana around his forehead, he was a walking canvas. Tattoos covered his neck, torso, arms, and legs. There was something written across his chest in blackletter font, but it was difficult to read as it rippled across his emaciated ribs. Blake surmised it said "Loyalty."

But it wasn't the ink that stood out. It was the revolver that Mr. Loyalty was pointing in Blake's general direction.

"You gotta lotta guts comin' up in here," he said.

Blake glanced at the cylinder. The copper jackets of the rounds were visible. The gun was loaded, there was no doubt about that. Blake was sure the old Smith and Wesson was fully capable of delivering a fatal blow. It was the capability of the operator Blake questioned.

Mr. Loyalty held the weapon canted at a ninety-degree angle. And worse than that, he held it above eye level. He was making a show of it, but it was clear he had no training or discipline. It was all Blake needed to know.

"I don't want any trouble." Blake raised his arms, bending his elbows and letting his hands drift out in front of him. The posture was intended to appear non-threatening, but Blake was actually preparing to strike.

"I'll bust a cap in your face, homey. Pow!" He dipped the revolver toward Blake's forehead.

Blake pivoted to the right, slapped Mr. Loyalty's wrist upward with his right hand and twisted the revolver free with his left. Holding the firearm by its frame, Blake drove the handle into Mr. Loyalty's face. It caught him in the crevice between his right eye and the bridge of his nose. He dropped to his knees.

"Damn, homey," he said.

Blake tossed the revolver from his left hand to his right and stretched it out in front of him. He moved past Mr. Loyalty and travelled down the hallway and into the kitchen. It was empty.

Blake checked the basement. The closets. The bathroom. Then moved on to clearing the upstairs bedrooms.

There was no one else in the house. There was no Lucy.

Blake returned to find Owen and Mr. Loyalty almost exactly where he left them. He lifted the revolver until the barrel hovered between Owen's eyes.

"If you ever try to contact Lucy again, I will come for you. If I find out you've lied to me, I will come for you. If I so much as hear your name again, I will come for you. Is that clear?"

Owen lifted his hands. It was like the gesture Blake had made a few minutes before except, in Owen's case, it legitimately signaled surrender. "I ain't gonna mess wit'er, man. Never again."

Blake turned and walked away. He moved through the roach-infested drapes, over the filthy linoleum and between the chain link gates. As he reached his rental, he stopped, flicked open the cylinder, and emptied the six live rounds into his hand.

He looked around. Noticing a storm drain along the curb about twenty feet away, he walked over and tossed the gun and bullets into the gap at the back of the steel grate.

Returning to his car, Blake couldn't help but worry. Owen had been telling the truth. He could see it in his eyes.

It was the worst-case scenario. The thing that neither Christa nor Gwyn had been able to even consider. Lucy hadn't run away. She was in real danger. And no matter the consequences, he would do whatever he could to make it right. If it wasn't already too late.

15

MONDAY, JUNE 1ST. AFTERNOON

ZOE GRASPED THE IRON BARS AND THREW HER BODY WEIGHT FORWARD AND back. The gate rattled but didn't move more than a fraction of an inch.

She had spent the past several hours pacing and plotting. She no longer felt like a teenage girl. No longer cared about the things she had a day prior. A primal feeling bubbled inside her. She was a caged animal. A rabid dog.

Getting her fear in check was the first step. The more she suppressed it, the clearer she could think. And the stronger her resolve.

Zoe figured it to be midday. The light carried a warmth that hadn't been there while the doctor was present and, although she had no way to keep track of time, she was sure at least six or seven hours had passed.

Shortly after the doctor left, she thought she heard the faint sound of a boat motor receding in the distance. She imagined the surroundings outside of the underground cell.

After she was abducted, she was transported by boat. The doctor seemed to have left the same way. *Was a section of the fort only accessible by water?* If that was the case, it was unlikely that anyone would happen by. The shores around Fort Wetherill were rocky and treacherous. And while the steep shoreline was accessible by land, it was off the beaten path. The chances of someone venturing into the dense brush and exploring the craggy coves were slim.

Then again, she thought, maybe she was smack-dab in the middle of the Fort Getty campground. Hidden in plain sight. She imagined campers tending to their fires. Children playing a game of tag only feet away.

There was no doubt she'd arrived by boat, but how far was she carried after they landed? No matter how hard she tried, she couldn't recall.

No. She was confident she had heard the boat motor when the doctor left. And she hadn't heard it since. The sounds of the ocean reverberated against the smooth walls. They were close to the water. Very close.

If they listened intently, they would be warned of someone's arrival. They could prepare themselves. To do what, she didn't know. At least not yet.

For a moment, Zoe hoped their captors wouldn't return at all. Maybe they would be arrested or would simply move on. Zoe physically shuddered at the thought. The doctor had left three bottles of water and hers was already more than half gone. *How many days could they survive without more? Two? Three?* As awful as both men were, they were the lesser of two evils. Being stranded, locked in a cage, meant certain death.

She had to assume they were completely alone. So they could talk to each other. They could put their heads together. She crouched down next to the blonde-haired girl.

"They're gone," Zoe said. "We're alone."

The blonde-haired girl turned her head away.

"Just tell me something. You don't have to speak, just nod. Do they always come at the same time? Late at night or early in the morning?"

The blonde-haired girl's head hesitantly nodded up and down.

It occurred to Zoe that their captors may have been trying to avoid detection by avoiding times when they might be spotted by other people. If there was a predictable pattern, they might be able to use it to their advantage.

"Have they ever shown up in the daytime?" Zoe asked.

The blond-haired girl shook her head.

"They're not here," Zoe repeated. "We can speak. No one can hear us. You have to trust me."

Zoe looked to the other corner. The short haired girl had perked up. Her eyes were brighter. More focused.

"Look," Zoe said. She put her face to the bars and yelled at the top of her lungs. "Hey! Assholes! Can you hear me?"

As the echo of her own voice dampened, nothing but the sound of lapping waves filled the space.

"See," Zoe said. She turned back to the blonde-haired girl. "I'm Zoe. What's your name?"

The girl's dry, cracked lips parted. "Leigh."

"Leigh. Okay. How long have you been here, Leigh?"

"Five days, I think."

"How about you?" Zoe turned to the short haired girl. "What's your name?"

"Lucy."

"Wait," Zoe said. "I know you. From school. You were two years behind me."

"I remember you," Lucy said.

Zoe turned to Leigh. "Are you from Jamestown too?"

"No. I'm from Connecticut. I go to URI."

"How old are you?" Zoe said.

"I'll be nineteen in August."

Lucy burst into tears. "I want to go to college. I want to get my license. I want to see my parents again."

Zoe hobbled over to Lucy on her knees and wrapped her arms around her. "We're all going to see our families soon. They're out there looking for us. They'll find us."

"I don't think my parents are looking for me," Leigh said. Her face was devoid of expression. "I have an apartment off-campus. I decided to stay for the summer. They probably don't even know I'm missing."

Lucy sniffled. "Mine probably don't want to find me."

"Stop that," Zoe said. "I bet they're freaking out right now. I know mine are. And I'm sure Leigh's family is looking by now, too."

"I was so nasty to them." Lucy broke down again. Mucus dripped from her nostrils and onto her lips.

"You've got to stop crying," Zoe said. "You're going to get more dehydrated."

Lucy wiped her eyes. "All the kids would make fun of me because I have two moms. I guess I was just mad. Like, why did they have to be gay? The worst thing is that I never told them that. I never told them so many things. I wish I could hug them and tell them I love them and that I'm sorry for being such a jerk."

"The most important thing we can do right now is have faith," Zoe said. "We are going to get out of here. We're going to survive. And then we can fix whatever regrets we have. But we can't just roll over and wait to die. We have to do something."

"There's nothing to do," Leigh said. "We're going to die in here. You might as well admit it to yourself."

"She's right," Lucy said. "Just like the other girl."

"What other girl?" Zoe said.

"When I got here, there was another girl," Leigh said. "I tried talking to her, just like you. But she wouldn't speak to me. I didn't know why until he caught me trying to talk to her. I remember him going to get the key and then unlocking the gate. He beat me bad. It was the most pain I ever felt in my life. The next thing I knew, it was daytime, and he was gone. I have no idea how long I was unconscious for."

"I'm sorry," Zoe said. What else could she say? She had also been brutalized at the hands of the Captain. She had experienced his frightening strength. But it was better not to dwell on past trauma. They were making progress, and the last thing Zoe wanted was for her two companions to clam up again. "What happened to the other girl?"

"She was here for a few days after I got here. She had a bad injury to her hand. I don't know what happened to her, but every morning, during the morning session or whatever, her bandages were changed. Then, one night after Lucy showed up, she was taken out. I knew as soon as I saw the flashlight and that stupid Captain's hat come around the corner, it was going to be bad. And it was. She never came back. He killed her just like he's going to kill us. Now you're here. I'm the next to go."

"You don't know that," Zoe said. "Maybe they let her go because she was too badly injured or something. Maybe she's being held somewhere else."

"If she got away," Leigh said, "wouldn't she tell someone where we are? Wouldn't she have gone to the police?"

Zoe didn't have a response. As much as she didn't want to admit it, Leigh was right. She changed the subject.

"We need to figure out what they want with us. We must have something in common. Some reason we're all here. What was this stuff the Doctor was saying about trying to cure us? Does he think we're all sick? Does he know something we don't? It makes no sense. It's like they know us. Or we're supposed to know them. Have either of you ever seen them before?"

"All the time," Lucy said. "Haven't you?"

"I don't think so, no. I mean, I wasn't able to get a good look at the Captain, but the Doctor didn't look familiar. Do you really know them? From where?"

Lucy and Leigh looked at each other. Both of their eyes widened as if sharing a telepathic moment of shock.

"You haven't seen the Captain's face?" Lucy said.

Zoe looked at Lucy. Then at Leigh. Then back at Lucy. "No, why?"

Leigh spoke first.

"There's something you should know."

16

MONDAY, JUNE 1ST. LATE AFTERNOON

BLAKE PULLED UP TO THE HOUSE. CHRISTA'S CAR WASN'T IN THE DRIVEWAY. Neither was Gwyn's for that matter, but that was no surprise. It was just as well. He wasn't looking forward to breaking the news that Lucy wasn't with Owen. Their absence would give him a little extra time before he would have to deal with it.

As he rolled along the gravel, Blake noticed Lucas standing in his usual spot. Blake waved, but Lucas didn't notice. He was engrossed in his wristwatch.

Blake got out and approached his new friend.

"Hi, Lucas."

Lucas looked up from the display.

"Hi, Mr. Blake. It's time for my walk." He directed his attention back to the display.

"I like to walk, too," Blake said. "Do you mind if I come with you?"

"Yeah."

Blake wasn't sure how to take the response. In Lucas's dialect, there were so many meanings to the word.

"Yeah, you mind? Or yeah, I can come with you?"

"You can come with me. Sheffield's cove. Nineteen seconds."

"Okay then," Blake said. "I'm ready."

Blake walked around the hedgerow and joined Lucas on his lawn. He hadn't noticed if the old woman was watching from the window. Now, he had no line of sight to the second-floor window where she usually planted herself. He preferred it that way. As ridiculous as it was, he wanted to avoid the visual scolding he would have received.

Without any verbal warning, Lucas dropped his arm and started walking.

The term *walking* was a bit of a misnomer. It was more of a shuffle. With the heel of each foot barely clearing the toe of the other. Blake kept pace but had to limit his steps to the point that he felt like he was mimicking a slow-motion movie sequence.

"I haven't gotten a chance to explore much," Blake said. "I'm looking forward to seeing this Sheffield's cove."

Lucas left the grass and stepped into the side street that ran along his property. He crossed to the right side of the road.

"Me too," Lucas said. "I like to walk."

Blake had to admit, it was nice to take a walk. And Lucas was good company.

They strolled in silence for a couple of minutes. As they reached the end of the street, the tall grass of a salt marsh was visible in front of them. Beyond that was a narrow body of water. Blake assumed it was Sheffield's cove.

"Now we go this way." Lucas turned right onto a dirt road that ran along the marsh. Blake followed.

The dirt road ended at a small beach, maybe ten feet wide. Blake could see why it attracted Lucas. It was gorgeous.

To the left was the body of the cove. The water was still. Sandbars protruded from the center of the saltwater pond. Ahead, across the water, was a lush, uninhabited landscape. Large bird's nests had been built atop tall man-made posts. To the right, the pier of the West Ferry and the outhauls along its edge were visible. From that angle, the low sun glimmered off the water between the moored boats of Dutch Harbor like a picture on a postcard.

"This is beautiful, Lucas. Thank you for showing it to me."

"Yeah. This is beautiful." Lucas looked at his watch, then gazed out toward the west.

Blake did the same, letting his mind wander. He thought of Haeli and how much she would have liked it there. In this moment of quiet, this serene setting, Blake realized for the first time since he arrived that he missed her. It wasn't Anja that permeated his thoughts, it was Haeli. He longed for her, the intensity of which took him by surprise.

Blake felt the urge to call her. To share the moment with her, even if it were by voice alone. But he was there for Lucas, and it would have been rude. He would call her when he got back to the house.

Lucas remained still, staring into the distance. Blake wondered what he was thinking about. What went on inside his head? Was it all numbers and figures? Deep existential pondering? Or was he simply punching the clock?

The pressure of the silence began to weigh on Blake. He felt the need to say something. Luckily, Lucas beat him to it.

"I like you Mr. Blake. You're my friend."

"I like you too, Lucas. And you're right, I am your friend."

"Do you live here now?" Lucas said.

"No, I'm still just visiting. I'm here to help with something, then I have to leave."

It was something Blake hadn't thought of before. By befriending Lucas, he may have been causing more harm than good. If he became attached, would he understand when Blake had to leave? Would he feel deserted?

Lucas looked at his watch, then turned and began shuffling away from the beach. Blake took an extra-long step to catch up with him.

"What are you helping with?" Lucas asked.

"I'm helping find something that's lost."

"Are you finding the girls that were stolen? Like Lucy?" Lucas said.

Wait, what?

Blake couldn't believe what he just heard. Did Lucas just say what he thought he said?

It wasn't just that Lucas knew Lucy was missing. It wasn't even that he seemed to know there was more than one. It was the fact that he used the word 'stolen.' What did he know and how in the world would he know it?

"Lucas, stop." Blake reached out and touched Lucas's arm.

Lucas stopped and faced him.

"We're going to be late." Lucas said.

"Listen to me. I'm your friend, right?" Blake said.

"Yeah."

"I need you to tell me how you know girls were stolen."

Lucas laughed loudly. "That's easy."

"Good. Then you can tell me?"

"My doctor told me," Lucas said. "He said the girls were mean and bad, and that's why they were stolen."

"Your doctor told you this?" Blake said.

"He said they do sex with boys. And that's bad."

"Okay, Lucas, this is very important." Blake looked Lucas in the eye and waited until Lucas's irises snapped toward his. "What is your doctor's name?"

"Doctor John."

"Good," Blake leaned in. "What's his last name? Doctor John what?"

"Doctor John." Lucas said. "He's nice, he helps me with my conditions."

"Is Doctor John the one you go to see in Newport?"

"Yeah."

"Do you remember where his office is?"

"Yeah."

"Where?"

Blake held his breath. If Lucas could tell him where to find this Doctor, it could mean finding Lucy. At the same time, how much faith could he put in Lucas's recollection of a conversation? It was possible that the doctor was talking about something else entirely. Or he had heard about the missing person cases and was spouting off some misguided conjecture, not considering that Lucas soaked it up. Whatever the case, he was so desperate to find a lead, he was willing to try anything.

"Lucas, where?"

"I go straight and right and right," Lucas said. "Then on the brown stairs. Then count five doors."

"Do you know what street?" Blake asked.

Lucas shook his head. "He's not on the street."

Blake reminded himself not to get frustrated. Lucas was trying. But Blake needed a different tactic. "You go every Tuesday and Thursday, right? So, you'll see him tomorrow?"

"Yeah."

"Can I go with you?" Blake said.

"No." Lucas answered. "Doctor John wouldn't like it if I brought a friend. He says it's private talking."

"Maybe he wouldn't mind," Blake pressed.

"No. No. No." Lucas closed his eyes. His voice rose in volume and pitch. "Doctor John will be mad at me."

"It's okay, Lucas. I won't come with you. I don't want Doctor John to be mad at you."

Lucas opened his eyes and settled down. "Here they come." He pointed over Blake's shoulder.

Two teenage boys on bicycles skidded around the corner, leaving a dust cloud over the dirt road. They slowed as they were about to pass. One boy hollered to the other.

"Hey, look, it's the retard."

The other boy answered back. "Don't get too close, you'll catch it," he laughed.

Blake stepped into the road and motioned to the two boys.

"Come here," Blake said. He pointed to the roadway in front of him.

The boys stopped their bikes ten feet short of Blake. Their mouths hung open. It was the look of someone who knew they were in trouble but were still holding onto hope that they could play dumb to weasel their way out of it.

Blake put his hands in his pockets and sauntered toward them.

"Now, is that the way to treat another person? Don't you think you owe this man an apology?" Blake said.

The boys looked at each other. One mustered the courage to speak.

"Who are you, his bodyguard?" the kid said.

Blake had to hand it to them. The kids around this town had no fear. Probably because they had nothing they needed to fear. Until now.

Blake walked between the two boys, who still straddled their bicycles, and pivoted so that he stood behind them. He wrapped a hand around the back of each of the boys' necks and pushed them together until their heads were an inch apart.

"Get off me," the mouthy boy said. "You can't touch us."

Blake leaned in between them and spoke. Soft enough that Lucas wouldn't be able to hear.

His message delivered, he let go. Their heads sprung apart under their own tension.

The two boys looked at each other in a nonverbal exchange of resignation. Then they pushed their bikes toward Lucas with their feet.

"I'm sorry," one said.

"We didn't mean anything by it," the other added.

"Are we cool?" the first asked.

"Yeah," Lucas said.

The boys looked back at Blake. Blake nodded. They stepped onto the pedals and pumped as hard as they could. And then, they were gone.

"We are cool," Lucas said with a giant, heartwarming smile.

"Yeah, we are," Blake said. "Whattaya say we walk?"

"Yeah," Lucas said as he started to shuffle along the pavement. "We are cool."

17

MONDAY, JUNE 1ST. EARLY EVENING

THE DOCTOR HOOKED THE HANGER TO THE TOWEL RACK AND RAN HIS HANDS down the polyester button-down to smooth out any remaining wrinkles.

He tugged on the mirror, swinging it open to reveal the medicine cabinet. He selected the small plastic container and swung the mirror closed.

As his face came back into view, he examined it. The lines on his forehead had grown deeper every day, he thought.

He tilted his head to try to get a glimpse of any hairs that may have been growing from his nostrils. There was one.

That wouldn't do. Not at all.

He pinched the single protruding hair between his thumbnail and index finger and yanked, extracting it by the root. The sensation made his eyes water. It felt good.

It's true that he always tried to look his best. Especially when going to work. But these were special times indeed. He was on the verge of a breakthrough. A medical marvel that would validate his genius once and for all. Its importance could not be overstated.

Equally important, in his estimation, was good oral hygiene. Healthy gums were a sign of a successful man.

He flipped the lid of the plastic box and unspooled a foot worth of floss. He wrapped each end through his fingers until only two inches of the waxy twine spanned between them. Pushing his thumbs against his top lip, he exposed his teeth to the mirror. He turned his head from side to side, admiring them.

A flash of movement in the mirror caught his eye. Startled, the Doctor spun around.

The Captain. I should have known.

"What are you doing here?" he said. "I'm not dressed."

"I hope you're not avoiding me," the Captain replied.

The Doctor was avoiding him. He was hoping, just once, he'd be left alone long enough to focus on his work without having to deal with the Captain's irrational mood swings and idiotic ideas.

The Captain would say that the Doctor needed him, and he wouldn't have been wrong. But it didn't change the fact that the man was more often a hindrance than help.

"That's preposterous," the Doctor said. "I'm not avoiding you. I'm running late. And you're not helping matters."

"Well, get on with it then." The Captain crossed his arms and waited.

"I can't floss with you watching. Wait outside, I'll be right out."

"So you can sneak out the window?" the Captain said. "I don't think so. You and I both know what today is."

"It's too soon. I've barely started."

"You agreed," the Captain said. "You know they all have to be disposed of. You gave your word that I can have her, and you wouldn't throw a tantrum."

The truth was, he had agreed, if only to appease the Captain. But that was days ago, and time had moved too fast. It seemed a shame to waste a perfectly good subject. On top of it, it would only mean that they'd have to recruit another to replace her.

"Give me a couple more days," he said.

"No," the Captain snarled. "You're wasting your time. And mine. They're not fixable. They're damaged goods and you know it. It disgusts me that I even have to deal with them. Just like you disgust me."

"You're wrong about them," the Doctor said. "Whatever you think of me, they can be saved. I can prove it to you if you'd give me the chance.

Look at the last one. We were making such great progress. She was on her way to being cured. But you took her anyway. Why?"

"Listen to yourself. What does it matter? We can't keep them. Even if you could fix the little sluts."

"Then why bother recruiting them at all?" the Doctor asked.

It was an honest question. It hardly seemed worth the trouble if he was just going to turn around and complain about the whole endeavor, day after day.

"To teach them a lesson," the Captain said. "Simple as that. Not to keep them as pets."

"They're not pets." The Doctor increased his volume. "They're patients."

"You'd better remember who you're talking to. Raise your voice to me again and I'll put your head through that mirror. Got it?"

The Doctor didn't respond.

"You wanna know the truth?" the Captain asked. "You're delusional. That girl admits she touched herself and you think cutting her fingers off is going to fix her. As if that's going to make her pure. Any less of a whore. It's a load of crap."

"It isn't! You don't understand the process. The minor amputation was only the first step. To stop it from spreading. There was more work to be done."

"Either way, tonight I'm taking the one you promised me," the Captain said.

"I won't let you." The Doctor had intended for the words to be assertive, but they came out as little more than a whisper.

"What did you say to me?"

He cleared his throat. "I said I won't let you."

In an instant, the Doctor felt the intense pressure of the Captain's grip on his throat.

"I'll kill you," the Captain said. His voice was strained and raspy.

The Doctor gasped for air through his compressed trachea. With his left hand, he clawed at the Captain's right. It would not budge.

The room began to undulate. Specks of light floated in front of his eyes. In the end, one hand was all it was going to take for the Captain to put an end to him. It was frightening and, in a way, awe-inspiring.

The world darkened and the Doctor began to slip into oblivion. The Captain squeezed harder.

Then he let go.

The Doctor collapsed to the floor and filled his lungs with the dry air. It felt cool, yet it burned at the same time. The tingle sent him into a coughing fit.

Once he regained his composure, the Doctor silently stood up and faced the mirror. He drew out a length of dental floss, then paused and closed his eyes.

"Fine. You can have her."

18

MONDAY, JUNE 1ST. EVENING

BLAKE CLOSED HIS LAPTOP AND STOOD UP FROM THE EDGE OF THE PULLOUT bed. He slid the computer into his bag and smoothed out the comforter.

The smell of garlic wafted in from beyond the closed door. His stomach grumbled. It was the first time he'd noticed hunger since he arrived.

As expected, the Rhode Island Department of Health database wasn't much help. A query revealed hundreds of licensed physicians and medical professionals with the first name of John. Narrowing it down to only psychology-related fields, and again to those within Newport, he still received a dozen hits, not including Jonathans, or any other variation of the name.

The only reason Blake assumed Lucas's doctor was a psychiatrist, psycologist, or other type of clinician that deals with purely cognitive disorders, was the frequency of Lucas's visits. Blake couldn't see a scenario where a neurologist or any other type of physician would require bi-weekly consultation. On top of that, Lucas seemed physically well.

The database was a start, but looking into each possible hit would be time consuming. If nothing else, the search validated his original idea as the best course of action.

Blake opened the door. A wall of luscious aromas engulfed his senses and compelled him toward the kitchen.

Both Christa and Gwyn toiled away at what was no doubt going to be an amazing meal.

Christa was standing at a cutting board, chopping a cucumber. She tossed the resulting slices into a large bowl of leafy greens.

Gwyn was at the stove. Hair pulled back and a bandana tied around her forehead, she juggled several pans over the flames of the gas range. She moved with dexterity and finesse, as if she were practicing martial arts.

"Smells delicious," Blake said.

He stood just outside the kitchen, in the attached dining room. The small kitchen already seemed crowded enough with just the two of them.

"I hope you're hungry," Gwyn said.

"One of the benefits of being married to a culinary master," Christa joked. "Just don't get in her way."

"Tell me you're not doing all of this on my account," Blake said.

"Not at all," Gwyn replied.

He knew she was. And he appreciated the gesture. But, more importantly, it was nice to see them taking their minds off their missing daughter for a moment. After he had filled them in about his encounter with Owen, the mood turned bleak.

Blake understood. Knowing now it was unlikely that Lucy had run away voluntarily, it was difficult to maintain a positive outlook. Visualizing a scenario where Lucy was returned to her family unscathed was harder still. It would take a mountain of blind faith.

Blake knew he would bear the brunt if that faith turned out to be misguided. And he had come to terms with it. He'd gladly accept the blame if it would prevent Christa or Gwyn from putting it on themselves.

As much as he didn't want to spoil the relatively stable moment, he needed to ask the question that had monopolized his thoughts for the past several hours. Consequences be damned.

"Can I ask you a personal question? About Lucy." Blake said.

"Of course," Gwyn said without hesitation, "we have no secrets."

Everyone has secrets.

"Was she seeing a doctor, by any chance? A psycologist, maybe? Anything like that?"

"No," Christa said. "There was a social worker involved, during the adoption process. But not since then. Lucy isn't mentally ill. She's going through a phase."

"You always do that," Gwyn said. "Downplaying everything. Maybe we should have taken her to see someone. Maybe she'd still be here if we had." She shook the pan. The hot oil flamed and sizzled.

"She didn't run away, Gwyn," Christa said. "Why can't you get that through your head?" She dropped the knife on the cutting board, stormed into the bathroom, and slammed the door.

It seemed that no matter how many times he received the lesson, Blake still hadn't learned when to shut his mouth.

Gwyn pulled the pan off the flame and placed it on a cork pad. She picked up a towel and wiped her hands.

"Why do you ask?" she said.

"I was thinking there may be a connection between the missing girls. Grasping at straws, that's all. I'm sorry I brought it up."

"It's just that Chief Hopkins stopped by earlier and spoke with Christa. He asked the same question. Is there something we need to know?"

Interesting. What did Hopkins know?

Blake could have told her what Lucas said. But for what purpose? Lucy hadn't been seeing a doctor. And tomorrow, if all went well, Lucas would lead him straight to the one person who could answer any outstanding questions. One way or another.

He shrugged. "He's probably thinking the same thing as I was. Trying to find a connection. I'm sure if he had anything substantial, he would have told you."

"I guess you're right," Gwyn said, returning to her work.

"Can I do anything to help?" Blake asked.

"You can set the table," Gwyn said. "Plates are in that cabinet there. Silverware in the drawer next to the sink."

Blake collected three plates and stacked the glasses, forks, and knives on top. He carried them to the dining room and set the stack on the table.

His phone rang. Blake checked the screen.

Haeli.

"I'll be right back," Blake said as he touched the screen to answer the call.

"Haeli, hi."

"I saw you called," Haeli said. "I was in the pool."

"Nice. Still at the gym?" Blake pushed through the storm door and walked onto the front porch. The door slammed behind him.

"I'm almost done. I think I'll hit the treadmill for a few minutes. I did extra laps today, so I won't stay much longer."

Blake sat and kicked his feet up on the wicker table. "I've been thinking about you a lot."

"Have you now? I was beginning to think you fell off the earth. Haven't heard from you in two days. You didn't even answer my texts yesterday."

"I know," he said. "I was distracted with this whole thing. I'm sorry. I should've called."

"So, are you on your way back?" Haeli asked.

"Not yet. It turned out to be more involved than I thought."

"You haven't found the kid?"

"No, not yet. Her name is Lucy, by the way. You know how we thought she ran away with her boyfriend? She didn't. And now there are others missing."

"Have you talked to the police? What are they saying?"

"Briefly. They're looking into it. But it's a small department, and I'm not sure they have the resources or the experience." He lowered his voice. "Something's not right, Haeli. I think this situation is worse than anyone realizes."

"How small can the department be? I mean, Providence is a pretty big city, isn't it?"

"I'm not in Providence. I'm on a tiny island. Jamestown. It's right next to Newport. I'm staying with..."

It hadn't occurred to Blake that Haeli didn't yet know about Christa. It was a critical piece of information. One that he should have led with.

"Harrison?" Haeli said.

"No." Blake said. "As it turned out, the friend that Harrison wanted me to help was actually…"

"Spit it out," Haeli said. "Was actually who?"

"Anja's sister, Christa."

Blake waited for Haeli's reaction. There was nothing but dead air.

"I didn't know until I got here. They were worried that I wouldn't come if I knew."

"So, you're saying you're with Anja's sister. And the girl who's missing is Anja's niece."

Blake sighed. "Yes."

Again, silence.

"Are you all right?" Blake said.

"Me? Yes, why wouldn't I be?"

"I don't know. I thought you might be upset."

"I'm not upset. But I am a little worried. What happens if you don't find her? Or worse? Then what? Are you going to carry that on your shoulders, too?"

"I'll find her." Blake said. "And I know what you're thinking. This isn't about Anja. It isn't even entirely about Lucy. Not anymore. There's a predator out here. I can feel it. And I can't leave here until—I don't know. Until it's safe."

"I'm not your mother," Haeli said. "Do whatever you want. Just be careful."

"I'm always careful," Blake said. His attempt at humor went unnoticed. "And when this is all over, I want to bring you here. I think you'll love it."

"If you still feel that way when it's all done, it'll be a miracle."

She was right. With every minute that passed, the more of a miracle they would need. If the situation took a turn for the worse, the little town would be the last place any of them would want to be, ever again. But none of this was the reason he had called her.

"Anyway, I was just calling to let you know I was missing you," Blake said.

"It's only been a couple of days," Haeli said. "I'm sure you'll survive."

Blake chuckled. "How's the homestead?"

"The plants are still alive," Haeli said. "For the moment, anyway."

"Are you good?"

"I'm good." The tone of her voice was ambiguous.

"I'll call you tomorrow, okay?" Blake said.

"Okay, we'll talk tomorrow. And try to answer your texts."

"I will," Blake said. "Bye."

"Bye."

Blake returned inside to find the table set and the food already plated. Christa carried a bowl full of sliced Italian bread from the kitchen and placed it on the table.

"Sit, eat," she said. "Before it gets cold."

* * *

"You sure you don't want more dessert?" Gwyn asked. "Coffee?"

"No, thank you," Blake said. "That was fantastic. Where'd you learn how to cook like that?"

"Hyde Park," Gwyn said.

The blank look on Blake's face must have tipped her off that he had no idea what she was talking about.

"The Culinary Institute," Gwyn added.

"Oh." Blake said. "Of course."

Christa reached over and took Gwyn's hand. "There's nobody better."

"Oh stop," Gwyn said. "No, keep going." She laughed.

"Seriously," Christa said. "When it comes to restaurants, whatever Gwyn touches turns to gold. Look at 'Ohana. You wouldn't believe how many awards she's won."

"Just good luck," Gwyn said.

"And an insane work ethic," Christa said. "The first time I laid eyes on Gwyn was at one of her restaurants in Maryland. It was right after she'd opened the fourth location. I remember watching her coming in and out of the kitchen, checking on guests, answering the phone, directing the staff. She was everywhere. I remember thinking, this woman's got a lot of energy. Even on our first date, she left in the middle of the movie to tend to some crisis. Do you remember that?"

"I do. The sous-chef up and quit in the middle of the dinner rush. I had to jump in."

"It paid off," Christa said. "All four restaurants were bought out by a major restaurant group."

"How did you end up here?" Blake said.

"Honestly, once I sold, I never thought I'd get back into the business. I figured we'd travel and enjoy an early retirement. But once we adopted Lucy, that all changed. An old acquaintance was retiring and looking to sell his restaurant in Newport. We thought it would be a great opportunity for Lucy. Small town upbringing. That kind of thing. We found this house. Christa was even able to find a job with the real estate agency in town. It all just kinda worked out."

"How long ago was that?" Blake said.

"Let's see, I opened the first restaurant in 2004, when I was twenty-five. The sale was in 2011. Christa and I had just gotten together. We got married in 2013. Pretty much the second it became legal."

"And then we got Lucy about a year later," Christa said.

"Thanks to Jannine," Gwyn added.

"Jannine?" The name didn't ring a bell for Blake.

"Jannine was a friend of mine growing up," Christa said. "She's a social worker in Baltimore. Or she was. I think she's a hairdresser now. Anyway, we happened to hook up on Facebook and she was telling me about her job. I mentioned Gwyn and I were thinking about adopting. She told me she just met the sweetest little girl named Lucy, who was a ward of the state and living in foster care after being removed from an abusive home."

Gwyn cut in. "Christa and I went to meet Lucy and instantly fell in love with her. She was eight years old at the time. Jannine wasn't exaggerating, Lucy was the sweetest little girl you'd ever wanna meet."

"And the rest was history," Blake said.

"Yep," Gwyn backed her chair out and stood up. "Came here in 2018 and you know the rest. Starts out as a happy story, doesn't it?"

"It's amazing what you two have accomplished," Blake said. "And what you did for Lucy. I'm sure she knows how lucky she is."

Gwyn grabbed her keys from the kitchen and walked back through the dining room toward the front of the house. "I've gotta go check on things at 'Ohana. I'll take a ride around on my way out, just in case." She hurried out the door.

"She does that when she gets anxious," Christa said. "Just up and leaves. She and I have been taking turns driving aimlessly around the island, hoping we'd somehow spot Lucy, as if she were just lost or something. I know how ridiculous it is, even while I'm doing it, but at least it feels like I'm doing something. I can't stand just sitting here while she's out there. I just don't know what I'm supposed to do."

"You need to stay strong. That's all you can do," Blake said.

"I can't lose her, Blake. I won't survive it." Her eyes glistened and her nose reddened. "Losing Anja almost killed me. I can't do it again."

"I know," Blake said. And he did. More than anyone.

"I think about it all the time. How those awful people killed her just for doing her job. How can such evil exist in this world?"

Blake felt the wave of guilt wash over him. What she didn't know, what no one knew, was that Anja's killers weren't there for her. They were there for him. Her fate was his fault. And it was something he had struggled with every day since.

"Lucy loved her so much. When we moved here, she came to visit a few times. She and Lucy would sit out on that porch and talk for hours. I never thought in a million years that I'd lose either of them. And now I'm afraid I've lost both."

"You've got to take your mind off it, thinking like that won't help anything." Blake grabbed his plate and stood up. "Here, let me clean this up. It's the least I can do."

"Wait," Christa said. "There's something I want to show you. Sit. I'll be right back."

Christa hurried around the corner. Blake could hear her feet pounding on the stairs. First up, then back down. She returned with a shoebox and set it on the table in front of Blake.

"What is it?" Blake asked.

"After the funeral, Gwyn and I went to Anja's townhouse to prepare for the estate auction. These are the few things I kept. Mostly pictures. Some trinkets. Open it."

Blake lifted the cover as if he were opening a rattlesnake cage. He reached in and pulled out a handful of pictures. He thumbed through them.

"These are incredible," Blake said. He held up a photo of two small blonde girls, sitting on the grass with their arms around each other. "Is this you?"

Christa took the picture and brought it close. She smiled. "Anja and me in Stuttgart. Anja was probably about six here."

Blake reached back into the box and pulled out a stack of folded papers. He separated one and unfolded it.

"My god," he said. "This is a letter I wrote her." He opened another. "Here's another one. I can't believe she saved these."

"I told you," Christa said. "I talked to her almost every day on the phone. She never got over you, Blake. When you came back into her life, it was like she was reborn."

"When I met Anja, she was visiting your parents in Stuttgart. After she returned to the States, and before I moved back, I wrote her a letter every week. I was such a cheese ball."

"I remember. She'd talk about it all week long. She was like a school-girl waiting for the mail to arrive."

"I'd love to read through them, if there's time."

"You can keep them," Christa said. "I've never read them. Wasn't my place. They're between you and her."

"Thank you," Blake said.

He set the letters aside and investigated the box. Amongst some random pieces of jewelry was a leather billfold. He retrieved it and opened it.

Inside was an ID card with Anja's picture on it and a gold shield that read *Federal Bureau of Investigation* and *Department of Justice*.

"Her credentials," Blake said. "How do you have these?"

"I found that in the laundry basket."

"I can't believe the Bureau didn't recover them," Blake said.

"They had already left before I found it," Christa said. "Was I not supposed to keep it?"

"Technically, no. But I'm glad you did. It gives me an idea."

"What?" Christa said.

"Do you happen to have a digital scanner?"

19

MONDAY, JUNE 1ST. NIGHT

THE CAPTAIN RAN THE BEAM OF THE FLASHLIGHT OVER ALONG THE WALL.

Where are you?

The chrome medallion would eventually reflect the light and make itself known. He had attached the shiny keychain several days earlier. It was a solution he only devised after enduring the frustration of a half-hour's worth of searching. The brass-colored key had blended into the graffiti covering the wall around the protruding piece of rebar from which the keyring hung. It wouldn't happen again.

The metal glinted. He snatched the key and pointed the light down the hallway. His excitement swelled. He could feel it in his loins.

As he neared the opening to the room, he paused and listened. Had they been talking to each other before he arrived? They were silent now. Of course, the clever little hussies would have seen the light well before he got close enough to hear their whisperings. The next time he would find his way in the dark.

Before turning the corner, he took a moment to picture their faces. The fear that would be written on them. His body vibrated with anticipation.

He inhaled, savoring the putrid odor that filled the dank chamber.

His temples pulsed against the rim of his hat.

Aside from when he slept, there wasn't a single moment he didn't wear it. The black and white lid served as a reminder of his authority. To everyone, including himself. This was his ship down here, just as much as his boat was. The Captain had the final say. The ultimate rule. Lest anyone forget it.

Mentally prepared, he turned the corner and shined the light through the bars.

All three girls sat slumped against the wall. Their eyes closed.

I know you're awake. All of you. Why do you play with me like this?

He inserted the key and swung the gate open. He walked to the blonde-haired girl and drove his toe into her rib cage. Her eyes sprung open.

There it is.

He stared into her eyes, soaking in the debilitating fear pinning them open and freezing every muscle in her body. It was a beautiful thing, fear. The driving force of all actions, or lack thereof. It was the reason the other two girls would sit quietly, pretending to sleep while peeking through parted lashes. If only he could capture it. Bottle it and save it for later.

But, in his experience, he knew that even this girl's fear would dissipate. Through fatigue, exhaustion, desensitization. It was an offering, put forward to protect the other senses. Given as a sacrifice, in the same way zinc anodes protects a ship. The zinc gives itself to the saltwater to protect the metals of the propeller, the rudders, and the rest. But eventually, when all the zinc has been eaten away, the sea gets what it wants.

Even now, as the young girl quaked and silently sulked, he could see her fear waning. If he looked deep enough into her wide eyes, behind the fear, he could see something else.

Lust.

Of course. It was in her nature after all. It was no surprise the filthy pig would come onto him. She couldn't help herself.

He grabbed her by the hair and pulled. Her limp body dragged across the floor.

"No, no, no," she cried.

The others remained still.

Once clear of the gate, he dropped her and directed the light to assist with the task of securing the padlock.

He shined the beam toward the hallway. "Walk."

The girl didn't move. Her upper body rested on her palms and stiff arms. Her legs laid overlapped behind her, like a mermaid sunning herself on the rocks. No, a siren. Trying to reel him in to her trap. To seduce him. To destroy him.

He grabbed her by the hair once again and dragged her into the hallway, parting the broken glass that littered the floor.

He moved quickly past the other rooms until he reached the last.

Shards of glass had embedded themselves into the girl's legs along the way, causing a grinding sound as he pulled. He lifted her to her feet and shoved her into the room. She stumbled and fell back to the floor.

The room was chosen for a reason. Although it looked the same as all the others, this one had a feature tailored for his purposes. Embedded in the floor and along the walls were iron plates. And on each plate was a thick iron ring.

When these forts were in operation, each iron fixture, track, and hinge had a practical use. But these functions were lost to history. Now, they would fulfill a new duty.

With the ropes already secured to the rings with a sturdy bowline hitch, he would only have to attach them to her wrists and ankles in such a way that the lines remained taut.

Last time, he had left too much slack, giving the girl too much range of motion. Not that it made much difference, but the constant squirming had become an annoyance.

"What are you gonna do to me?" she said.

He provided an answer. Not in words, but in action. It was easy enough. A quick swing of his leg told her all she needed to know.

He paused while she worked the loose teeth to the front of her mouth and spit them onto the floor. Blood and spit covered her chin. She cried.

It was the crying that he hated most. It was a plea for pity. The victim card. But she was no victim, and she knew it. She was a dirty whore and no amount of crying would change it.

He grabbed her by the shoulders and pinned her to the floor. He put his knee on her chest and let his weight settle through her delicate frame, toward the concrete below her.

He pulled the line tight and secured it to her right wrist. Instead of the fisherman's slipknot, this time he stuck with the bowline. He moved on to her right wrist and then each leg, ignoring the feeble protests and attempts to escape.

Once secure, he stood and held the light high, pointing the beam directly down on the splayed girl. No, she couldn't be saved. He stood by that. But in this moment, she transcended her former self. A literal five-point star, offering herself to him in atonement.

He placed the butt of the flashlight on the floor, pointing its beam at the ceiling. It provided enough ambient light to easily work.

The girl gurgled, then turned her head to spit a mouthful of blood.

"Please," she said. "Please."

From a leather pouch affixed to his belt, he pulled a folded knife with a teak wood handle. A useful tool when on the water, it never left his side.

He dropped on one knee and brought the point of the knife to her neck. She instinctively dropped her chin to protect her throat. He slid the blade under the neckline of the sundress and ran it downward, opening the fabric like a zipper and exposing her breasts and white cotton bikini underwear.

He ran the point along her abdomen with just enough pressure to scratch but not cut. Her supple nineteen-year-old skin depressed and then bounced back behind the blade. Her body shook as he slid the blade over her hip bone and under the thinnest section of fabric. He pulled, snapping the panties loose.

"Relax," he said. "I'll be gentle."

20

TUESDAY, JUNE 2ND. EARLY MORNING

THE CAPTAIN LEANED INTO THE THROTTLE. HE LIFTED HIS HAND AND DROVE the heel of his palm into the L-shaped handle. It didn't budge.

"It's at its maximum," the Doctor said. "You're going to break it if you keep pushing."

"You insisted we come all the way out here. It's getting late and we're moving way too slow. We should already be back by now."

The sun had broken the horizon and now illuminated the eastern side of the Beavertail lighthouse, about two miles behind. The Captain's concerns were legitimate. There'd be more traffic on the water as it got later. But once they got rid of their cargo, it would no longer be as much of an issue.

"You should be thanking me," he said. "Without me, you would have dumped her in the bay like you did the last time. And we know how that turned out."

The Captain didn't respond. He held the wheel steady, keeping the boat on a southwesterly course.

"Another mile," the Doctor said. "Then it should be safe."

"I'll decide where we'll do it. This is my vessel. My rules."

The Doctor wasn't so sure. The first time he'd accompanied the Captain, only two weeks prior, it was as if the man had never operated the boat in his life. He fiddled with the controls, flicking switches on and off to see what they did. Finally getting the motor started after five minutes of trying, he spent another ten minutes working out how to put it in reverse.

If he had to guess, he'd say the boat was stolen, or at least borrowed. Knowing the Captain, stolen seemed more likely.

"Did you bring something to weigh her down with like I told you to?" the Doctor asked.

"No need. By the time she pops up, she'll have been swept so far out to sea, no one will ever find her."

"That's what you said the last time. What if she's carried back toward shore?"

"She won't be. I know these currents like the back of my hand."

A gust of wind tore through the cockpit. The captain laid his hand on his head to prevent his hat from flying off.

"This should be far enough, then," the Doctor said.

The Captain disengaged the throttle and killed the motor. "It is. But not because you say it is. Help me bring her up."

"I'm not helping you with anything. This is your problem. I'm only here to make sure you don't get us caught."

The Captain slid the hatch board from the companionway and stepped down. He grabbed the girl's ankles, dragged her to the base of the ladder and propped her feet against its rungs.

He climbed onto the deck, then reached down, wrapped his hands around her ankles and hoisted her body topside.

"The bitch is heavier than she looks."

"Her name is Leigh," the Doctor said. "Not that you'd ever cared to ask."

"What do I care what her name was?" He motioned toward Leigh's mangled corpse. "You want to do the honors?"

He didn't.

The Captain squatted down, slid his arms under her and lifted. Leigh's head hung heavily from her fragile neck. Then, without further ceremony, he tossed her into the murky green ocean.

The Doctor watched as another viable subject receded into the depths.

"Cheer up." the Captain said. "I can get you another one. Just say the word. Do you want me to find you a new one?"

The Doctor bowed his head in shame. "Yes. Please."

21

TUESDAY, JUNE 2ND. MORNING

HOPKINS DUG INTO HIS DESK DRAWER AND PULLED OUT A PAD OF PAPER WITH a spiral binding across the top. He tucked it under his arm and headed into the hallway. Turning into the only other corridor, Hopkins saw Fuller standing outside the door to the Department's single interrogation room.

Equipped with video and audio recording equipment, the room was the standard location for all criminal interviews.

Hopkins approached. "Excellent work, Charlie. Where'd ya end up finding him?"

"On his boat." Fuller said. "I took Alvarez out this morning, just to check it out one more time. Wouldn't ya know, there he was."

"Did he say anything? How was he acting?"

"He's pretty much playin' dumb," Fuller said. "He was below deck when we boarded. Working on his motor. That's why his hands are dirty."

"Did you look at them closely?" Hopkins asked. "His hands? Arms? Any defensive wounds?"

"He does have a few scrapes. Maybe a minor laceration. But he was elbow deep in that V8."

"Very good. Do we have anyone sitting on the boat?"

"I left Alvarez there. Had the Harbor Master bring me, Walton, and Walton's buddy to shore."

"His buddy?" Hopkins said.

"Walton had a friend helping him out. John something. Strange guy. Not much of a talker."

"Where is he?"

"Don't know. Home, I guess. You said you wanted Walton, I didn't think—"

"Did you at least get his information?" Hopkins asked. "Did we positively ID him?"

"Sure. Alvarez has the info. He ran him for warrants. No hits."

"Okay." Hopkins said. "That's fine. I'm going to sit down with Walton myself. Has anyone given Miranda yet?"

"No," Fuller said, "but I left the forms in there."

"Thanks. Do me a favor? Stay close. In case I need you to do some digging."

"I'll watch from my office," Fuller said.

Hopkins straightened his uniform and opened the door.

Doctor Edward Walton, born November 18, 1970, sat with his hands folded on the stainless-steel table. He had a neatly parted head of thick brown hair and a square jaw. His body language was relaxed. Too relaxed.

"Doctor Walton." Hopkins offered his hand, "I'm Chief Hopkins."

"I recognize you," Walton said. "Do you mind if I ask you what I'm doing here?"

"We'll get to that," Hopkins said. "Just have to take care of a few housekeeping items."

"Not a problem," Walton said. "I was just kind of in the middle of something. Not to be a pest, but if we could hurry this along."

"I'll do my best, Doctor," Hopkins said. "Or should I call you Edward? Ed? What do you prefer?"

"Ed's fine."

"Okay, Ed." Hopkins picked up the Miranda Rights form and set it down in front of Walton. "I know you're anxious to get on with your day, but before I can ask you any questions, I have to go over your rights with you? It'll only take a minute."

"My rights? Am I being arrested?"

"No, you're not under arrest. It's just standard procedure. What I'm going to do is read each line aloud. You can read along if you'd like." He handed Walton his pen. "I'll have you initial each line as we go over it. Then I'll have you sign, confirming that you've been advised of these rights and you wish to talk to me, okay?"

Walton paused. His face flushed. "Am I a suspect in something? Should I have a lawyer?"

"That's up to you, Ed. If you've done something wrong and you think you should have a lawyer, by all means, you're certainly entitled to call one. But I can't say more until we go over these, okay?"

Walton nodded.

"You have the right to remain silent. Anything you say can and will be used against you in a court of law. Do you understand?"

"Yes."

"Okay, initial here."

Hopkins read through each line. He watched Walton to gauge his reaction. Walton initialed every line without hesitation.

"Do you understand these rights as I have read them to you?"

"I do," Walton said.

"Sign here."

Walton signed and dated. Hopkins flipped the document over and pushed it aside. There was no need to continually remind Walton of his right to stop talking.

"Look," Hopkins said, "I'm going to be straight with you, okay? I'm not here to trick you or put words in your mouth. I'm here to listen. To understand. The only thing I ask of you is honesty. I'll be honest with you, and I expect the same respect in return. Deal?"

"Of course."

"And I want to assure you that in my decades of experience as an investigator in Providence, I've seen and heard everything. I say that because I want you to know there's nothing you can say that will shock me. I'm not one of those guys who judges. We all make mistakes, right? We're all human."

"I guess so," Walton said.

It was a good sign. The ability to admit fallibility.

Touting his credentials wasn't a narcissistic trait, it was a tactic. Primacy, as it's called in Law Enforcement circles. The establishment of one's preeminent skill goes a long way in dissuading a suspect from attempting to match wits. Or, at least, that's the theory.

"Misty Brighton," Hopkins threw the words out there and then sat back in his chair. He watched Walton's eyes, his hands, his legs. Looking for any sign of tension.

"Misty," Walton said. "Yes. She was a patient of mine. What about her?"

Was.

While the news of Misty's death was widespread, her identity hadn't been released. Yet Walton referred to her in the past tense. The subconscious slip was an important verbal cue, and it boosted Hopkins's confidence that he was on the right track.

"*Was* a patient?" Hopkins asked. "Did she go somewhere?"

"No," Walton said. "I don't think so. Why?"

"It's my understanding that she's a current patient of yours." Even for Hopkins, it took a concerted effort to use the present tense.

"Unfortunately, no. A couple of weeks ago, during our session, Misty informed me it would be her last. She said her parents were sending her to a different doctor."

"Did you confirm with her parents? I think that'd be news to them."

"I didn't. At first, I wondered if Misty was making it up. Trying to goad me, like they do. But when she didn't show up the next week, I assumed she was telling the truth."

"And Zoe Morris?" Hopkins said.

"Zoe? What about Zoe?"

"Is she a former patient as well?"

"She's a current patient. Funny kid, tough as nails. I have a session with her on Thursday."

"Can I ask," Hopkins said, "what type of treatment were you providing Misty and Zoe?"

"You know I can't talk about my patients. That's privileged. I can tell you, in general, there are many reasons why families turn to therapy. I specialize in working with teenagers and young adults. Sometimes parents are concerned about destructive behavior. Other times, the kids just need someone to talk to who won't judge. I've heard it all as well, and judging isn't a part of the job description."

Hopkins scribbled in his notepad. He hadn't heard anything particularly noteworthy, but Walton didn't know that.

"Why are you asking about my patients?" Walton asked. "Have they said something? Accused me of something?"

"Would that surprise you?" Hopkins said.

"Of, course. I mean, Zoe can be manipulative, but I don't see her going so far as to make up lies about me. Misty... no, she would never."

"Do you have children, Ed?"

"No. We... My wife probably wouldn't like me saying this, but she can't have children. Not that we wouldn't have liked to."

"I'm sorry about that," Hopkins said, "How long have you been married?"

"Fifteen years."

"Congratulations, that's quite a feat," Hopkins said.

"It has its moments. How about you, married?"

"I was. She passed away."

"I'm sorry," Walton said. "I shouldn't have..."

"It's fine." Hopkins hated the idea of revealing information about his own life. But it would go a long way into establishing rapport. They were just two men, having a conversation. For the moment, anyway. "Tell me about your practice. I'm told you have an office in Newport as well as Jamestown."

"Technically, yes. My partner Doctor Grenier and I started our practice in Newport. When we added the second office in Jamestown, I moved over. John stayed there. Even though we're equal partners in both, we pretty much run it like two separate practices. It wasn't the plan, but that's how it worked out. Turned out to be a good arrangement. He has his patients, I have mine. We share the bills and the profits. Actually, your people met John this morning. He was giving me a hand with the motor."

"They mentioned it." Hopkins said. "Do you ever see each other's patients?"

"Only in an emergency, if one of us is unreachable. Our records are intertwined, so if there's a crisis, like a committal for a suicide attempt or something like that, the other can easily bring themselves up to speed and step in. But that rarely happens."

"What's your schedule? Do you keep normal office hours? Nine to Five? How about weekends? Do you ever see patients on weekends?"

"Again, only in emergencies." Walton sighed and slid his chair back from the table. "I don't know why you're so interested in my work, but if you're not going to tell me why I'm here, I don't know how I can be of any help. I should be getting back to the boat."

"You're here because of Misty's murder, Ed." He paused. "But you already know that, don't you?"

It took a moment for the words to register on Walton's face. Before Hopkins's eyes, the hue of Walton's skin turned a pale white, as if all the blood had drained away from his face. "Hold on. You're saying Misty's dead? That she was murdered?"

"You can drop the shocked routine. We're well past that, don't you think?"

Hopkins tried his best to emit confidence. To show Walton that denying his involvement would be futile because he had already figured it all out. But the truth was, he hadn't figured anything out. If Walton was guilty, he wasn't acting it.

"You think I had something to do with it?" Walton said.

"No, Ed. I know you did."

Walton stood up and backed away from the table. He pointed at Hopkins. "No. No. No," he repeated. "Don't you try to pin this on me. I had nothing to do with it."

"Sit down," Hopkins bellowed. "We're not done talking."

Walton looked Hopkins in the eye and then slinked back into his chair.

"I'm going to need to know where you were last weekend. Everywhere you went. Everything you did. Everyone you saw."

"I wasn't even here last weekend. I left last Wednesday and didn't get back until last night. I'm telling you I didn't do what you think I did."

"Where did you go?" Hopkins asked.

"I was…" Walton hesitated. "I was at a conference. In Toronto. You can ask my wife."

"Where did you stay?"

"The Marriott."

"What street was it on?"

Walton closed his eyes. "I don't remember."

"Of course you don't. But it's not a problem. I'll just give a call to Homeland Security. Have them verify when you crossed. Ask them to send the video. Then I'll call every Marriott in the area so I can confirm when you checked in and out. How does that sound?"

Walton's eyes shifted toward the table. His confident veneer showed signs of cracking. Hopkins had him in his clutches.

"Okay," Walton said. "I wasn't in Toronto."

"I know," Hopkins said. He softened his voice and rolled his chair closer to Walton. "This is your chance, Ed. Your one opportunity to tell your side of the story. You made a mistake, people will understand that. But you have to tell me what happened."

"It's not like that," Walton said. "I wasn't in Toronto, but I was away. I was… meeting someone."

"Who?"

"Samantha. A psychologist I met at the PSA conference in Fort Lauderdale last year. I told my wife I was going to Toronto, but I went to Niagara Falls." Walton covered his face with his hands and then slid them toward his ears. He tugged on his earlobes. "You're not going to tell her, are you?"

"That depends," Hopkins said. "Where did you stay?"

"The Red Coach Inn. It's on Buffalo Ave. I have the receipts. I can give you my credit card statements. I'll give you Samantha's number. I'll give you whatever you want. Just don't tell my wife, please, it would kill her."

If this was true, it meant Hopkins had been barking up the wrong tree the entire time. It had been so promising. Such an unlikely coincidence. But if Walton had been gone for the week, he couldn't have been Misty's killer. Back to square one.

"Sit tight," Hopkins said. He stood up and opened the door. "I'll be right back."

"You believe me, right?" Walton asked. "I might be a horrible husband, but I didn't kill anyone."

Hopkins didn't answer. He stepped into the hallway and closed the door behind him.

Damn it.

Walton was telling the truth.

Hopkins walked to Fuller's office. "I need you to call the Red Coach Inn, in Niagara Falls—"

"Already done," Fuller said. "Walton checked in on Wednesday afternoon. One room, two occupants. He was with a Samantha Reed. Checked out Sunday."

"That's what I was afraid of," Hopkins said.

"What are we going to do with Walton?" Fuller asked.

"The only thing we can do. Let him go."

22

TUESDAY, JUNE 2ND. LATE MORNING

Blake glanced over his right shoulder. Just long enough to get a peek at the receding shoreline, but not so long as to run the risk of veering from the precariously thin lane.

Two hundred feet above the Narragansett Bay, the Newport bridge offered a bird's eye view of Jamestown's East Ferry. From that height, the port looked like a self-contained cluster, marked by the castle-like turret of the Bayview Condominiums building. The miniature row of shops led his eye to the wooden pier where he encountered Goldilocks and the others.

He had studied the map in preparation for his task. While he still allowed the GPS to guide him, the homework would give him a better bearing. Stronger situational awareness should the need arise.

As he crested the two-mile span of roadway, suspended by cables from its two soaring towers, landmarks began to jump out at him from below. The Naval War College to the left. Rose Island and Goat Island to the right. Fort Adams in the distance.

Blake checked the time on the navigation system display. If Lucas kept to his schedule, as Blake had no doubt he would, he would board the ferry in just a few minutes.

Verbal instructions preceded each turn. The route took him by an old cemetery, a small train station, and a baseball field reminiscent of a miniature Fenway Park.

On Thames Street, it was as though he had travelled back in time. Cobblestone streets cut through crowded wharfs, lined with historic buildings.

He could picture what the place would have looked and felt like in centuries past. Whalers, traders, pirates. Grand wooden ships with large crews of hardened men, pouring into the cobblestone streets for a night of debauchery.

Whatever its history held, today the town was a mixture of upscale swank and stalwart function. The result was downright captivating.

He would have loved to explore. To take in the sights and sounds. But there was a timeline to keep, and the clock was ticking.

Around a bend, Thames Street straightened and constricted. The navigation warned of the approaching destination.

The sign for Ann Street came into view on his left. It marked the start of the one-way street leading up the hill, away from the water.

Moving along at only a few miles an hour, Blake scanned the right side of Thames Street. A few feet ahead, under the street sign that read, "Ann St Pier," a sandwich board sign bore a familiar logo.

Jamestown Newport Ferry.

Yellow block letters read, "Boarding," and an arrow pointed to the right.

Blake came to a stop at the junction. By the looks of it, Ann Street Pier was more of an alley than a roadway. Just wide enough for one car to pass, the short street led directly to the water.

A curt honk of a horn from behind urged him to move along. With no room to park a car on Thames, and most definitely no place to stop on Ann Street Pier, Blake took his next left onto Brewer, then snaked his way through the side streets until he found a gap in the row of parked cars large enough to fit the Nissan.

He checked the time. Eight forty-two.

More time had been eaten up by finding a place to park than he had anticipated. He would need to hurry if he were to beat the Ferry.

Blake jogged down the hill, turned onto Thames and then onto Ann

Street Pier. He hustled to the end of the asphalt strip, stopping where it met the wooden pier.

Just in time.

The blue and white boat was just coming to a stop. A young woman wearing a polo and khaki shorts stood on the gunwale. With the looped end of a rope in hand, she stepped onto the dock, secured the line to the cleat, and stepped back on board.

In a matter of seconds, he assumed, Lucas would be walking the dock, right toward him. He looked around for a place where he could observe but avoid being recognized. Spotting a section of weathered stockade fence protruding from the side of a brick building, he casually slipped behind it.

Peeking around the edge, he watched as Lucas emerged and shuffled along the dock toward the alleyway. The fence offered little cover to the side and rear, and Blake hoped Lucas would be too preoccupied to notice him as he passed.

Only he didn't pass. Instead of continuing toward Thames Street, Lucas stopped at the base of the pier and climbed down to a small beach between the docks and an apartment building. The structure itself jutted out into the water atop a long concrete pier.

Blake hugged the fence as Lucas moved across the sand, weaving between the red plastic kayaks beached there. His movements were traced by the tracks he left in the wet sand. They looked as though they'd been created by wheels rather than feet.

Glancing over his shoulder, Blake noticed a tall man with a square jaw and sunken eyes standing at the entrance of the alley. With both hands, he held out his cellphone as if he were taking a picture or a video. For a moment, Blake had an uncomfortable sensation that he was the subject of the strange man's interest, but his concern waned as the man raised the phone to his ear and moved along onto Thames Street. Blake turned his attention back to the task at hand.

Upon reaching the far side of the beach, Lucas stepped onto the concrete slab.

Whichever direction Lucas travelled from there, it would only be a matter of moments before Blake would lose sight of him. He would have to move fast to close the distance before that happened. Even though, in doing so, he would be exposing himself.

The level of risk came down to whether Lucas would happen to look behind him. Luckily, during his few previous encounters, Blake had found Lucas to be a man of singular focus. A one-track-mind, so to speak. He decided it was worth it.

Blake sprinted to the edge of the pier and dropped down onto the sand. Straight ahead and above, a woman wearing a blue tankini stood on the balcony of one of the apartment units. It was hard to tell if she was looking at him from that distance, but she was definitely looking in his direction.

He strolled along the sand in a wavy line. His head down as if perusing the assortment of seashells that littered the beach. All the while, he continued to peer across his brow toward Lucas.

Maybe it was the nosey woman, or the fact that he promised Lucas he wouldn't come, but the whole scenario made him feel guilty. Creepy, even. In a comical way. This was likely a fool's errand, after all.

But he wouldn't be slinking around all over town, at least. To his surprise, Lucas had made a beeline for the apartment building. Before Blake realized it, Lucas entered through the glass door.

Blake dropped the Sunday stroll routine and darted for the building. He planted his palm, vaulted himself onto solid ground, and ran toward the door.

As he arrived, he pressed himself against the side of the building, staying just out of view. He leaned over to peek through the glass.

Inside, about ten feet from the door, was a staircase. Lucas was just rounding the first landing.

Blake pulled the handle slowly and quietly slipped inside. He climbed the short set of stairs. With each deliberate step, he paused and listened. As he reached the first landing, he snuck a peek up the next set. The coast was clear.

As he hit the top of the second set, he poked his head around the corner and into the long corridor. Just in time to see Lucas disappearing into one of the units.

Blake counted the doors. *Fifth one on the right.*

Now, there was nothing to do but wait. He climbed a few steps toward the third floor and took a seat on one of the treads.

Blake figured it would be an hour, maybe an hour and a half, before Lucas would head back to the ferry. It was worth the wait.

Regardless of how long Lucas's appointment was, Blake knew he had some time to kill. He took out his phone, called up the text messaging thread with Haeli, and stared blankly at the screen. His fingers hovered over the image of the keyboard while his mind wandered.

WHAT SHOULD HE SAY TO HAELI? WHAT WOULD HE SAY TO THE DOCTOR when he confronted him? How far was he willing to go to extract information?

For all he knew, this guy John had nothing to do with any of this. And even if he did, it wasn't likely he'd be forthcoming. If he could at least identify him, he could bring the information to Hopkins. Surely the doctor would have no objection to giving Blake his name. Right?

As much as Blake tried to remind himself there was a good chance the excursion would be a dead end, he couldn't shake the feeling that this doctor might hold the key to figuring out what happened to Lucy. And it wasn't just what he told Lucas. Hopkins had asked if Lucy saw a doctor as well, something that could hardly be a coincidence. And then there was this peculiar location. Why was this doctor seeing patients at a residence? Or was this Newport's version of an office building?

As far as Blake could tell, there were no signs posted, nor any indication of commercial use. The rows of balconies were indicative of apartments, or condos, and the woman he had seen was wearing a bathing suit.

No, this was residential. But was it his home? Did he even have a legitimate office? Was he even a real doctor? Lucas probably wouldn't know the difference.

Blake took a breath and tried to reign in his thoughts before they spiraled farther into speculation. What he needed to do was sit tight. To call upon any patience still buried deep within himself. It wouldn't be long until all of his questions would be answered.

* * *

THE SOUND OF THE DOOR OPENING TRAVELLED THROUGH THE QUIET hallway and into the stairwell where Blake had set up camp. It was followed by the sound of shuffling feet.

Lucas.

Blake glanced at his phone. Two hours and nine minutes.

He waited until he heard the steps transition from the rough carpet to the rubber matting of the stairs before popping his head around the corner to confirm that it was, in fact, Lucas.

A few moments later, the exterior door opened and closed. Blake waited a few extra seconds to be sure he was gone.

Blake moved into the hallway and approached the fifth door on the right. He knocked, then took a step backward and posed for the peep-hole, a friendly smile on his face.

There was no answer.

Blake knocked again.

Nothing.

He pressed his ear to the door. He could hear the creaking of the floorboards.

It was clear the occupant of the unit was not coming to the door. He was probably hoping Blake would simply go away.

But there was too much on the line to turn back now. He needed a new plan. A ruse to get him through the door.

He tried the handle. The door cracked an eighth of an inch.

Unlocked.

Blake thought back to the revolver he had taken from the junkie in Cranston and discarded in the storm drain. He wished he had kept it.

Now or never.

"Maintenance," he said as he pushed the door open. "Anyone home?"

Ahead, the sliding glass door that led to the balcony was wide open. The curtains flapped in the breeze.

Damn it. He's running.

Blake ran to the balcony and looked down toward the beach. Below, a slender man wearing a white ball cap was limping across the sand. His footsteps led away from the building.

Blake looked to the concrete below. Although the one-story drop was manageable, he wasn't surprised that the man seemed to have been injured. It wasn't easy to land gracefully on such a hard surface.

Blake watched as the man hoisted himself onto Ann Street Pier, hobbled over the deck of the waterfront restaurant to its north, and disappeared through the gap between two buildings.

Blake's instinct was to give chase. But the man had too much of a head start. By now, he'd have blended into the crowd of pedestrians roaming the area of Thames Street.

Blake returned inside. He checked the rest of the apartment for good measure, although he had not expected to find anyone.

It was a strange setup, this place. The bedroom was empty aside from some cardboard boxes and a few jackets hanging in the closet. There was a small table with two chairs in the kitchen, but the counters were bare. For the most part, the unit hardly appeared lived in. With one glaring exception. The living room.

The living room was lined with bookshelves filled with tattered books and other junk. There was no couch, no television. Just three chairs that sat in a triangle in the middle of the room.

Blake inspected the contents of one of the shelves. The collection of titles included an eclectic mix of medical subjects. Blake pulled out a leather-bound volume and read the title engraved on its cover. *Psychosurgery. Intelligence, Emotion and Social Behavior Following Prefrontal Lobotomy for Mental Disorders by W. Freeman and J.W. Watts.* He flipped through the pages, then returned it to the shelf.

He ran his finger along the row, skimming the titles as he went. Many were surgical manuals, medical journals, or pharmaceutical references.

He moved to another shelf.

There, stacked one on top of the other, were piles of notebooks. Blake peeled one from the top of a pile and opened it.

What the hell?

He turned the page. Again and again. Nothing but illegible scribbling.

Large, swirling loops and jagged, angry scratches. But not a word to be found.

Blake tossed the book onto the chair and picked another from the top of the pile. It was the same. Page after page.

He lifted off three quarters of the largest stack and set it down on the floor. He grabbed the next notebook down and cracked it open.

No way.

Dozens of notebooks, thousands of pages. Nothing but scribble.

Whoever this man was, he was sick. And, while he didn't know how or why, there was no doubt in Blake's mind that this doctor was involved in Lucy's disappearance. A girl had already been murdered, and he'd bet anything that he had been a few seconds away from catching the man who was responsible.

He took a step backward and contemplated the impressive scale of the macabre library. For some reason, it sent an icy shiver down his spine.

On the top shelf to the far right was a plastic human skull. Blake walked over and touched it just to make sure it wasn't real. At this point, it wouldn't have been out of the question.

Below the skull was an old, faded eight-point hat. Blake picked it up and read the patinated brass hat badge. *Jamestown Police.*

For a moment, Blake wondered if the doctor had used the thing to impersonate an officer, to possibly gain the trust of the girls. But it was covered in a layer of dust, and the greening badge wouldn't have fooled anyone. Besides, as far as he could tell, there was no uniform to accompany it.

It all amounted to one thing. It was time for him to involve Hopkins. As Chief of Police, Hopkins would have the resources to solve this thing once and for all.

Getting Hopkins to trust him, on the other hand, would be another feat. But desperate times called for desperate measures. Hopkins would come around. Of that he was sure.

23

TUESDAY, JUNE 2ND. AFTERNOON

BLAKE PUSHED HIS WAY THROUGH THE GROUP OF PROTESTERS. HE HAD figured they would have tired by now, but their numbers had increased.

He got the impression that, from his conversations with Christa, Gwyn, Chief and others, many of the locals were being displaced and thus replaced with the wealthy class. Blake couldn't blame the old timers. Property values were so high, it made sense for them to sell and move to a cheaper part of the state, or country. It also explained how so many people had the time to stand out in front of the Police Department and hold signs for days on end.

Blake approached the desk officer.

"Hi. Is Chief Hopkins here? I have some information I need to relay to him."

"If you'd like to make a report, I can take your name and we'll send an officer to speak with you."

"No, sorry, you don't understand," Blake said. "This is important, it's about the missing girls."

"What about them?"

"Just call Hopkins, please. It will only take a minute."

"Chief Hopkins isn't available at the moment," the officer said. "Like I said, if you'd like to have a seat, we can take your report when someone becomes available."

Blake hadn't planned on playing his only trump card. Not yet, anyway. But arguing with the guy wasn't going to get him anywhere. He reached in his pocket and pulled out the leather billfold. He opened it and pressed it against the glass.

The officer leaned forward and squinted at the credentials. His stern expression slackened.

Without Blake having to say another word, the officer picked up the phone and pressed one of the buttons.

"Chief, yes, sorry to bother you. There's a Special Agent Brier from the FBI here to see you. Says it's about the missing girls. Yes, sir. I'll bring him back."

The officer got up and left the glass bubble. A second later the door to the lobby opened, and he waved Blake in.

"Thank you," Blake said.

"Sorry about that. We've had reporters coming from as far as Boston looking to weasel their way in here. Can't be too careful."

"I totally understand," Blake said.

The officer approached an open door. He knocked and announced Blake's presence.

"Come in." Hopkins looked up from his paperwork.

The officer walked away as Blake entered.

"Thank you for seeing me," Blake said.

"Hold on, I know you." Hopkins's face contorted. "You were here with Lucy's parents. Friend of the family, right? What's this about the FBI?"

Blake opened the credentials and laid them on Hopkins' desk.

Hopkins picked them up and examined them. He looked at Blake, then at the picture on the ID card, and then at Blake again.

Blake held his breath. He thought he had done a pretty good job at doctoring Anja's identification. But then again, he hadn't counted on any real scrutiny.

"I apologize for not introducing myself properly before," Blake said. "I was only here to support Christa and Gwyn, not to interfere."

"So, what's this, then?" Hopkins said. "The FBI's trying to get in this case?"

"No," Blake said. "Not at all. I work out of D.C. I'm not even here in an official capacity. In fact, I'm on leave."

"Then what? Coming to get an update? Or just give me some pointers on how it's done."

"Look," Blake said, "I don't know anything about that circus out there. You're in some hot water, I get it. But that doesn't mean anything to me. I take one look at you and I can tell you're a capable investigator. Probably with more experience than all these people put together, myself included. I'm coming to you because I need your help and you're the best chance Lucy's got. Just hear me out for five minutes."

Hopkins leaned back in his chair. He stretched his elbows out to the sides and ran his hands through his hair. Then, he sat forward and motioned to one of the chairs at the opposite side of his desk.

Blake sat. "Gwyn told me you stopped by and were asking if Lucy was seeing a doctor. Why?"

"We thought we had a lead. Turned out to be nothing."

"I wouldn't be so sure," Blake said. "Are you familiar with Christa's neighbor Lucas?"

"Sure. I know who he is. I see him around town now and then."

"So, I talked with him and he mentioned he sees a doctor twice a week, in Newport. No big deal there. But then he says that his doctor told him that there were several girls that were stolen. Stolen, he said. Then he says that his doctor told him the girls brought it on themselves, or something like that."

"You do realize who you're talking about here, right?" Hopkins said. "Lucas? No offense, but the guy isn't exactly a solid source."

"That's my point. He doesn't have the capacity to make something like that up. Plus, how would he even know the girls are missing?"

"Fine," Hopkins said. "Did he say who his doctor is?"

"He only knows him as Doctor John," Blake said.

Hopkins perked up. "John? In Newport, right? Would it be John Grenier by any chance?"

"No idea. Who's John Grenier?"

"Someone who came up in conversation today. Never mind. Go on."

Based on Hopkins's body language, it seemed Blake had at least gotten his attention. If he thought that was interesting, the next part was bound to knock his socks off. The only problem was, Blake wasn't sure how he'd react to the breaking-and-entering portion of the story. None-the-less, it needed to be told.

"I asked Lucas if he would mind letting me come along to his next appointment, which was this morning. He threw a fit about it. Said Doctor John would be angry if he brought a friend with him."

"So you followed him. Didn't you?"

"How'd ya guess?" Blake smiled. "I did follow him. And right from the beginning, it was strange. The appointment was at a residential condo near the Ann Street Pier. One of those multi-unit buildings. I waited until Lucas left and then I went and knocked on the door."

"Did you make contact?"

"Not exactly." Blake thought about the best way to spin it. He had already lied about being a federal agent. What were a few more small fibs going to hurt? "When I went to knock, the door was partially open. I could see a man inside. When I called to him, he ran onto the balcony and jumped off. Naturally, I was concerned for his safety, so I ran through the door and onto the balcony to make sure he was okay."

"And?"

It was clear that Hopkins was now tracking every word. He had become as invested as a toddler in a story-time circle.

"He was fine. Maybe rolled an ankle or something, but he was well enough to run away before I had any chance of catching up to him."

"Easy enough, give me the address and I'll look up who owns the unit," Hopkins said.

"Already did. It's a holding company out of New York. Bogus contact info. But that's not all of it. While I was inside, I happened to notice a few things."

"What kind of things?"

"Books, mostly. Hundreds of them."

Hopkins chuckled. "Oh. Books. We'd better lock him up, quick."

"You'd have to see it to understand," Blake said. "It's like a thrift store. Stacks of archaic manuals about surgical procedures, electroshock therapy, lobotomy, genital mutilation. Most of them from the forties and fifties."

"So, he's a collector," Hopkins said.

"Maybe, but if you look at the totality of the circumstances—"

"What circumstances?" Hopkins said. "The guy's a weirdo. Which he's entitled to be. Especially in his own home."

"That's just it," Blake said, "it's not his home. It's not even much of an office. There are no personal belongings, no food in the kitchen, and nothing with a name on it. No mail, or anything like that. Not even a business card."

"And you just *happened* to notice all of this while you were passing through."

"I may have done a little snooping," Blake said. "I know, it isn't exactly by the book. But these are exigent circumstances. A couple of young girls' lives are on the line. Anyway, if I hadn't poked around, I wouldn't have seen the notebooks."

"Don't tell me you read his notebooks. Seriously? What could be more confidential than a doctor's notebook? I don't think I want to hear any more."

"Don't worry," Blake said, "there wasn't anything confidential in them. In fact, there wasn't anything at all. Just scribbling. Books full of it. Now you tell me, what kind of mad man fills up notebook after notebook with pure nonsense?"

"Okay, I'll admit, that's creepy," Hopkins said.

"We have to get back in there," Blake said. "Legally."

"And how do you propose we do that?"

"I don't know. But if you could set your own eyes on this place, I know you'll agree with me. This is our guy."

"As much as I'd love to, we're going to need more to convince a judge to issue a search warrant. We could go with the plain view doctrine, except you weren't in a legal position to see what you saw. If you were a private citizen, it would be a different story."

"You think I don't know that?" Blake feigned indignation. He was supposed to be an FBI agent, after all. The truth was, Blake was well versed in criminal procedure. He just didn't care.

"Don't get your panties in a bunch," Hopkins said, "I'm just thinking out loud."

"I could give you a sworn statement," Blake said. "You could use it in the affidavit."

"Couldn't let you do that," Hopkins said. "As soon as it came out that you're a federal agent, you'd open yourself up to all kinds of lawsuits. No, I'll go and talk to Lucas, try to get a statement from him. If he can tell me something I can corroborate, maybe I've got a shot at a warrant."

"I'm coming with you," Blake said. "I've established a pretty good rapport. It'll save you a lot of time."

"Fine," Hopkins relented. "You can ride with me."

24

TUESDAY, JUNE 2ND. AFTERNOON

"J<small>UST PULL IN HERE</small>," B<small>LAKE SAID</small>.

Hopkins drove onto the gravel driveway in front of Christa and Gwyn's house. Neither of their cars were there.

"I don't understand it," Blake said, "he's always outside at this time. Standing right there in the front yard."

"How long have you been staying here?" Hopkins asked.

"Only a few days. Long enough to know that Lucas lives by his schedule. It's a compulsion. And, where else would he be?"

Hopkins got out of the car and walked around the bushes. Blake followed him to the front door of Lucas's house.

Hopkins knocked. After a minute or two, there was still no answer.

"Hang on." Blake jogged around the bushes into Christa's yard and looked up at the side of the house.

"Hi." Blake waved to the old lady in the window. He would have called her by name, but he had already forgotten it. "Is Lucas home?"

She shook her head. Her wrinkled face scrunched up into a disapproving scowl.

"Do you know where he is?" Blake asked.

Another shake. Same dirty look.

"Thanks," he said. Mostly to himself.

Hopkins had made his way around to the driver's side of the car. "We'll have to try back another time."

"I'm a bit worried about him," Blake said. "Maybe showing up at the condo right after Lucas left wasn't such a good idea. If he thinks Lucas tipped us off..."

"Let's not get ahead of ourselves," Hopkins said. "I'm sure Lucas will be back shortly. In the meantime, there are other avenues we can explore. I have my Lieutenant working with Newport PD on locating John Grenier as we speak. You said you got a look at the guy before he jumped out the window, right? Would you recognize him if you saw him again?"

"I don't know, it was quick. He was older. Very thin. I didn't get a good look at his face. Why? Who is this Grenier that you keep mentioning?"

"Let me back it up a bit. Yesterday, we found out that Misty and Zoe were both seeing the same doctor, a psychologist here on the island. Walton is his name. That's why I was asking about Lucy. I thought she may have been seeing him as well. Anyway, we brought Walton in for questioning, but it turned out he had an alibi. John Grenier is Walton's partner. Unlike Walton, he has an office in Newport."

"An office or a condo?" Blake said.

"No, an actual office. We checked it out. It's on Bellevue. But that doesn't mean he's not doing a little moonlighting. We made contact with him briefly before I spoke with Walton. Afterward, we tried reaching out to him again, and we couldn't locate him. If Grenier is tied to that condo somehow, we'd really be onto something."

"Do me a favor," Blake said, "let's take a ride over to Newport. We'll do a simple knock and talk. Nothing illegal about that, right? If it turns out to be Grenier, problem solved. If no one answers, well, it was worth a shot. Whatta ya say?"

Hopkins paused. His head rocked slightly from side to side as if the proverbial angel and devil on each shoulder were each pleading their case. "Just a knock and talk. No cowboy shit."

Blake smiled and lifted his hand, palm out. "Scout's honor."

25

TUESDAY, JUNE 2ND. LATE AFTERNOON

"You've got to stand up, Lucy." Zoe dipped into a squat and then sprung upward so her feet left the ground for a moment. She shook her hands at her sides. "You've got to move around. Get some blood flowing to your legs. And, no, getting up to take a shit doesn't count as exercise."

"I'm tired," Lucy said.

"Uh. You can't be tired. You haven't done anything. All you do is sleep." Zoe moved to the corner, opposite Lucy. She leaned against the wall and slid until she was in a seated position. She kicked her legs out in front of her and bent forward, touching her toes with her fingertips.

"That's Leigh's spot," Lucy said. "You can't take her spot."

"Are you serious?" Zoe said. "Leigh's not coming back, Lucy. She's never coming back."

"Don't say that." Lucy fought back the tears. "She has to."

"She's dead," Zoe said. "He killed her, and we just sat here and let it happen. You and me. We did nothing."

"What were we supposed to do?"

"I don't know, something. If we all fought, all at once, maybe she would've had a chance."

"I don't know how to fight," Lucy said.

"Yes, you do. It's like an animal instinct." Zoe pushed herself to her feet, walked over to Lucy and then dropped back to her knees. She looked Lucy in the eyes. "The Captain will be back. He will try to take one of us. You have to promise me we'll stick together. No more hiding in the corner. No more pretending to sleep. Promise me?"

"What do you want me to do?"

"I want you to go for his eyeballs. If you—"

"That's so gross," Lucy said.

"I know it's gross, but you want to get out of here, don't you? We need to both try to blind him. We need to dig our fingers into his eyes, no matter how disgusting it is. It's what my dad told me to do if I was ever attacked."

"I'll try," Lucy said.

Zoe wasn't convinced.

"If it's the Doctor, we've gotta try to get him to let us out," Zoe said.

"He's not going to just let us out."

"Have you listened to what he's been saying to us? He loves us and all this crap. What if we pretended to love him too? What if we promised him we'd marry him or something? I don't know, whatever he wants. I think it could work if you and I are on the same page. There's something in him we can get to, ya know what I mean? You said yourself he was always a nice guy, so there's some bit of normal person in him, don't you think?"

Lucy shook her head. "He's lost his mind, none of that is gonna work."

"Please!" Zoe said. "We have to try. If the Captain shows up and opens that gate, we fight. If it's the Doctor we work together to try to get him to open the gate, then we fight. Okay?"

Lucy dropped her gaze and nodded.

"Promise?" Zoe said.

"Promise."

"Pinky swear?" Zoe extended her pinky finger and held it at Lucy's eye level.

Lucy wrapped her own pinky around Zoe's.

Zoe squeezed it tight. Like her life depended on it.

26

TUESDAY, JUNE 2ND. EARLY EVENING

HOPKINS PARALLEL PARKED THE CHEVY IMPALA AT THE TOP OF THE HILL, NOT far from where Blake had parked that morning.

Now the streets were even more crowded with pedestrian traffic. And despite being a weekday, the bars and restaurants were teeming with patrons.

Blake stepped onto the sidewalk and waited for Hopkins.

"Lead the way." Hopkins cut through the tight space between his bumper and the vehicle parked behind it.

The two headed down the street, toward the water.

"So what's with all the controversy, the paper saying you're a drunk and the rest of it?" Blake asked. "They tryin' to railroad you or what?"

"Nope. I am indeed a drunk."

Blake was taken aback by Hopkins' bluntness. He liked it. No excuses. No apologies.

"Okay, then," Blake said. "Screw 'em if they can't take a joke."

Hopkins laughed. "It's weird. After my wife Linsey died, I had gotten to the point where I didn't care about this job. I didn't care about anything. But now that I'm about two days from being booted on my ass, I feel like I need more time."

"I know exactly how you feel, man. Someone close to me was

murdered. It's been a while and I'm just now coming to terms with it. Really since I've been here, to tell you the truth. I don't know, somethin' sort of clicked. Like I finally got my head screwed on right."

"Yeah," Hopkins said, "I know what you mean. I was going off the deep end. Drinking from morning 'til night, and then some. But believe it or not, since all of this started, I haven't had a drop. It's almost like my own problems are insignificant, ya know? Puts it in perspective."

"Exactly." Blake tapped Hopkins on the arm to get his attention. "It's this way." He turned onto Thames Street and crossed to the other side. "Do you mind me asking what happened to your wife?"

"Car accident," Hopkins said. "Drunk driver, ironically enough. She was an amazing woman. One of a kind."

"Mine too."

Both men walked in silence for a block. Blake thought about how peculiar life could be.

It was funny how much he and Hopkins had in common. And he liked him. So much so that he felt a twinge of guilt about lying to him. But Hopkins wouldn't be there opening up to him if he hadn't. There was an unbreakable bond between lawmen. A secret society in broad daylight. It was the same for the men in Blake's line of work. Brothers in arms. Only in this case, he was nothing more than an imposter.

"So, Lucas comes over here by himself?" Hopkins said. "Didn't think he had it in him."

"I assumed the same thing until I got a chance to really talk with him. He got the shit end of the stick, ya know, but he doesn't seem to let it get him down. He keeps plodding along. Should be a lesson for all of us. Talk about making your own problems seem insignificant."

"Amen to that," Hopkins said. "This is Ann Street Pier, we headed down here?"

"We can cut through further up." Blake said.

Hopkins followed Blake through a private parking lot toward the building.

"If you want to knock," Blake said, "I can hang out by the beach in case he decides to take a flying leap again."

"Sure," Hopkins said, "where am I going?"

"Through that door. Second floor. Fifth door on the right."

"Got it," Hopkins pulled out his phone. "What's your number, I'll call you if I make contact." He punched in the digits as Blake gave them, then headed inside the building.

Blake hopped down to the beach and scanned the balconies. There was no movement on the fifth balcony.

The smell of fried fritters filled the air. Blake figured it was coming from the restaurant a few hundred feet behind him. It seemed to be a popular place. A line had formed on the pier and every table on the patio was occupied.

He put his newly discovered hunger aside and focused on the task. If the man, Grenier or whoever, came over the railing of that balcony, Blake was going to make sure he regretted it.

But he never came. After a few minutes, Blake's phone rang.

"You in?" Blake said as he brought the phone to his ear.

"There's no answer. I don't hear anyone inside. Looks like we're coming up empty all around."

"Stay there," Blake said. "I'm coming to you."

Blake hung up the phone and hurried into the building and up the stairs. He found Hopkins outside the fifth door on the right.

"You sure you don't hear anything?" Blake said. "Because I think I heard someone yelling for help."

"Don't even think about it," Hopkins said. "I'm already on the cusp of losing my job."

"Lucas could be in there," Blake said. "Shit, the girls could be in there at this point. I want you to look me in the eye and tell me your job is worth more than the lives of those girls. More than a mentally disabled man."

It wasn't a question of whether Blake's guilt trip had hit home. Blake could already see it in his eyes. All he needed to do now was give Hopkins a minute to catch up.

Hopkins let out a frustrated growl. He cocked his head in a sideways nod. "Well? Do it already."

Blake smiled. He backed up so he would have enough space to kick the door with enough force to break the lock in one shot.

"Wait." Hopkins held up his hand toward Blake. Then put it on the doorknob and turned. It cracked open.

"Good call," Blake said.

Blake pushed the door all the way open. Instead of rushing in, he stood in shock.

The room, full of books and other junk that morning, was completely empty.

"This can't be," Blake said. He took a step backward again, this time to count the doors from the stairwell.

Five.

Hopkins walked into the empty room.

"This room was completely full when I was here," Blake said as he followed Hopkins inside. "I swear to you."

Blake sped into the kitchen. Empty. The bedroom. Empty.

"You're telling me that since this morning, someone came in here and cleared out this entire apartment?" Hopkins ran his finger along the kitchen counter. "It's spotless."

"He's cleaning up after himself," Blake said. "He knows we're on to him."

Blake felt the need to defend himself. He could only imagine what Hopkins was thinking. That he was playing games? Leading him on a wild goose chase?

"Are you hearing me?" Blake said. "He's cutting his losses. That means Lucy, Zoe, Lucas, they're all liabilities. God damn it, we're too late."

"Blake," Hopkins shouted. "I agree with you. We need to get back to the car. We're going to Newport PD. We need to know who was in this condo and we need to know now."

27

TUESDAY, JUNE 2ND. LATE EVENING

BLAKE REACHED UNDER THE SIDE TABLE AND WITHDREW THE THREE BUCKET candles and the long butane lighter. He spaced the candles along the ledge, lighting each as he placed them. Beyond the covered porch, the last bit of light drained from the sky.

The sunset had been a spectacular one. An orange and red backdrop broken up by well-defined clouds, rimmed by purple light. There was an awful serenity to it. The universe playing out a masquerade.

In Blake's personal universe, there was no such calm. Since leaving Newport empty-handed, his desperation had spiraled into a feeling of impotence. He fully understood Christa and Gwyn's guilt in wasting any single minute without doing something, anything, to further the cause. But action required information. Otherwise, it was simply going through the motions.

He thought of Haeli and how much he wished she were there. Not only because of the help she could offer, which would have been considerable, but also for moral support.

She had been right, in a way. He was too invested.

Blake had never met Lucy. But under the circumstances, he considered her family. Lucas was only a recent acquaintance, but his kindness and fragility had endeared him to Blake.

But above any personal connections, justice drove him. Justice for the girl who was killed. Justice for all of them.

Pacing alone on the front porch, he wondered how Christa and Gwyn were holding up. He pictured Christa driving around aimlessly, as she no doubt was, wallowing in her own despair. He imagined Gwyn pouring herself into her work to drown out the negative thoughts.

Surely they would both be home soon. And when they returned, he would tell them the truth about everything that had happened. It was time to bring them in. No shielding, no mincing of words.

He would do the same for Lucas's aunt if she would answer the door. After trying several times, he finally gave up. But maybe it was better that way. What would he be able to tell her?

There was no real indication that Lucas had been taken. Just as there was no hard evidence that Lucy and Zoe were victims, themselves. Even if Blake believed it to be true. And he did, with conviction.

He could have called it a hunch, but it was more than that. It was a deduction. Drawing on everything he had ever experienced.

Still, it wouldn't serve anyone to rule out other explanations, however implausible. Lucy wasn't with Owen, but she still could have run away. It was possible that Lucas had gotten hurt or lost. He could have gotten off at the wrong ferry stop and was still wandering around Newport. He could have fallen in the water on one of his walks and drowned, for all he knew.

Blake knew little about Lucy's movements and less than nothing about Zoe's. But Lucas was a walking day-planner. Tracing his steps should have been easy.

The last place Lucas would normally have been was Sheffield Cove. Blake considered taking a walk to check. But doing so would be the same as Christa and Gwyn driving around in circles. Busy work.

Then again, he thought, *what would it hurt?*

His decision made, Blake left the porch, cleared the bushes, and cut through Lucas's yard toward the side street.

As he started to walk, he noticed movement in the roadway, about fifty feet ahead. There was just enough light to make out a shape.

Skunk.

Blake paused and waited for the animal to saunter away. Some confrontations were better avoided.

In the short time he had been there, he had seen all kinds of critters. Skunks, opossum, fox, and even coyote. As soon as the sun went down, the place became Wild Kingdom.

As he continued, two more shapes came into view. Two teenage girls. They sat in the grass in front of a bungalow style house, just off the road. Two bicycles laid on their sides next to them.

Blake listed toward the center of the road to give the teenagers a wider berth. He didn't want to frighten them.

As he passed, the girls were engaged in what seemed to be a jovial conversation. One of the two briefly turned towards Blake, then smiled and waved before turning back to her friend.

They really did have no fear.

Where Blake was from, a large man approaching two teenage girls in the dark would have sparked at least some apprehension on their part. But not here. Here was a utopia, where nothing bad ever happened.

Blake reached the end of the paved road and turned right. Ahead, racks of kayaks and rowboats on either side of the path marked the last stretch before the water.

It was there he heard the first scream.

Blake spun in a circle, trying to get a sense of where the sound was coming from. It was distant. And somewhere behind him.

He hurried to where the dirt road met the pavement.

The screams got louder. Their source became apparent.

One of the two young girls was running toward him, screaming at the top of her lungs. Behind her, the silhouette of a man was hoisting the petite frame of what Blake assumed was the other girl over his shoulder.

Blake sprinted past the first girl, mustering enough breath to say, "Don't stop. Keep running."

The man took off toward the north. His unruly cargo encumbering him just enough that Blake was able to begin closing the gap.

Blake called out, "Stop." It was no surprise that his command was not obeyed.

Reaching the wooded lot at the corner, the man darted between the trees and disappeared.

Blake kept his eyes trained on the spot where the man entered the woods. He pushed his legs until he could no longer feel them. Until he seemed to be floating above the pavement.

He didn't slow as he approached the wood line. He ran headlong into the brush. Branches scraped at his face, some snapping clean off, others bending and bouncing back behind him.

It was darker inside the quarter acre of forest. Much darker. At the far edge, the lights from homes across Narragansett Avenue shone through the gaps between trees. It served as the only source of orientation.

Blake stopped for a moment. He could hear footsteps. And then the panicked voice of a young girl.

"Help," she said. "Somebody, please."

The chilling words sent Blake barreling through the brush once again.

As he swerved to avoid smashing into the trunk of a tree, he nearly collided with flesh and bone. It was the young girl. And she was alone.

She swung, striking him in the shoulder. She swung again. Blake caught her wrist.

"It's okay, I'm not going to hurt you," Blake said. "You're safe."

The girl dropped to her knees and began bawling.

"Where is he?" Blake said.

"He dropped me on the ground and kept going," she blubbered.

Blake scanned the tree line. There, silhouetted by the faint light that outlined the edge of the woods, Blake could see the man emerging toward the street. He was running west, down the hill toward the marina.

"Go home," Blake said. "Run."

The girl began pushing through the woods. Blake did the same, in the opposite direction. He popped out onto the street and sprinted down the hill.

In the distance, the lights of the marina reflected off the faceted surface of the parking lot. Its white color provided contrast, allowing all other objects to stand out. Like watching a film negative, Blake could see his shadow streak across the landing.

He's trapped. There's nowhere for him to go.

Blake sprinted down the hill, all the while keeping sight of the dark figure.

The man darted to the left, leaving the illumination of the lot and breaking Blake's visual contact.

Did he jump in the water?

Blake's lungs burned. With every breath, his determination became stronger.

Feet away from where the man had disappeared, and a few seconds from finally getting his hands on him, he heard it. The sound of the motor, roaring to life.

Blake banked to the left toward the edge of the pier. His muscles tensed as he came to a stop just before careening over the side.

Ten feet away, the boat slid out of its slot in the line of outhauls. Fifteen feet. Twenty.

Blake thought about jumping. Maybe he could have made it if he hadn't hesitated. But now it was too late.

As the boat turned to face the direction of the channel, Blake could almost make out the man's profile. He was wider, heavier than the thin man he had seen in Newport.

He wore a white hat, but not a baseball cap. It was the hat of a naval officer.

Blake looked around to make sure he hadn't mistaken the pilot of the boat for the man he had been chasing. There was no one else but him.

Blake pulled his phone from his pocket and dialed 911.

"Jamestown Police, what's your emergency?" the operator said.

"I'm calling to report an attempted kidnapping," Blake said.

"We've received the complaint. Officers are en route, sir."

Blake spoke quickly, "The suspect is traveling west in a small boat from the West Ferry. You've got to get someone out there right now."

"Where are you, sir?"

"I'm at the marina, the suspect fled a minute ago, there's still time to intercept him."

"Sit tight, sir. I'll have an officer come and speak with you."

He should have known. The protocols by which the dispatcher and police officers operated were too slow to be of any use to him. Short of commandeering a boat of his own, what he needed was the Coast Guard. If they could only stop the suspect before he left the bay, this would all be over.

He opened the recent call list. Hopkins had called him while they were in Newport. His number was first on the list.

Blake tapped the entry and put the phone to his ear.

"It's Blake," he said. "I need your help. He's getting away."

28

TUESDAY, JUNE 2ND. LATE EVENING

GWYN SIFTED THROUGH THE PILE OF PAPERWORK COVERING NEARLY EVERY inch of her desk. Run sheets, inventory reports, invoices, work orders, job applications.

Initially, it had all been organized, even if only Gwyn understood the scheme. But over the past week, the system had gradually evolved toward a state of maximum entropy.

Not five minutes prior, Rupert had handed her the sales report from the previous night. She, in turn, made the mistake of throwing it on her desk.

It's here somewhere.

Despite the inefficiency of it, Gwyn insisted that all computerized reports be printed out and provided to her daily. In her opinion, it was easier to digest the numbers that way.

As General Manager, it was Rupert's job to handle day-to-day operations. But Gwyn made it a habit to review every figure, every day. It wasn't that she didn't trust Rupert. She did. But it had become somewhat of a compulsion. One that had only gotten worse since Lucy's disappearance.

'Ohana was her business. She had to set an example. To be a strong and informed leader.

It was the same at home. There, it was on her to be the "Man with the plan," as Christa would often say.

She was trying to hold it together for her wife's sake. To be the rock, their family had always leaned on. But it was hard to put on a tough exterior when, most of the time, all she wanted to do was curl up in her bed and cry.

Instead, when she felt the urge to feel sorry for herself, she'd hide away in the modest little office at the back of 'Ohana's busy kitchen.

Unlike the ornate dining room, her private space wasn't anything to look at. With bare cinder block walls and a tile floor, it was more of a repurposed janitor's closet than anything else.

Just outside her open door, the kitchen buzzed. Pots and pans clanged. Wire whisks whipped the sides of metal bowls. Knives clicked against butcher blocks. And then, of course, there was the chef. Barking and snapping at the kitchen staff like an ornery dog whenever any of his requests took more than a half second to be fulfilled.

A commercial kitchen was by no means a Zen garden. But Gwyn found comfort in the chaos. Her mind felt quiet in comparison.

Gwyn rifled some more.

How am I supposed to find anything in this mess?

She shuffled a random stapled packet to the top of the pile and skimmed it. Then, another. And another. Frustration mounted.

"Stupid son of a—" She swiped both hands across the desk, sending an avalanche of documents and pens and paperclips to the floor. She fell back into her chair. As satisfying as her tantrum was in the moment, she already felt a twinge of embarrassment at her inability to control herself.

She surveyed the damage. The computer keyboard and mouse hung suspended off the side of the desk by their cords. The only items left standing were the computer monitor, and a framed five by seven photograph of her, Christa, and Lucy, taken at the Fourth of July fireworks event, a year prior.

There were no decorations in the office. No wall hangings, no knick-knacks. There weren't even any personal items aside from the two framed photographs she kept on her desk. The one that remained, and another one, of her parents at Oloʻupena Falls, which had apparently been swept up in Hurricane Gwyn.

Oh, no.

Gwyn slid out of her chair and onto her knees. She dug into the debris and pulled out the other half of the matching set.

As she had feared, the glass had fractured. A single crack ran from one corner to the other, passing through her father's face.

She brought it to her lips and gave it a peck, then pulled out the cardboard kickstand and set it down on the opposite side of the monitor.

"Sorry, Pop."

In her eyes, Gwyn's mother and father, Patrick and Alana Lawson, were the patron saints of the place. They were the reason she had gotten into the business to begin with.

When her parents met, her father was a twenty-two-year-old Marine stationed on Oʻahu. Her mother, a nineteen-year-old native Hawaiian, was working at a local restaurant in Honolulu called ʻOhana. The way her father told it, he would visit the restaurant every day until she agreed to let him take her out. Luckily for Gwyn, she finally gave in. They were married by a Justice of the Peace, three months later.

After Gwyn was born, they left the base and bought a modest little house in a working-class neighborhood. Her father remained in the military and her mother became the manager of the restaurant.

Gwyn had a vague recollection of the neighbor who babysat her during the day while her parents were at work. Her name was Nana. She was big and fat and old and scary. And she had whiskers on her chin. But Nana was good to her, and Gwyn distinctly remembered being distraught when she died.

Then, when Gwyn was nine years old, her mother's employer, already in his eighties by that time, decided to retire. He put the business on the market and half their family's livelihood with it. But her mother saw it as an opportunity. A chance to fulfill her dream. To build a legacy to pass down to Gwyn and future generations.

By investing their life savings, leveraging the little bit of accrued equity from their home, and securing an additional loan through the

Department of Veteran Affairs, they were able to purchase 'Ohana. Her mother would later say it was one of the proudest moments of her life.

Her father retired from the Marines to help with the business, and for the next year, they both devoted every waking moment to making it a success.

Every day after school, Gwyn would go help at the restaurant. Even at nine and ten years old, she learned the fundamentals of the business. She expanded her horizons. But, most of all, she had fun. 'Ohana was her playground. And the waiters, waitresses, bartenders, busboys were all her playmates.

In Hawaiian, the word, "'Ohana," means family. And it couldn't have been more fitting.

But the dream was short-lived.

About a year in, a Kona storm, a type of seasonal cyclone, caused heavy flooding and structural damage to the building, along with many others on Waikiki. To afford the insurance, her parents weren't able to buy a policy to cover a natural disaster. In debt, with nothing else to leverage, they couldn't afford to make the necessary repairs. 'Ohana was forced to close its doors forever.

Although they were eventually able to sell the property to a developer, they took a significant loss. It was a financial blow from which they never fully recovered.

When Gwyn received the big check, after selling off her original chain of restaurants, the first thing she did was pay off her parents' house in Honolulu. The house she grew up in. The house they still lived in.

That was Gwyn's proudest moment.

The reincarnation of 'Ohana in Newport paid homage to the risks and sacrifices her parents had made. The values and knowledge instilled in her from a young age set her on a path to the life she now enjoyed.

But if 'Ohana was to honor family, why did she feel as though it was driving a wedge into hers? It wasn't the same for Lucy as it was for her. Neither Christa nor Lucy showed any interest in being involved. They seldom even visited.

Part of her wondered why she opened the place after she told herself she was done. She didn't need the money. Not really.

If she could go back and do it over again, they could stay in Maryland where Lucy was happy and innocent. And safe. She could reclaim the lost time with her daughter and devote herself to what mattered most.

But there was no going back. The best thing she could do, the only thing she could do, was push the notion from her mind and focus on the present. If, for the love of God, she could only find that report.

On a mission, Gwyn left the office, stormed through the kitchen, and pushed through the swinging door toward the dining room. She ducked in behind the bar.

Alex, the bartender, was pouring a concoction from a shaker into three lowball glasses he had lined up, rim to rim.

Most of the stools were occupied with patrons. Busy for a Tuesday night.

Gwyn snuck behind Alex and headed to the touchscreen interface at the far end. The point-of-sale terminal would allow her to print out another report, if she could remember where to find it.

She pawed through the administration menus for a minute before resorting to the golden rule of business. Delegation.

"Alex," she called, "do you know how I get to the screen for the dailies?"

She was going to mention that computers aren't her strong suit. But anyone who had ever worked with her already knew that much.

"Of course." Alex shoved the pint glass and spoon under the flowing Guinness tap. "Give me a sec, I'll show you."

"I've got it." Rupert seemingly came out of nowhere. He placed his hand on Alex's back as a warning that he was passing behind him and joined Gwyn at the terminal.

"What do you need?" he asked.

"Yesterday's run," she said.

"I just handed it to you," Rupert said.

"I know. It's gone. Can you just print me another one?"

Gwyn stepped back and Rupert moved to the screen.

Behind her, a young man and a woman sat at the last two stools against the wall. The adjacent stool was vacant, but a fresh beer sat on the bar top. Gwyn figured it was previously occupied by the man who stood behind the couple.

The trio was engaged in enthusiastic conversation. Judging by the labored enunciation and the volume of their voices, it was fueled by more than a few rounds.

Normally, the drunken drivel would have been of no interest to Gwyn. But one of the men said something that caught her attention. Her ears perked up.

"Swear to god," the standing man said, "she's a cop in Jamestown. She said it wasn't an accident. The girl was a runaway, and she was killed."

"No way," the other man said, "I heard she fell off a boat and got chopped up by the prop."

"I don't know. That's what Andrea told me. She said she was a teenager who ran away and got stabbed up. I'm not supposed to say anything."

"That sucks," the woman said. "You know who I blame? The parents. Like, did they even know where their kid was? If I had a kid, she wouldn't be running around doin' whatever she wanted."

It hit a nerve. Gwyn could feel her cheeks heating up and her temples starting to throb. She spun around to face the group.

"Get out."

The woman smiled, at first. Then her expression changed to one of confusion. "What?"

Gwyn raised her voice. "I said, get out of my restaurant."

"What's your problem, lady?"

"You don't know anything about it," Gwyn yelled. "You don't know shit! Now get out! Now!" Spittle flew from her lips.

The group sat frozen in shock.

Gwyn's peripheral vision darkened. She fought back tears. She hated them. She hated all of them.

Rupert's hand clamped around her upper arm. She could feel him pulling her. Dragging her along the rubber mats. Past the rows of bottles, perched along glass shelves. Past the gawking patrons.

She saw Alex's face. He looked horrified. At her? It was those bird-brained cretins that should have appalled them. Not her.

"Get them out of here, Alex," she said, as Rupert continued to pull her around the corner and through the kitchen door. Rupert let go with a slight push.

"What the hell was that, Gwyn?"

She pressed her fingers against her temples. "They don't understand."

"You can't just flip out on customers."

"I know." Tears rolled down her face. Her breath was rapid and shallow.

"Go home, Gwyn. Be with your wife." He put his hand on her shoulder. "I've got this, okay? I've got this."

"Thank you." She wiped the bead of snot from just below her nostril. "I think I will."

29

TUESDAY, JUNE 2ND. NIGHT

Zoe's eyes snapped open. She listened.

The incessant lapping of waves filled her ears. It was an ever-present soundtrack. A torturous, looping meditation soundtrack, threatening to push her over the brink of madness.

But another noise infiltrated. The sound of footsteps.

The Captain.

The soft, distant glow of the flashlight appeared and began to define the square archway separating the room from the hallway. Black bars cut through the faint picture.

Zoe tucked her legs under her and rose to her knees. She crawled toward the opposite corner. She winced as her ankles cracked. The snapping sound echoed through the chamber like firecrackers. She paused and listened.

The footsteps had stopped.

Zoe stretched her arm out in front of her. She leaned forward until she felt something soft, then gently ran her hand along the contours of the flesh until she was able to identify the body part she was touching.

Shoulder.

Clasping both her hands together, Zoe ran her right hand towards Lucy's face while her left traced downward, toward Lucy's hand. At the same time, she pressed her palm over Lucy's mouth and squeezed her fingers. She gently shook until she could feel Lucy's muscles tense and pull, and then relax.

Zoe waited an extra few seconds before letting go to let Lucy's groggy mind process what was happening.

Slowly, Zoe released the pressure on Lucy's mouth and placed her index finger vertically across Lucy's lips. Lucy seemed to get the message.

Zoe carefully backed away and returned to her own corner.

The footsteps came again. With each thump, the light flickered and became brighter.

There was no way to know what time it was, but she hadn't fallen asleep for several hours after dark.

Just like with Leigh, he was coming in the middle of the night to claim one of them. In a few moments, the Captain would open the cage and it would be time for them to make their stand. Zoe hoped Lucy was ready.

The light consolidated from a general glow to a discernible circle that jittered along the floor. The footsteps were just outside the room now. They should have brought terror, but they didn't. Not because Zoe had all of a sudden found some inner warrior, but because it wasn't the Captain.

Zoe had learned to tell the difference by sound alone. If it were the Captain, the footsteps would have been heavier, as if each foot flopped onto the ground. Like he was killing a spider with each step. The Doctor's were softer, and each step was preceded by a scuffing sound, like he was walking on his toes.

As the figure appeared, Zoe's suspicions were confirmed. Not that she could see him clearly behind the flashlight, but she could see his outline. The rounded shape of his head was enough to identify him. She had yet to see the Captain without that awful hat. But aside from that, it was the shape of his body. The Captain's posture was straighter. His shoulders were broad and sat high beside his neck. The Doctor's shoulders slumped downward.

Just by the way the Doctor stood, it was clear he was weaker than the Captain, more unsure of himself.

The light hit Zoe in the eyes, then moved across the cell toward Lucy. Through floating white spots, Zoe could see that Lucy's eyes were open.

"How are you feeling?" the Doctor asked. "I brought you some food. Fresh water."

"We're okay." Zoe yawned and stretched her arms to her sides as if she were just awoken. "Is it morning already?"

The Doctor scoffed. "No, it's not. But I thought we'd get an early start." He pushed two bags of potato chips and two bottles of water between the bars.

"I'm glad." Zoe smiled. She bit her bottom lip. "I was just having a dream about you."

"Is that so? Did I die in this dream of yours?"

"What? No. It was a happy dream. We weren't in here. Somehow, we were at the water, only it wasn't around here. It was like Italy or something. We were having lunch at a little restaurant. There were white tablecloths and music. You were holding my hand. It was romantic."

"Interesting," the Doctor said. "I wouldn't worry about it. I think it's a good sign. It's just your impulses trying to escape from your subconscious. It's the disease fighting against your progress."

"But don't you think it sounds nice? Just you and me, somewhere away from all of this. Away from *him*. We could be so happy."

"Why would that sound nice to me? I'll admit, the last day I ever have to see the Captain again will be the best day of my life. But being in a romantic setting with you? I couldn't think of anything more repugnant. No offense."

"But... you said you loved us. I thought..."

The doctor laughed. "I do. A doctor loves all his patients. You wouldn't understand this, but I've taken an oath. To care for those who can't care for themselves. Even people like you." He shined the light on Lucy. "How about you? Are you having fantasies about me as well?"

She shook her head.

Zoe closed her eyes and took a deep breath. Lucy had been right. It was a stupid plan. The Doctor wasn't going to be swayed by a little flirting. In fact, it seemed to have the opposite effect. But there had to be a way to get him to open the gate. Maybe if she faked a seizure. Maybe if she were to injure herself.

The inside of her eyelids lit up as if they were on fire. She opened them with a flurry of blinks.

"Cheer up, Zoe," the Doctor said. "You're a very lucky young lady."

She didn't want to hear his sick reasoning for why she could possibly be lucky. Locked in a cage. Starving. In pain. It wasn't exactly hitting the lottery. But even if she ignored him, he would tell her anyway.

"Go ahead. Why am I lucky?" she asked.

"Because it's me here, instead of the Captain. He heard you, ya know? He knows you've been talking to Lucy. That you've broken his one rule. He wanted to handle it himself. But I convinced him to give me one last chance. I assured him I could address it my way. That it wouldn't happen again. You should be grateful."

"I am," Zoe said, and she was. The alternative likely meant death.

"I wasn't quite prepared for it, but we're going to have to bump up your treatment. I'm going to need you to come with me. We're just going to go into the other room. The treatment is quick, you'll be back in no time."

Zoe gasped. There was a chance, after all. He was going to open the gate. He was going to give her and Lucy the opening they needed. She needed to play it cool.

"Don't worry, I'm not going to hurt you. But please don't do anything stupid. I'm going to help you, but you have to work with me. Promise?"

"Yes." She swallowed hard. "I promise. I'll do whatever you want if it's going to keep the Captain away."

"Great. I'll be right back."

Before the light completely left the room, Zoe made eye contact with Lucy. She mouthed the words, "Get ready." She saw Lucy pulling her legs under her before she receded into the blackness.

The Doctor returned and trained the light on the padlock. He inserted the key.

Zoe stood up. She let her hands dangle at her sides. While her body remained still, her muscles vibrated from adrenalin surging through her veins.

The door swung open, and the Doctor stepped backward.

Zoe took small, tentative steps towards the open gate. For the first time, she was about to cross the threshold. The feeling was like no other she had ever experienced. It was as if she was being reborn. Squeezing out of the suffocating womb into the bright, wide world.

As she cleared the iron bars, she gathered all her energy. She channeled her hate. Her fear. Her regret. And put it all into one lunging movement.

Fingers outstretched into claws, she thrust her untrimmed fingernails toward the Doctor's face. She let out a guttural yell as she threw all her weight behind the attack.

The Doctor grabbed her by the wrists and pushed.

She slammed into the wall and fell to the ground.

"You promised.," he said. "I don't want to have to hurt you."

Zoe lifted herself to her hands and knees, then struggled to her feet.

The Doctor flipped the metal flashlight around and cocked it high above his shoulder. "I will, Zoe. Don't make me do it."

Zoe panted. She wiped the drool from her mouth and bent her knees. Then she lunged again.

She heard the clank of the metal as it contacted her skull. The searing pain followed behind it. She hit the ground hard.

As the room grayed, and just before she sunk into unconsciousness, she saw Lucy through the opened bars. Curled up in the corner with her eyes closed.

30

TUESDAY, JUNE 2ND. NIGHT

BLAKE SPOTTED HOPKINS. HE WAS STANDING IN THE STREET SPEAKING WITH the girl who had been carried into the woods. A man and a woman stood with her. Blake figured they were the girl's parents. Next to them, the two bicycles still lay in the grass.

Blake kept his distance. It was important they got the victim's story without him interfering.

The flashing lights of the police car, positioned to block access to the side street from Narragansett Avenue, turned every reflective surface into a strobe light. Mailbox numbers, license plates, even the traffic vest that one of the officers wore.

Along the row of dense trees bordering the empty lot, the flashing lights oscillated the shadows within the deep lines of the tree bark. The whole parcel became a living, breathing creature. A hungry leviathan angered that its meal was plucked from its mouth.

The red and blue strobes had also caused the shitshow that occurred when Christa returned home. Assuming Lucy's body had been found, she threw herself into the middle of the street and had a complete mental breakdown. Blake had just about calmed her down when Gwyn showed up and the process started over again.

After hearing the story, they had agreed to go inside. Blake went with them, just to get them settled. He promised he would explain more when he returned.

Selfishly, he hoped they would pop a Valium and be fast asleep by the time he got back. But something told him that sleep wouldn't be possible for them.

Blake looked back toward Hopkins and noticed that the young girl was pointing at him. Hopkins looked over his shoulder, and with a smile, waved Blake over.

"This is Special Agent Brier," Hopkins said. "Agent Brier, this is Mikayla."

Mikayla sprung forward and wrapped her arms around Blake's arms and torso.

"We don't know how we could ever thank you," her father said.

"It's nothing," Blake said. "Just glad Mikayla's all right."

It was true. He had saved the girl. If he hadn't been giving chase, the suspect would never have dropped her. But he felt as though he had failed her, just as he had failed Lucy and Zoe and Lucas. He wasn't able to stop him from getting away and now their lives were in danger, more than ever. If he hadn't killed them already.

"Charlie," Hopkins said.

Fuller left the plainclothes officer he was speaking to and joined Hopkins.

"This is Lieutenant Fuller," Hopkins said. "He's going to take the three of you to the police station for a statement. Are you sure you don't need any medical attention?"

"I'm sure," Mikayla said.

"Okay," Hopkins said. "I'll check on you later."

Fuller escorted the three toward his car.

Hopkins turned to Blake. "Unbelievable. He's getting more and more brazen. Right out here in the open."

"This pretty much seals the deal that the others were taken against their will." Blake said.

"I agree. I think I'm going to have to bite the bullet and get the State out here. It's too much for us. The Coast Guard is setting up off Beavertail and by the bridge. But I don't think they're going to be in time. If he made it through the passage, he could be anywhere by now. I put out a bulletin but, with only a clothing description and a generic boat description, I'm not sure how much use it'll be. Arlene and the council were right, I should have called them in sooner."

"We didn't really know what we were dealing with until today," Blake patted the back of Hopkins's shoulder. "At least now, we've got some information to work with. We know how he travels and how he operates. And what do you make of the Naval Officer cap? There's a naval station nearby, isn't there? Can we reach out to the Master-At-Arms over there?"

"We can. But every damned charter and ferry boat captain in the area wears one of those caps. The crew of those big ritzy yachts. Yep, they wear them. Tugboats, sunset cruises, all of 'em."

"Still, it's an important clue," Blake said. "Why would he be wearing it while he's out trying to kidnap a kid? Maybe he thinks it conveys some type of authority. Which I guess it would, to an extent. But it's not like a police uniform."

Blake thought back to the condo and the old eight-point hat he'd found on the bookshelf.

"There was something else," Blake said, "I'm not sure I told you. In the doctor's place, there was a hat with a Jamestown Police badge. It wasn't the same design as the one you're wearing, though. The thing looked ancient."

"Hmm. You think this guy may be posing as authority figures in order to get close to his victims?"

"The thought did cross my mind, originally," Blake said. "But the guy I saw running from the condo is definitely not the same guy I saw tonight. Totally different build. The guy at the condo was skinny. This one wasn't. And the guy I was chasing ran like the wind. Unless his ankle healed up real fast, I'm afraid I put us on a wild goose chase this morning."

"Unless the two guys are related somehow. Let's do what we have to do here, and then we'll regroup. I'll call Newport and find out if there was any progress on Grenier." Hopkins called one of the officers. "Can I borrow your flashlight?"

The officer delivered a Maglite to Hopkins, who handed it to Blake.

"Walk me through it," Hopkins said. "The suspect was here, then took off this way."

Hopkins began walking north. Blake walked beside him.

"He had the girl on his shoulder and ran to about there," Blake said, "then went into the woods."

Blake moved ahead. Guessing the approximate spot, he led Hopkins through the wood line.

"Go slow," Hopkins said. "Watch for any footprints or anything he may have dropped."

Blake moved further in. In the light of the flashlight, it didn't look familiar. He pressed the Maglite to his body to dampen it and used the backlit trees to gauge if he was in the right place. He used this method several times. He pointed the flashlight at the ground to move, then shut it off to check his surroundings.

"Around here," Blake said, "this is about where I ran into Mikayla." He pointed toward the far edge. "And that's where I saw him pop out to the road."

Hopkins scoured the ground. Besides some dirt that looked like it might have been disturbed, there was nothing. No discernible footprints. Not even Blake's.

"It's too dry," Hopkins said.

Blake moved forward. He moved the light from side to side, scanning the widest area he could. Something stood out, about five or six feet to his right. He pushed through the brush to investigate.

"I've got something," Blake said.

Hopkins joined him. "Christ Almighty."

On the ground was a brown burlap bag, large enough to fit a human being. Beside it was a pile of rope.

No words needed to be exchanged between the two men about what they had found. Its implication was obvious.

Hopkins unclipped his radio from his belt. "Bobby, come into the woods. Follow my light."

"Roger," the radio squawked.

Hopkins held his flashlight high and rotated it back and forth until the plainclothes officer reached their position.

"I'm going to need you to collect these items," Hopkins said. "We're going to continue checking for more evidence."

"No problem," the officer said.

"By the way, this is Blake Brier from the FBI," Hopkins added. "This is Bobby, our one and only Detective."

"We met a little earlier," Blake said.

Hopkins backed away from the evidence. "Where'd he go next?"

Blake trudged toward the north and then pushed through to Narragansett Avenue. He waited for Hopkins to catch up. "He got to about here, and then he ran straight down the hill."

They both began walking in that direction.

"When he hit the bottom, I thought I had him." Blake let out a frustrated snort. "I forgot there were boats lined up that close to the side of the pier. When he went over the side, I thought he was going to try to swim. I actually thought, 'Yeah, now you're mine.' Man, was I wrong."

"You did as much as you could," Hopkins said.

Blake understood that Hopkins was placating him. But he appreciated it anyway.

They reached the marina and walked to the south edge of the pier. There, several sets of grated stairs, positioned every twenty feet or so, led from the jetty on which they stood, into the water. Ropes attached to pulleys stretched from wooden posts on shore to pilings twenty or thirty feet out. The purpose of the pulleys was to allow small boats to be floated away from the edge during low tide, then pulled in to be accessed from the stairs when the depth allowed it.

The outhauls, as they were called, were a convenient way to store a small boat and still have instant access to it when needed. And, as it turned out, each slot was registered to an individual. As Hopkins pointed out, the permits were only available to island residents.

It wasn't difficult for Blake to identify the exact slot from which the suspect had fled. It was the only empty slot. The loose rope sagged toward the water.

Hopkins picked up his phone and dialed. "Charlie. I know you're in the middle of something. I need you to look in the outhaul book."

Hopkins provided him with the slip number and waited. He twisted the phone so the microphone side faced behind him.

"You may not have physically caught him, but this might be the next best thing," he said.

Fuller must have come back on the line because Hopkins twisted the phone back toward his mouth and nodded to himself several times. Finally, he spoke. "I see. Okay, I'll keep you posted."

"Well?" Blake said.

Hopkins' brow scrunched inward, toward his nose. It was the first time Blake had seen Hopkins with such a quizzical expression.

"It belongs to a guy who lives a few houses up from here. I know him. Everyone does. They call him Chief."

"Sure, we've met," Blake said. "He used to be the Chief of Police back in the day. I've spoken with him a few times. That can't be right, though. Doesn't make sense."

The man he chased was definitely not Chief. The old man was slight, extremely slender, and he could barely walk with his bad knee, never mind run.

"Come on." Hopkins started back the way they came. "We're going to pay a house call."

Blake followed.

Could Chief really be involved in this? He had seemed such a meek man. Personable and likable. Then again, Ted Bundy had often been described the same way.

It was possible, based solely on description, that the man he saw fleeing the condo was Chief.

But was he physically capable of emptying the contents of the condo? What if he had help? Not one, but two suspects. Or more.

It was as if the more they learned, the less they knew.

Hopkins reached the door first. He knocked loudly and then rang the bell.

The house was dark, which was expected this late at night. Although, with the racket Hopkins was making, the whole neighborhood should have been awake already.

The thought occurred to Blake that if the Chief had rented the condo in Newport and was posing as a doctor for whatever reason, Lucas would have recognized him. Lucas saw the Chief daily. Once while Blake was present.

Wouldn't Lucas have mentioned it? He thought back to Lucas's words. Lucas said he went to see Doctor John in Newport on Tuesdays and Thursdays. He never said Chief wasn't his doctor. Because Blake never actually asked.

Lucas was a man of few words. He answered questions directly and took things literally. It was possible that Lucas was telling him who the doctor was the whole time. Blake just wasn't listening.

His mind swirled. Chief's thick accent rang in his ears.

The old man had been strangely unconcerned about Lucy's disappearance. And then there was the fact that he seemed so confident the dead girl was not Lucy, even before Christa and Gwyn were able to determine that it wasn't her.

Lucas trusted him. Lucy would have also trusted him.

A rage churned inside of him. He had sat there, having a pleasant conversation with the very man he was after. It burned in his gut. How could he be so stupid?

Blake's frustration came flying out of his mouth as an involuntary snarl. "That son of a bitch."

"He's not here." Hopkins ignored Blake's outburst.

"Of course he's not here." Blake said. "He's out there."

"Shouldn't his wife be answering?"

"Who knows," Blake said, "she's probably dead too."

"Shit." Hopkins took out his phone again and placed a call. "Charlie, I need you to put out a teletype. John Perrington. Yes, that's right. Chief. Yes, all surrounding states. And hurry." He hung up.

"So?" Blake pointed to the door. "Are we or aren't we?"

Hopkins' jaw tensed. "Oh, yes. We are."

31

TUESDAY, JUNE 2ND. NIGHT

BLAKE STEPPED ONTO THE FRONT PORCH. WARM LIGHT SHONE THROUGH THE gaps around the opaque blinds. Christa and Gwyn were still awake.

The purr of the Impala's engine increased in pitch. Blake turned toward the street and watched as Hopkins drove by. He was the last of them.

As the taillights faded, they left behind a magical calm. As if a reset button had been pushed and the tiny section of the world returned to the way it had been before.

But it hadn't. And it probably never would.

Blake cracked the door, trying to be as discreet as possible. If they had fallen asleep, he would wriggle into his room and try to do the same.

As difficult as it would be, he would need at least a couple of hours of shuteye if he were to operate at full capacity.

Over the years, Blake had become an expert at catching a few Z's whenever and wherever the opportunity presented itself. Even standing up on one occasion. Hidden in a three-by-three blind, essentially a broom closet, in Amran, Yemin, there wasn't much room to sprawl out. No matter the circumstances, sleep is a toll that eventually has to be paid.

Blake peeked his head into the living room. Christa was there, sitting on the edge of the couch cushion and staring into space. Gwyn wasn't with her.

"You okay?" Blake moved into the room and sat beside her.

"She's dead." Christa pushed her forehead into Blake's shoulder. Tears dropped, leaving dark dots on Blake's pants and the tan cushions.

Blake reached over and rubbed her back.

At this point, it was a safe assumption. They now knew that the monster was physically overpowering these girls, binding them with rope and carting them off to God knows where. He was getting more brazen. More prolific.

It was unlikely he was keeping them all alive. He had already killed once, so they knew he had no aversion to murder. The logistics of containing multiple abductees, feeding them, keeping them subdued, it didn't seem likely. And it didn't fit the profile.

From what he had seen and what Hopkins had told him about the murder and rape of the one victim they'd found, they were dealing with a serial killer. People like that didn't usually keep multiple prisoners. The selection of a new victim typically marked the death of the previous one.

It was pure luck that the one girl—Misty, he believed Hopkins said her name was—washed up in a place where she could be discovered. But it would not likely be the case for the others. There was a good chance that Lucy was lost at sea forever.

"There's something I need to tell you," Blake said.

Christa pulled away and wiped her cheeks.

"We think we've identified one of the suspects," Blake said.

"There's more than one?"

"Maybe," Blake said. "But as of right now, we have reason to believe that Chief may be involved."

"What?" Christa scoffed. "No way. No freakin' way."

"I know, it's hard to wrap your head around, but—."

"How? Why? He stops by almost every day. We talk for hours sometimes. Even Lucy would." Christa raised her voice. "You're telling me we let a murderer onto our porch? Into our house? Into our lives, for Christ's sake?"

Blake understood the rage. He had felt it too, even if he had only had a few interactions with the man. It was a betrayal. And it made it all the worse.

"We haven't found him yet, but we will. There will be justice, Christa, I promise you." It was the most he could offer.

Christa stood up and slammed the meaty side of her fist into the wall. "I don't want justice! I want my baby back!"

A flurry of footsteps came rolling down the stairs. Gwyn appeared, wearing a silk robe and fuzzy pink socks.

"What happened?" Gwyn said. Everything about her face was wide open. Her eyes, her mouth. Even her nostrils flared. "No. No. Don't tell me."

"It's Chief," Christa said.

"Chief died?"

"No! Chief killed Lucy."

"What?" Gwyn stood stunned.

"Christa, stop," Blake stood up and faced Gwyn. "We don't know that Lucy's dead. We don't know what Chief did or didn't do. We only know that he was involved."

"How do you know that?" Gwyn said.

"You know how I told you I chased a man, and he fled on a boat? The boat belongs to Chief. Hopkins and I searched his house, there's no one there."

Gwyn's mouth closed. Her eyes squinted. "You were chasing Chief? John? From down the street? We're talking about the same person, right?"

"It wasn't him I was chasing. It was someone else. But we think they're working together. I saw some weird shit in Newport, Gwyn. Chief was there. I was so close to catching him."

"How did you know he was going to try to take Mikayla?" Christa asked.

"I didn't. I was out looking for Lucas and I just happened to be in the right place."

"Mikayla is lucky you were," Gwyn said. "She's a sweet girl. She was always good to Lucy."

"And now her parents have her. Alive and well." Christa said. "Why does she get to be saved and Lucy doesn't? It's not fair. It should have been Mikayla. Not Lucy."

"Come on, Christa," Gwyn said. "You don't mean that. We don't want anyone to go through what we're going through."

"What do you care?" Christa said. "You're too busy with that damn restaurant to give a crap about the rest of us."

Gwyn moved toward Christa. "Don't give me that. I'm not the one who smothered her. With all your rules, it's no wonder she spent most of her time out of this house. She wouldn't have been out there if she wasn't trying to get away from you."

Christa yelled. Not words, but a guttural noise that made the hair on Blake's arms stand up on end.

Blake wedged himself between them. "Both of you, sit!"

It took a moment of deep breathing, but they eventually gave in to Blake's well-intentioned, albeit forceful, suggestion.

"Listen," Blake said. "There is no blame to go around. Both of you have loved and cared for that little girl. You took her in. Rescued her from a desperate situation. You are amazing, loving people. Don't turn your anger and your pain on each other. Trust me, it's easy to let it tear you apart."

Blake pulled the ottoman away from the couch and sat, facing Christa and Gwyn.

"Look at each other," he said. "Go on, look in each other's eyes."

Bloodshot eyeballs shifted and locked on to one another.

"The woman in front of you is your strength. She is the one and only thing that will hold you up. Remind you to let go of the anger, the need for revenge. Because revenge doesn't work. Believe me. Be good to your-selves by being good to each other."

Blake surprised himself. He didn't know where all of this squishy psychobabble was coming from, but in the interest of keeping the peace, he ran with it.

It wasn't that he wasn't telling the truth, or that he didn't mean what he said. In his own life, it had been Fezz and Khat that he leaned on during the worst of times. Now, it would be Haeli. But no matter who it was, it was next to impossible to do it alone.

Christa reached out and stroked Gwyn's face. Gwyn squeezed her hand.

"Do you remember when we first brought Lucy home?" Christa asked. "We had bought cute little furniture and decorated her room. The first night, when we put her to bed, she freaked out. She was afraid of the dark. Afraid someone was going to come into her room and do bad things to her."

"She slept in our bed for an entire year," Gwyn said.

"Right between us. It was where she felt safe."

Gwyn took Christa's other hand and held both in front of her. "Don't think I don't cherish every moment I get to spend with her. With you."

"I know," Christa said. "I'm sorry. I'm just exhausted. I love you. And we will get through this."

"It's late," Gwyn said. "Come up to bed with me. Try to get some sleep. Tomorrow, I'll take the day off. I'll stay here with you."

Gwyn stood up, leaned over, kissed Blake on the top of his head, and headed up the stairs. Christa walked to the stairway, then looked back at Blake.

"Thank you," she said.

Blake sat on the ottoman for a moment. He heard Christa reach the top of the stairs and close the door.

He kicked his shoes off, flopped on the couch and stared at the ceiling.

It was only a few hours until morning, but Blake had a feeling it was going to be a long night.

32

TUESDAY, JUNE 2ND. NIGHT

Lucy's body shuddered.

Alone. In the dark. Waiting for the bad man to come. It was her worst fear. The thing that kept her up at night.

Everything she was had been stripped from her. Her family, her future, her dignity. Zoe was the only thing she had left in the world. Now she was gone.

Lucy cursed herself for her cowardice. She had promised Zoe. She had made a pact. But when the time came to act, she froze. Unable to fight. To move. Even to scream.

She longed for her Mama and her Mommy.

When she first met Christa and Gwyn, she remembered calling them by their first names. It was how they'd introduced themselves. Lucy couldn't remember exactly when, but at some point, she'd started to call them both Mommy. At home with Christa most of the day, while Gwyn was at work, Mommy morphed into Mama. Organically, it became a way to differentiate between the two. And they had been Mama and Mommy ever since.

Now, she would never call them anything, ever again.

She wished she could take back the past year of her life. That she could do it over again.

The second time around, when she met Owen on that pier, she would see him for what he was. She would tell him she had no interest in dating a loser.

But that wasn't what happened in real life.

At the time, she thought she was in love with him. She knew she wasn't. Deep down, she knew it all along.

Owen was a horrible person, and he treated her badly. Now, with hours of lonely silence to reflect, she couldn't remember what she had seen in him to begin with.

But she did remember how anxious she had been to lose her virginity. Not because of peer pressure, but because of some stupid idea that she needed to prove it to herself that she was straight. That she wasn't like her Mama and Mommy. That she was normal.

In a way, it *had* been peer pressure. She let other people's opinions control her. Force her to go against her own sensibilities. But those people were wrong. There was nothing 'not normal' about her parents. They loved each other. And they loved her. She wanted nothing more than to be like them in every way that mattered.

The sound of movement snapped Lucy out of her own head.

He's coming.

She knew the time would come. But she hadn't thought it would be so soon. She needed time to prepare herself.

The glow of the flashlight came next.

Not yet. Not yet.

Lucy peered at the opening. In a matter of a few seconds, she would know if it was the Captain or the Doctor. At this point, it didn't matter which.

But, as the figure appeared, Lucy could see that it was neither. This person was much smaller. More feminine.

Zoe!

She wasn't dead. The Doctor had been telling the truth. It was the last thing Lucy expected.

Behind Zoe, the Doctor appeared. Zoe stood by the gate, waiting for the Doctor to insert the key into the padlock and let her back in. Neither of them said a word.

The gate swung open. Zoe stepped in and stood facing him. Her hands at her sides and her spine erect.

He closed and locked the gate.

"See, all better." He turned and walked toward the entryway.

As the Doctor rounded the corner and just before the light faded away, Zoe turned and looked Lucy in the eye. She reached into the back of her waistband and flashed Lucy a shiny metal object.

A knife. She found a knife!

Lucy was typically slow on reading between the lines, but in that moment, she understood. Zoe could have already tried to use the weapon to free herself. But she returned. She came back for her. Or she came back for her help. Either way, there was a chance for survival. For both of them. And she would not let her down again.

33

WEDNESDAY, JUNE 3RD. LATE NIGHT/EARLY MORNING

BLAKE CHECKED HIS PHONE. HOURS HAD PASSED AND STILL, SLEEP HAD NOT come.

After moving to his bedroom and crawling into bed, the chaos in his mind worsened. He thought of Harrison and wondered if he should ask him to come. Under the circumstances, Harrison might be able to now release resources. But Hopkins would see it as a slight if Blake did it behind his back.

He thought of Fezz, Khat, Griff, and Haeli. If only they were there, they could have acted more swiftly. At a minimum, they would have been able to spread out and cover more ground.

It didn't even matter that they had yet to organize their own operation. Fezz, Khat, and Griff remained at the Agency, but they would have found a way to be there. They always did.

And what about Haeli? Why hadn't he asked her to come the moment he realized there was more to the case than a runaway kid? Did it have anything to do with Anja?

The reality was, he hadn't planned on encountering the type of threat they now knew existed. As far as he knew, he was stopping in for a day or two to help a friend with a family issue. The situation had devolved incrementally, never plummeting fast enough to set off the panic alarms. Until now.

It was like having an important conversation while driving. After arriving at your destination, you can't remember how you actually got there.

Although he was transplanted into the ongoing drama, the current situation rested on his shoulders. If he had been more aggressive in his approach, if he had done what he was trained to do, what he spent half a lifetime doing, he could have limited the damage. Instead, he flitted about, acting like a normal person in an ordinary world.

These were uncharted waters, for sure. But instead of navigating, he had been letting the current take him.

No more.

He made a resolution. Starting at that moment. He was done staying in his lane. Done playing by the rules and conventions of society. It had never worked for him before, and it wasn't going to work now.

Half a year ago, he had broken every law of man and nature in the name of justice. He and his crew had taken lives. Begged, borrowed, and stolen to complete their mission. Hell, they commandeered not one, but two helicopters.

Was that it? Was it the fact that he didn't have his team? Was he not capable of acting alone?

No. He was more than capable. He had his own contacts, his own methods, people that owed him favors. Just as any of them did. And he had the skill and training to back it up.

In the morning, he would equip himself with what he needed to complete his mission the way it should have been done from the beginning. He'd need weapons and, most importantly, a fast boat.

Blake was no stranger to the sea. Most of his insertions were done by water. Typically, along with the team, rigid-bottom inflatable boats were dropped by helicopter, or in some cases by parachute. While he never piloted these crafts in combat, he knew his way around them well enough.

It was settled. Hopkins, the FBI agent schtick; all of it would need to be cut loose.

Blake sat up and felt around for the wooden chair over which he had draped his jeans. He pulled them on and headed out to the living room to recover his shoes.

Lying awake and stewing over his mistakes did not help him any. Not that walking would fix anything, but moving might settle his mind.

Slow and methodical in his movements, he left the house without waking Christa and Gwyn, he hoped.

As he left the porch and approached the road, he started to turn left. Then he stopped. The purpose of his jaunt was to clear his mind, not to rehash. He turned right and headed east on Narragansett Avenue. It was the first time since he had been there, he realized, that he had gone that way on foot.

Within two minutes, he was under the canopy. There, the night was so black he could barely see his feet touching the pavement.

About a quarter mile down, he came upon a side street on the right. He made the turn. If he had his bearings, the road should take him closer to the water.

As he moved between the row of dark houses, a dog began barking. The sound traveled throughout the entire block.

He hoped the dog would settle. Given everything that had happened, a man lurking around in the middle of the night would be sure to cause some concern, should anyone be awake to see him.

As he reached the end of the pavement, the road transitioned to dirt and veered off toward the right. He recognized the road as the one that skirted the cove and led to the small beach where Lucas would make his daily pilgrimage.

Between the road and the cove was what looked like a field of tall grass. A postcard-sized sign was attached to a thin metal post that poked out of the thicket. Blake got close but, even a few inches away, he couldn't read what it said.

He took out his phone. The light from the screen was enough to illuminate the printed words. It was a notice, designating the salt marsh as a protected area.

Earlier, before the mayhem, he had intended to search the area for

Lucas. Seeing the tall grass, he realized that a thorough search would have been more difficult than he originally considered.

The landscape on the island was dense. Aside from the water, there were few open spaces. On much of the east coast, there weren't many places humans didn't trample on a daily basis. Here, so much of nature was off limits.

Christa had mentioned as much. She talked about how conservation was a priority and the many areas designated as preserves. Bird sanctuaries, estuaries, and salt marshes, like this one.

Blake wondered if these protected places should be a focus. If he were a kidnapper, a rapist, a serial killer, and he had just abducted a victim, he'd be looking for a place where people didn't go. A place to operate without fear of being stumbled upon. A place he could get in and out of without being spotted.

It wasn't out of the realm of possibility. But not this place. The thin strip of grass provided some visual cover, but it was too small. Too close to the road. Somewhere else, maybe. Somewhere out of the way.

Blake continued along the road until he reached the sand of the small beach.

The term 'beach' was one of convenience, used only because it was a spot that gradually touched the water. Other than that, the location had little in common with what most people would think of when they heard the word.

The term 'sand' was just as much a misnomer. It was more a mixture of sticky sediment and finely ground shale stone.

Blake got as close to the water as he could without getting wet. As he walked, his shoes sunk deep into the muck. Each step accompanied by a suction sound. Its smell was reminiscent of old shellfish or rotten eggs. Only not as unpleasant.

To the left, the outline of the causeway separating Sheffield's cove from Mackerel cove was barely visible, despite his eyes having fully adjusted.

To the right, about a quarter mile down the coast, the lights of the West Ferry made the marina landing stand out against the otherwise darkened landscape like Shangri-La.

From that angle, he could see the line of boats tethered to their outhaul rigging. The sight of it, a reminder of his failure. He clenched his jaw against the flood of anger.

Then he noticed something. Something he would have noticed sooner if he hadn't been brooding.

There were no gaps. A boat in every slot.

Could he have returned to the same place he was nearly captured? Could he be that careless? Or cocky?

Blake climbed over a few large rocks and pushed through a patch of tall grass before finding another thin strip of beach. He followed the shoreline toward the pier to get a better look.

Passing through the yards of several beachfront homes, he zeroed in on the slip from which the suspect had made his earlier escape. It looked like the same boat.

As he got close enough for the spill of the flood lights to reach him, he stayed to the shadows. He scurried along the rocky terrain until he could climb into the wooded area at the base of the pier.

Blake scanned the parking lot. There was no movement.

Leaving the cover of the trees, he walked along the edge, passing the first set of grated stairs, then the second.

Nearly upon it, there was no longer doubt. It was the same boat. He was sure of it. And the door to what Blake assumed was a small cabin was open.

If the suspect were below deck, he would be trapped. But Blake would have to move quickly.

He sprinted to the stairs and descended, his feet hitting only two of the risers before he leapt. He landed on the boat's deck with a thud. It bobbed and rocked under Blake's weight and the force of gravity.

He dove toward the open companionway and peered inside. There was nothing but random garbage below. Some rope, a few gas cans, a box of tools. But no suspect.

Unsure if the tiny cabin extended aft underneath where he knelt, Blake gripped the fiberglass around the edges of the opening and leaned further into the cavity. Behind and to the sides of the short ladder there was a solid fiberglass bulkhead. What he could see was all there was. And it was clear, no one was there.

Blake pushed with his arms to slide his body back so he could extract himself from the precarious position. Before his head cleared the top of the opening, he felt the deck shift from side to side.

Although he intuitively knew what it meant, he never saw the man. He never saw the butt of the Maglite careening toward his head or the man's foot as it thrust into his back, forcing him further into the bowels of the boat.

The last thing he did see, before losing consciousness, was the floor of the cramped cabin coming up to meet him.

34

WEDNESDAY, JUNE 3RD. MORNING

Hopkins pulled to the side of the road in front of the yellow cape. He blocked most of the lane, but he didn't care. Two cars had already taken up the gravel driveway, and he was happy to see that Blake's rental was one of them.

Hopkins walked onto the porch and touched the doorbell button. It didn't move. Covered in a thick coat of paint, it probably hadn't been functional in a long time.

He drew back the storm door and rapped on the inner one.

Christa answered. Wearing a pair of white pajamas, she pawed at her hair in a perfunctory attempt at making herself presentable.

"Good morning," Hopkins said. "I hope I didn't wake you."

"No, not at all," Christa said. "What's happened?"

Christa was expecting news. He had news, but not the kind that Christa was hoping for. Nothing about Lucy.

"Nothing yet," Hopkins said, "I just stopped in to speak with Blake."

"Oh, he's not here," Christa said. "Do you want to come in? Can I get you a cup of coffee?"

"No, thank you. Do you know where he went? His car's here."

"I don't know," Christa said. "When I woke up, his door was open, and he was already gone. Maybe he went into town for breakfast or something. I'm sure he'll be back soon. You sure you don't want to come in and wait?"

"No, I really can't stay. Can you just pass a message to him?"

Hopkins didn't want to say too much. One of the reasons he had come was to let Blake know Chief was located in Bristol. That he and his wife had been visiting their daughter there and had been for two days.

But he didn't want to tell Christa as much. The fact that he had even considered the Chief a suspect at all was somewhat embarrassing, in retrospect.

"Just tell him the person we were looking for has been found," he said, "and that it wasn't what we thought."

"Chief?" Christa asked.

Of course, he told her.

"Sorry, didn't realize you knew about that. Yes, Chief."

"But the boat? The outhaul?" Christa asked. "And Blake said he saw him in Newport."

"I'm not sure who he saw in Newport, but it wasn't Chief. He's been away visiting his daughter. We confirmed it with his wife, his daughter, his son-in-law, even the neighbors. As far as the outhaul goes, it's registered to him, but he hasn't had a boat on it for the past two years. The harbor master confirmed that as well."

Christa sighed. The corners of her mouth drew up in the beginnings of a smile. "That makes so much more sense. I've gotta tell Gwyn."

"Tell Gwyn," Hopkins said. "But if you could please keep all of this to yourselves. I don't want the local rumor mill getting hold of it."

Christa's half-smile expanded into a full-blown grin. "Chief *is* the rumor mill."

Hopkins laughed. How right she was. They had put out bulletins. Broken in his front door. Tracked him down to his daughter's house. He was going to have a story to tell. A story about the inept Tom Hopkins. And it would most certainly be told to anyone and everyone within earshot, for all of Chief's remaining days.

"Thanks," Hopkins said. "I'll take a lap around the area to see if I can catch up with him. Did you happen to notice if he left his phone here?"

"I didn't, but I can look. Why?"

"He wasn't picking up, that's all." Hopkins said. "That's okay. Just have him call me when he gets back. I need his help with something."

"I will," Christa said.

Hopkins let go of the storm door. Christa withdrew into the house, leaving the inner door open. He headed back to his car.

It was bad timing for Blake to be unreachable at that critical moment. Not because they had located Chief, but because they had located Doctor Grenier.

Unlike his partner Doctor Walton, Grenier was considerably less cooperative. Nonetheless, he was currently being transported to Jamestown by Newport PD.

Hopkins was hoping to bring Blake in on the interview, hoping he would recognize the man. But if he couldn't find Blake in the next twenty or thirty minutes, he'd have to move forward without him.

This was Hopkins' last chance to crack the case. One day before the hearing that would decide his fate, he was about to go head-to-head with the potential killer in a battle of wits and will.

More than any other time in his life, he hoped he didn't screw it up.

35

WEDNESDAY, JUNE 3RD. MORNING

BLAKE'S SENSES BEGAN TO RETURN. FIRST THE THROBBING PAIN BEHIND HIS temples. Then the awareness of his body, sprawled out on the hard surface.

The stench was nauseating.

His tongue touched his lips. They were dry and coated in grit.

He opened his eyes and rocked himself onto one elbow.

What is this place?

The soft glow of cool sunlight filtered in from beyond the opening to the room. Through blurry vision, he took it all in. The iron bars, the graffitied concrete walls. It was as if he'd been transported to another time and place. A post-apocalyptic world.

Blake sat up and shook his head to clear the cobwebs from his brain.

Was he hallucinating?

He turned to his right. The sight of the young girl in the corner behind him sent his pulse skyrocketing. He jumped to his feet and spun around. There, in the other corner, was another one.

Both girls sat completely still, their doe-like eyes fixed on him. Dried blood was caked on their gaunt faces. For a fleeting moment, he thought they might be dead. Propped up in a sick exhibit. But no. They were broken, to be sure, but they were alive.

He could hardly believe it. After all this time, they had somehow survived.

It was a stroke of luck that he ended up there, with them. He had never been so happy to have been captured in his life.

The last time he had been knocked unconscious, he was shoved into a trunk of a car, held captive and tortured for hours on end. He had vowed to never let it happen again. Now, he thanked the gods of stupidity that he'd failed to make good on his promise.

Blake rushed to the petite girl with the short, boy-like hair. He dropped to one knee and reached out his hand. She flinched.

"You're Lucy, right?" Blake said.

Lucy nodded.

"I'm a friend of your moms'. I'm going to get you out of here."

Lucy squeezed her knees in toward her chest. She didn't trust him. And he didn't blame her.

"I know you and I have never met," Blake said, "but I've known your mom Christa for a long time. And your Aunt Anja, too. Your mom called me to help find you. They're worried sick."

Lucy's eyes glistened. "The Captain," she said. Her voice was thin. Barely audible. "He's going to kill us. He's going to kill you too."

The Captain. She was talking about the man in the Naval cap.

Blake forced a smile. It intensified the pain behind his eyes. "No, he won't. He's never going to hurt you again, I promise you."

Tears streamed down Lucy's face. She looked so small. So fragile.

Blake reached out again and stroked her hair. Instead of retreating, she leaned her head into his hand.

"You're so strong, Lucy. Your parents will be so proud of you." Blake looked over his shoulder. "Both of you." He shifted his body to face the opposite corner. "You must be Zoe."

Zoe nodded, then shuddered and covered her face with her hands.

Blake understood her fear. He could have been just another threat, as far as she knew. But she wasn't reacting to him. She had heard something, and now Blake heard it too. Someone was moving.

Blake stood up and darted to the gate. He stuck his hand through the bars and grasped the padlock. The shiny metal lock was an anachronism.

A modern tool in an otherwise archaic setting. He pulled on it. It was securely locked.

The clasps through which it was threaded were heavily rusted, but they were thick. There was no way Blake was going to be able to break them with his bare hands.

Outside the cell, the nondescript rustling consolidated into a discernible sound of rubber soles scuffing against the concrete floor.

Blake stood with his legs apart and his fists balled and away from his sides. He waited for the man to appear. To finally come face to face with his adversary.

Blake glanced to either side, as if to send a message to each girl saying, 'I've got you.' And he did. Whatever happened, he would die before letting anyone lay another finger on either of them.

Then, like the finale of a grand stage illusion, a figure appeared in the backlit opening. The concrete proscenium framing the star of the show. Only, it wasn't who he expected. Not in a million years.

In a crazy and beautiful twist of fate, the universe had sent them all the gift of salvation.

A combination of excitement, amazement and relief washed over him. A flood of emotion took over his body.

"Lucas! Am I glad to see you buddy," Blake said. "Are you okay?"

"Yeah," Lucas said.

"We have to hurry. I need you to look around for a key. A small key that can open this lock. Okay? Can you do that for me?"

Lucas shrugged. "Okay, Mr. Blake." And with that, he shuffled off.

From the second Lucas left Blake's view, Blake could feel the anxiety balling up in his stomach.

What if Lucas became distracted? What if he wandered off in search of his next scheduled event? What if he forgot about them?

Blake took a breath. Lucas was child-like, but more capable than he seemed. Blake had faith in him. Confidence that he would complete the task.

"Lucas?" Blake called out. He pressed his head against the bars with his ear facing out.

There was no response.

"Lucas? Buddy? You still there?"

"Yeah." Lucas came around the corner, the key gripped in his raised hand.

"Fantastic job," Blake said. "Who's better than you, Lucas? Bring it here."

It was ironic. For all of Blake's pity, it was Lucas who would end up saving them. He was an unlikely hero. But a hero, nonetheless.

Lucas handed Blake the key. He popped open the padlock and let it fall to the ground. Then he swung the gate open and stepped toward Lucas.

"I was worried about you, Lucas. Where the hell have you been? How did you find us? Is there anyone else here?"

"No," Lucas said.

"Okay, you can tell me the rest later. Let's go find our way out of here," Blake looked back at the girls. They remained curled up in their respective corners. He waved them toward him. "Come on, we've gotta go now. Can you walk?"

Lucy stood up slowly, then looked at Zoe.

Zoe rose to her feet.

"I know you're scared," Blake said, "but we need to get you two—three —somewhere safe before he comes back. I'll deal with him after we figure out where we are."

Blake stepped back and waited. Lucy started to move. She took short, tentative steps, eventually joining Blake outside the cage.

"It's okay, Zoe." Blake held out his hand toward her. "You can do it. I need you to be strong. Take my hand. We'll go together."

Without warning, Zoe launched herself toward Blake. She barreled through the opened gate, knocking Blake's outstretched hand away with her body. She raised her arms above her head and threw herself forward.

As her arms drove downward, Blake caught a glimpse of the blade that protruded from her two-handed grip, just before she plunged it into Lucas's chest.

Lucas crumpled to the ground. Zoe stood panting like a rabid dog, still clutching the blood-soaked knife.

Blake grabbed her wrist and wrenched the blade from her hands. He dropped to his knees and placed his hand on Lucas's chest. Blood gushed from the wound. It flowed over Blake's fingers and pooled on the floor.

Lucas gurgled and gasped. A second later came another sporadic breath. Blake knew what it meant. The agonal breathing was familiar to him. It was called the death rattle, and it meant Lucas was not going to make it.

"No! Come on, Lucas. Stay with me."

The next breath did not come.

Blake turned to Zoe. He yelled in anger and confusion. "Why? Why did you do that?"

Zoe stood silently, without the slightest hint of emotion.

"She can't answer you," Lucy said. "He cut out her tongue."

Blake could feel the blood rushing away from his face. He looked at Zoe in horror. She turned her head slightly, looked him in the eye and snapped her mouth open wide.

The grotesque mutilation he saw shocked and enraged him. "Who? Who did this to you?"

Zoe closed her mouth, lifted her arm, and pointed at Lucas.

36

WEDNESDAY, JUNE 3RD. MORNING

"I'M GLAD YOU'RE NOT GOING IN TODAY," CHRISTA SAID AS SHE FLUSHED THE toilet.

"It's probably better for everyone," Gwyn shouted through the shower curtain. "I was getting a little frazzled."

Christa chuckled under her breath. "You don't have to yell. I'm right here."

"What?" Gwyn shouted.

Christa could picture the goofy look that was probably on her face. The coy grin she always had when she thought she was funny.

Christa pulled back the edge of the curtain and stuck her face through the gap. Droplets spattered her face.

Gwyn's hair was sudsy and piled on top of her head. Goofy look confirmed.

Christa puckered her lips. Gwyn answered with a kiss.

Christa closed the curtain and headed to the scallop shaped sink basin to wash her hands. "I was thinking we'd take a ride around together. Figure out if there's any places we didn't check."

"Whatever you want to do," Gwyn said.

Christa's phone buzzed.

Harrison.

"Harrison's calling." Christa opened the door and moved into the kitchen. A puff of steam followed her.

"Hi, Andy," she answered.

"Good morning," Harrison said. "How are you?"

"Hangin' in there."

"I'm glad. I was just calling for an update. Is Blake there? I've been trying to call him. He's not picking up."

"You're the second person who said that in the last hour," Christa said. "He went out. I'm not sure where."

"He usually calls me before nine, that's all. Last I talked to him was yesterday morning. He told me he was going to check something out in Newport. That there was a doctor who might have had some information. Do you know what came of it?"

"Oh. You don't know?" Christa said. "Something happened last night. A girl was almost abducted right around the corner from us. We think it's the same guy who took Lucy."

"What do you mean 'took Lucy?'" Harrison said.

Christa could feel the emotion building up. But she managed to keep the tears from coming.

"Didn't Blake tell you?" She asked. "Lucy wasn't with Owen."

"He did. But... I figured..."

"It's bad Andy." Christa's composure began to slip. "I'm afraid she's—"

"She's not. Blake would not let that happen. Trust me. Did the police get the guy? From last night?"

"No," Christa said. "Blake saw him. He chased him, but the guy got away. He thought it might have been one of our neighbors, but that turned out to be wrong."

"Jesus H, I'm coming down there," Harrison said. "I told Blake to keep me in the loop."

"I'm sure he wanted to. He and Hopkins have been working so hard to try to find her. He—"

"Still, he should have called me. And who's Hopkins?" Harrison asked.

"He's the Chief of Police. Blake's been working with him for the past few days."

"Chief of Police. Okay, I'm going to call him. If there's any indication that this guy crossed state lines, it becomes a federal case and I can get my people involved. All I've gotta do is get him to say it's a possibility."

"Thank you, Andy. Anything you can do. I appreciate it. But there's one thing you should know before you talk to Chief Hopkins."

"What's that?"

"How Blake got Hopkins to give him access."

"Let me guess," Harrison said, "I'm not gonna like it."

37

WEDNESDAY, JUNE 3RD. MORNING

"What is Zoe trying to say?" Blake said. "That Lucas did that to her?"

"He did do it," Lucy said. "He locked us in here. And he was going to kill us. Just like he killed the others."

Blake looked at the lifeless body that laid at his feet. He tried to wrap his brain around what Lucy was telling him. Maybe she was mistaken. Maybe the shock of everything that happened had messed with their minds.

Zoe stood in a daze. Her entire body quivered.

"Lucy, listen to me. Both of you. This is Lucas. The mentally handicapped man who lives—lived—next door to you. He's not the person who abducted you."

"I know who Lucas is," Lucy said. "Only, it's not really him. I mean, he was different. He wasn't, you know, slow. He was acting crazy. Pretending to be other people and making us call him different names. Sometimes he wanted us to call him Doctor and then, if he was angry, he said he was the Captain."

"The Captain?"

"Yeah. He put on this hat, like boat captains wear, and his voice would get all, I don't know, rough, I guess. We knew when we saw the Captain it was gonna be real bad. Like, if we talked to each other, he got really, really angry. He was evil. You've gotta believe me."

My God, the hat.

He did believe her.

The man he chased wore the hat she described. He was Lucas's build. He had Lucas's profile. Blake could have kicked himself for not making the connection sooner. But there was no way his mind would have made that leap on its own. How could he ever have considered that the imposing man who threw a teenage girl over his shoulder and ran like the wind was the same man who shuffled around town, waving joyfully at strangers.

Then there was the Doctor. Yes. It was all starting to come together.

"I believe you," Blake said. "Zoe. Listen to me. You did what you had to do to protect yourself. To protect all of us. You're a strong young lady."

Blake knew his words wouldn't make much of a dent in the guilt she must have felt. And he knew it would only get worse as the horror of what she did set in. Taking a life is never easy, even for him. But at the moment, they needed to move, and he needed her to snap out of it.

"We've gotta get you two out of here. Is there anyone else besides Lucas?"

"No," Lucy said.

"Okay, we're going to walk. Stay behind me and stay close. Can you do that?"

Lucy nodded.

"Zoe?"

Zoe looked at Blake with wide eyes. She rocked her head up and down.

"Good. Let's go. And don't touch anything." Blake started around the corner.

As he walked, he held the bloody knife out in front of him, ready to defend his cargo at all costs. After a few steps, he paused and checked behind him. Both girls were there.

Ahead, daylight streamed in from the top of an L shaped, concrete staircase. They continued toward it.

On the left, there was an opening to another room. Blake visually cleared the interior. It was like the room they had come from. This one had the same iron bars, except the door section was missing. Otherwise, it was empty.

Blake moved on.

There were four more openings along the left wall before they would reach the stairs. Each room was closer to the source of the light, making each brighter and easier to clear with a quick glance.

As Blake peeked into the last room, he stopped and spun around toward his two shadows.

"Close your eyes," he said.

They did.

Blake guided them the last few feet to the base of the stairs.

"Stay right here for a minute."

Blake returned to the last opening. He peered in from the hallway to avoid contaminating the scene.

A large splotch of crimson covered the floor, obscuring the graffiti. It was as if someone had spilled a gallon of lumpy red paint and then tried to wipe it up. Only it wasn't paint. Blake knew blood when he saw it. The way it congealed. The color it turned as it dried. And then there was the telltale metallic smell. So potent he could taste it in the air. Blake assumed it was Misty's. But, one thing was for certain. Whoever it once belonged to hadn't survived.

This room was different from the others. There were no bars. A number of rusted iron rings were embedded in the concrete along the walls and the perimeter of the floor. A few of them had ropes attached, the ends of which had soaked up the blood where they laid.

And then there were the tools.

In a pile by the corner was an assortment of old hand tools. A few saws. Pliers. Snippers. A hammer. A hand-cranked drill. Blake winced at the thought of what the tools were used for. Misty's fingers and Zoe's tongue, for starters.

It was hard to imagine that Lucas was capable of using such instruments of torture. Both philosophically and literally.

Blake rejoined the girls and started up the stairs. When they reached the top, they emerged at ground level, in a dirt clearing surrounded by dense trees and brush.

The crumbling concrete steps continued upward toward the top of the monolithic structure. Blake had the girls wait once more while he bound up the steps to take a quick look.

Along the flat roof were three enormous circular pits, each with huge bolts protruding from their bases.

Cannon mounts.

This was an old military installation. One of the forts that Christa had spoken about.

Blake looked eastward. Through the trees he could see the shimmer of water. It was a bearing, at least. Somewhere to start.

He scuttled down the stairs, hopping from left to right to avoid the sections that had broken away.

"Do you have any idea where we are?" he asked as he reached the bottom.

"I think it's Fort Wetherill," Lucy said. "I've never seen this part. It looks the same, except it's not buried. And there's a lot more trees."

"I could see water over this way," Blake said, "follow me."

As they pushed through heavy growth, Blake used the knife to help him break off the smaller branches to make it easier for the girls to follow.

As they reached the edge of the wood line, all three emerged onto the rocky shore. At that moment, it became obvious where they were.

A low-lying fog lingered over the water, not yet burnt off by the advancing sun. Across the water, and less than a mile away, a structure poked through the haze. A big tan building with big block letters affixed along its top. They read, "Dutch Harbor."

"That's the West Ferry," Blake said.

"We're on Dutch Island." Lucy gave a nervous laugh. "We're not at Fort Wetherill, we're on Dutch Island."

Blake felt a tugging on the back of his shirt. It was Zoe, trying to get his attention. She pointed toward the north, along the shoreline.

"What is it?" With a glance, Blake was able to answer his own question.

A hundred feet away, tucked along what looked like an old sea wall or the remains of a dock, was Lucas's boat.

Blake started toward it, hopping from rock to rock. One of the boulders was covered in a green slime. His foot slipped, but he recovered before losing his balance. He looked back. The girls were expertly traversing the terrain. "Careful, the seaweed's slippery over here."

Blake reached the boat first. He waded into the water and climbed on board. There, sitting on the pilot's seat, was the naval cap.

Before helping the girls on, he checked the cabin to be sure no one was lying in wait. No one was.

He picked up the cap by pinching the fabric along the top, avoiding the parts that would have come in contact with Lucas's head. He tossed it down into the cabin.

Zoe dropped down to the deck and crossed her legs, Indian style. Lucy sat down next to her.

The key was not in the ignition.

Blake popped open the glove compartment. Inside was the key, and his cell phone.

He picked it up and tapped the screen. It didn't respond. He pushed the power button. It came to life.

The battery indicator showed a twenty percent charge, exactly where he last saw it.

Thanks Lucas.

Blake searched up the number for the Jamestown PD and dialed.

As it rang, he inserted the key in the ignition and twisted. The engine sputtered to life.

"Police Department, Officer Braidon speaking."

"This is Blake Brier. Get me Chief Hopkins. I found them."

38

WEDNESDAY, JUNE 3RD. MORNING

HOPKINS SLAPPED THE PHOTOGRAPH OF MISTY'S SHREDDED FACE ON THE steel table in front of Doctor John Grenier. He circled around behind Grenier's chair and brought his mouth to his ear.

"I'm going to ask you again, where were you last Friday and Saturday."

Grenier flashed his crooked teeth and looked over his wire-rimmed glasses, which had migrated halfway down his nose. "And I'm going to tell you again, it's none of your goddamn business where I was or what I was doing." Grenier placed his fingertips on the photograph and shoved, sending the glossy paper over the edge and onto the floor.

Hopkins picked up the picture and slammed it down on the table once more. "No. You're going to look at her. You're going to face what you've done."

"I don't know what your problem is," Grenier said, "but I don't have the slightest clue who that is—or was. Do I need to get my lawyer in here?"

Lawyer. The magic word. The mere mention of it sent shivers down the spine of even the most experienced interrogators. The moment a person in custody asked for an attorney, all questioning would cease. Or else any information gleaned after that point would be inadmissible in court. Fortunately, Grenier hadn't asked for a lawyer. He'd asked if he needed to get one. And Hopkins wasn't in the business of providing legal advice.

"This young girl, Doctor," Hopkins tapped the photograph with his pointer finger, "was one of your patients. Misty Brighton." Hopkins walked around the table, flipped open the file folder and withdrew a sheet of paper. He slid it across the table toward Grenier. "This is a portion of a log, provided to us by your partner, that shows you accessing Misty Brighton's records two weeks ago. Ring a bell now?"

Grenier pushed his glasses toward his nose and brought the printout to eye level. "This shows my office accessed the record, not me. You'll have to ask my receptionist about that. This girl is Ed's patient. I've never seen her before in my life. Now, can I go?"

"Sure you can. As soon as you tell me where you were last weekend."

"For Christ's sake, man. I was at the casino, all right? I was at Foxwoods like I am every weekend. If you were any kind of detective, you'd already know that. Look, I've got my own problems, all right? I'm up to my eyeballs in debt. I've got loan sharks looking to break my thumbs or whatever they do, and now you're coming at me with this. I don't need it."

There it was. The angle. Somehow, this all came down to money. Was this a human trafficking scheme? Were the girls being provided to settle a debt? To be sold on the black market?

Hopkins grabbed the chair from the opposite side of the table and placed it a foot away from Grenier. He sat down and scooted forward so that his knee touched the side of Grenier's leg.

"Look, you've gotten yourself in deep. I get it. I'm sure you never meant for this to get so out of hand. Let me help you fix it. We'll make this right. You and me together. All you have to do is tell me how it works. What happened to the other girls?"

"What other girls?" Grenier replied. "You're out of your mind. How many times do I need to tell you, I don't know what you're talking about? And, frankly, I don't care. Read my lips. I. Don't. Give. A. Shit."

Hopkins' entire body tensed. The deluge of rage-filled adrenaline sparked by the flippant statement surprised and overwhelmed him.

Before he knew what he was doing, he had sprung from his chair, grabbed Grenier by either side of the head and pushed.

Grenier's chair slid and slammed into the wall. The five strands of hair that he had combed over his shiny dome flipped up and stood out in different directions. His glasses slid off his nose and sat perched on his upper lip. He was the picture of patheticism. But his eyes. His smug eyes remained defiant and expressionless.

Hopkins grabbed Grenier by the jaw and cocked back his right fist.

"Go ahead," Grenier said, "hit me."

Hopkins' tricep flexed and stretched as his fist coiled back an extra inch.

Then, the door flew open.

"Stop," Fuller said.

"Get out of here, Charlie," Hopkins ordered.

"That's enough, Tom. Let him go."

Hopkins reluctantly lowered his fist.

"Agent Brier just called. We need to go. Now."

39

WEDNESDAY, JUNE 3RD. LATE MORNING

BLAKE BACKED OFF THE THROTTLE AS HE REACHED THE EDGE OF THE channel and entered the mooring field.

Lucy and Zoe sat huddled together on the deck, next to where Blake stood at the controls. Despite the warm breeze, Zoe was hugging herself and shivering as Lucy rubbed her back.

"Almost home," Blake said. "Hang in there."

He scanned the area for any incoming vessels. There were none. He looked back at Dutch Island, the dense, uninhabited jungle that had served as Lucy's prison for the past week.

In a twisted way, it was satirical how close the girls had been. Since Blake arrived, the small island was a constant fixture. Always looming in the background. Only three-quarters of a mile from the West Ferry, it stung to think that the entire time, they were so close that he could have swum to them.

After calling the Police Department and speaking with Charlie Fuller, Blake called Christa. Instead of telling her the good news, he put Lucy on the phone. He wished he could have seen her reaction.

When Lucy passed the phone back, Blake told her they were headed to the West Ferry. He had no doubt that Christa and Gwyn were already at the dock waiting for him. And Hopkins wouldn't be far behind.

Every night at six o'clock, Jamestown Fire Department tested their emergency response horn. The blast could be heard throughout town and was a signal to volunteers to tune into their radios or muster at the station for emergency response. Weaving through the stationary moored boats, Blake heard the tone in the distance. It meant the cavalry was on their way.

There was about to be a lot of attention on the island, the likes of which most residents had not seen in their lives. Blake found himself wishing it wasn't so for the two young girls in his charge. They had been through enough already. But no matter what happened from that point on, they were never going to be able to simply slip back into their lives like nothing happened. National press or not.

Unfortunately for everyone affected, the story would never be fully behind them. It would be a topic of every true-crime and investigative reporting franchise for years to come. Dateline, 20/20, and the rest.

Despite having been there, having seen it all unfold, Blake still had a hard time believing it. He'd thought he had seen it all. Horrible atrocities committed in the name of power, religion, politics, and money. He thought he had looked into the face of evil. But he had never seen anything quite like this.

Lucas, the endearing young man who'd greeted everyone with a wave and smile. Who propelled himself through daily life by clinging to his simple schedule. Who could barely form a sentence with more than a few third-grade words. How was it even possible?

As Blake approached the public dock, he could see Christa and Gwyn descending the gangway. When they reached the floating platform, Christa was covering her mouth with both hands and hopping up and down with elation.

Blake turned the boat and coasted until the starboard side contacted the rubber strip along the edge of the platform. He shut off the motor and tied off to the cleat.

"My baby!" Christa held her arms out wide for a hug. She and Gwyn sobbed openly.

Blake helped Lucy to her feet and onto the dock. She was swallowed up by both women's embraces.

Blake crouched down beside Zoe. "Here, let me help you."

Zoe took Blake's hands. He hoisted her to her feet and helped her onto the dock.

Hopkins' Impala streaked across the parking lot. It skidded to a stop, displacing a strip of crushed shells beneath its tires. Hopkins and Fuller rushed to the top of the gangway. The shock was evident on their faces.

Christa, Gwyn, and Lucy started up the ramp, as one bundled unit.

Blake and Zoe approached the others.

"I'm sure your family will be in here in a few minutes," Blake said.

Zoe nodded.

As they reached the top, a medic fly-car pulled in, followed by a Jamestown Fire-Rescue ambulance.

The circus had begun.

"We are so glad to see you two," Hopkins said.

The understatement generated a moment of awkward silence.

"Let's get these young ladies over to the ambulance," Blake said. "See if they have a couple of bottles of water on board."

Blake handed off Zoe to Gwyn, and the four started walking. Blake hung back and watched as the group was met by the paramedic and a couple of EMTs from the ambulance.

"Lucas is dead," Blake said.

"They told me," Hopkins said. "Actually, Charlie played me the recording of your call on the way over here. Was it really Lucas behind this whole thing? He must have had help. And what about his doctor? Grenier could still be part of this, right?"

"Maybe," Blake said. "I've been trying to replay everything that happened in my mind. Lucy said that while they were being held, Lucas was role-playing as a doctor. I wonder if there ever actually was a Doctor John in the first place. Lucas left that apartment in Newport and when I got in there, there was no one inside."

"You said you saw the guy jump out the window."

"I may have misspoken. The window was open and when I looked out, I saw someone heading away from the building. I figured the guy had to have jumped out, 'cause he wasn't inside, right? But what if there was no one else but Lucas?"

"I don't know," Hopkins said. "I don't see how he could have managed any of this."

"I don't know either," Blake said. "But I believe Lucy. And everything matches up. She said he was calling himself 'The Captain,' and would wear a captain's hat when he would get particularly violent. If you look in that boat, you'll see that hat. I think I was chasing Lucas last night."

"I was so sure Grenier was my guy," Hopkins said. "How could I have been so wrong? If you hadn't called when you did, I'm afraid I would have done something I would have regretted."

"Well, I'm glad I found them in time." Blake smiled. "Wouldn't want you getting fired, again."

Hopkins snickered. Then his face contorted as if he had a revelation. "But how did you end up finding them?"

"It's a long story," Blake said. "But it turned out they were right there the whole time." He pointed toward the west. "Locked up in some old underground bunker."

"Unbelievable," Hopkins said. "Right under our noses."

"What the hell is that place, anyway?"

"Dutch Island?" Hopkins said. "Now, it's designated as a wildlife management area, but it used to be a military installation. During World War II, it housed enemy POWs. After the war, the big guns were scrapped, and it was abandoned. Transferred back to the State. The fort went to ruins and then, years ago, they made it off-limits due to safety concerns. No one should have been out there. That's probably why we didn't think to look."

"I'm sure that was the whole idea."

A second ambulance arrived. It looped around and parked next to the first.

Blake could see Lucy and Zoe, sitting in the back of the open ambulance. One of the EMTs appeared to be checking Zoe's blood pressure, while Lucy guzzled a bottle of water. Christa and Gwyn stood outside with Fuller, looking in.

As the second crew extracted their stretcher, the paramedic helped Zoe down and led her to the waiting gurney. They strapped the girl in and loaded her into the back of the bus. Fuller got in with her. Blake knew her injuries would require immediate intervention. He figured Zoe's parents were meeting her at the hospital.

"He cut her tongue out, you know," Blake said.

Hopkins tilted his head. His mouth parted, but he didn't speak.

"Zoe," Blake clarified. "Complete hack job. I'm surprised she didn't bleed to death."

"My God," Hopkins said. "That poor girl."

"There's a lot of blood in one of the rooms. And there are tools. It's a pretty horrific scene over there, Tom."

"So, it looks like the murder happened there, then?"

"I'd say it's likely. Whose jurisdiction is Dutch Island?"

"It's ours," Hopkins said. "Jamestown is actually made up of three islands. The one we're standing on is Conanicut. Then there's Dutch and Gould. Conanicut's the only one inhabited. Which means we've got our work cut out for us."

"You certainly do. It's going to be quite an undertaking, processing that scene. The fort, the boat. And what about Lucas's house?"

"Of course, Lucas's house and that condo in Newport," Hopkins said. "If you don't mind, I'll have you head over to the station and put your account on paper. This way Bobby can get started on the search warrants. I've already got everyone coming in. We should be able to handle it all if we plan it right. I'm going to hold off on notifying his aunt until we get an official ID on the body. I'll put Charlie on coordinating the rest once he's relieved from the hospital."

"No problem," Blake said. "Let me check on Lucy for a minute, then I'll grab my car and head over."

Hopkins paused, then extended his hand. They shook.

"Thank you," Hopkins said. "If you hadn't been here..."

"Well, I was," Blake said. He slapped Hopkins on the shoulder and headed toward the ambulance.

Lucy was safe. And, at that moment, it was all that mattered.

She and Christa and Gwyn would have a second chance. A new chapter, with a new perspective. They would go forward knowing what truly matters.

Blake had gained a new perspective of his own. It was as if Christa and Gwyn's journey through blame and regret had allowed him to release his own.

Blake slid in between Christa and Gwyn and put an arm around each of them. They both turned to him with huge grins and tears of joy.

Lucy reached out her hand toward Blake. Blake released one arm and took her hand. Lucy squeezed, and for the first time since he met her, she smiled.

Maybe bringing Lucy back safely had somehow set things right. Reset the balance of fate. Maybe just spending time with Christa was the closure he needed. Or maybe his own cheesy words had resonated within himself. Whatever the case, Anja's death would no longer have a hold over him. Not like it used to. And he had all of them to thank for that.

40

WEDNESDAY, JUNE 3RD. LATE AFTERNOON

BLAKE PULLED ONTO THE GRAVEL AND PUT THE NISSAN IN PARK. AS HE stepped out, he glanced up at the second-floor windows of Lucas's house. The old woman wasn't there.

In a few moments, Hopkins would be there to serve the search warrant. He figured he had just enough time to find an aspirin and maybe suck down a cup of coffee.

At the station, Blake had typed out his statement himself. He had tried to be as thorough as possible, accounting for every moment from the time he saw the boat at the outhaul, to his arrival at the dock with Lucy and Zoe. It hadn't been easy. The pounding migraine behind his eyes had only gotten worse with every keystroke.

While he typed, Detective Berret ran back and forth to his desk. He came to look over Blake's shoulder, then returned to his own keyboard to add the next tidbit of information into the search warrant affidavit. It turned out to be enough detail to suit his purposes, but Lucy and Zoe's accounts would provide a clearer picture.

When Blake left, the judge was signing the search warrant. Hopkins was gathering a few officers to help serve it, once they got word back from Berret that it was all set. Lucy had just gotten medically cleared and begun giving her official account. Christa and Gwyn stayed with her. It would be some time before Zoe would be asked to do the same.

Blake went into the house and headed for the kitchen. He pushed the power button on the Keurig coffee machine, inserted a pod, retrieved a mug from the cupboard just above it, and placed the mug under the nozzle.

While the water heated, he went into the bathroom and opened the medicine cabinet above the sink in search of an aspirin or a Tylenol. He felt weird about being in there. For some reason, going through someone else's medicine cabinet felt like an invasion of privacy, even though he had spent nearly a week in the house. But having located a bottle of Excedrin, it was well worth it.

Blake popped two pills, then walked over and started the machine brewing. As it sputtered its last drops, he swiped the mug and headed to the front porch.

As he took a seat on the settee, waiting for Hopkins to arrive, he wished there had been reason to visit under better circumstances. He knew Christa and Gwyn wouldn't mind if he were to stay a couple of extra days, but he needed to get back to Haeli, and they needed their space to deal with the aftereffects of everything.

Thinking of Haeli, he took out his phone and, using the voice activated feature, said "Call Haeli." He hit the speaker button and took a sip of his coffee.

"This is Haeli," the recording answered, "go ahead and leave a message, if people still do that kind of thing. Bye." *Beep.*

"Hi, it's me. Just wanted to let you know I'm okay. And that I'm coming home. I'll try to grab a flight out in the morning. You will not believe how things turned out. I mean, you literally won't believe me when I tell you. The good news is we found Lucy, and she's safe. Miracle, right? Anyway, see you soon. Bye. I'm gonna text you right now too. Okay, bye."

Blake hung up, then brought up the text messaging application. "Just left you a message. All set here. Heading back tomorrow. See you then."

Hopkins' Impala appeared, followed by two marked cruisers. Hopkins pulled into Christa's driveway. The cruisers pulled onto the grass, one in front of Lucas's house, the other in front of Christa's.

Blake gulped his coffee as Hopkins got out of the car.

"You coming with?" Hopkins asked,

"Damn skippy," Blake said. He finished the last swig, put the mug down and headed to the yard to meet Hopkins. The other two officers filtered over. One of them carried a Halligan tool. The multifaceted crowbar had many uses, not the least of which was breaching locked doors.

"Try not to scare the old woman," Hopkins said. "From what I understand, she's not going to like us being in her home."

"You're about to tell her that her nephew was a psychopathic killer," Blake said. "Oh, and that he's dead. I'm sure she'll get over us being in the house." He laughed.

"Point taken," Hopkins said. "We'll give the knock one more try. If she won't answer, we'll pry it. Let's go."

The group moved around to Lucas's front door. Hopkins banged on the door with the side of his fist. "Police Department with a search warrant," he yelled. "Open the door Cathy."

Cathy. That's what her name was.

Hopkins put his ear to the door. "It occurs to me this is the first time we're going to break in with the actual legal authority to do so." He grinned.

"Not as fun," Blake said.

Hopkins backed up from the door. "Cathy. Last chance. You need to open the door."

There was no change.

"Do it," Hopkins said.

The officer with the Halligan stepped forward, inserted the pick end, and torqued the bar until the door popped open.

The smell that emanated from inside the house was nauseating. Worse than the smell of excrement that filled Lucy and Zoe's cell at Dutch Island. Blake could only imagine how bad it would be inside.

Hopkins went in first. Then Blake. Then the two officers.

"Cathy," Hopkins called out again. "Are you home?"

It was a silly question.

The front entrance opened into what would have been a living room.

Now, only a three-foot wide path cut through the room and forked off toward the kitchen and the stairway. The rest of the room was full of junk and trash, piled head high.

They moved slowly, watching where they stepped. Blake wasn't sure what he was walking on, but it wasn't a solid floor. It seemed to be a matted layer of decaying garbage that squished underfoot. Each step releasing new and more potent odors.

Along the edge of the path, about halfway into the room, was the melted remains of what looked like a cat.

"How could anyone live like this?" Blake said. He kept his voice low in case the old woman was in ear shot.

"She's not staying here," Hopkins said. "We can't leave her in this."

Hopkins made his way toward the staircase. Blake followed him as the other two officers peeled off toward the kitchen.

They climbed the stairs, staying in the middle of the narrow path and avoiding contact with anything on either side.

At the top of the stairs was a bathroom. Its condition was inde-scribable.

There were two closed doors on either side of the hall. Hopkins chose one and headed toward it. He paused to take a pair of blue rubber gloves from his pocket and put them on. Then he turned the handle and pushed the door open.

Even with Hopkins obscuring most of his view, Blake was floored by the condition of the room. Not because it was disgusting, but because it was just the opposite.

They entered the large master bedroom and looked around.

"Lucas's room," Blake said.

The hardwood floors were clean and polished. There was hardly anything inside the room but a twin bed and a single bedside table. The closet was open, displaying about a dozen articles of clothing, neatly hung, and evenly spaced across the wooden dowel. The attached bath-room was equally spotless.

Blake walked over to the nightstand. He reached out for the knob of the small drawer.

"Don't touch anything," Hopkins said. "Not yet. We'll come back to it."

Hopkins moved back to the hallway and toward the remaining closed door. Blake joined him.

The stench from inside was already worse than they'd encountered up to that point.

Hopkins pushed the door. It opened about two feet before being stopped by whatever was behind it. From the seven-foot-tall mounds of trash visible through the gap, it was clear what stopped it from fully opening.

Hopkins squeezed through and into the path. It was so tight, Hopkins was forced to cant his body on a diagonal while he moved. Blake had to turn completely sideways.

Ahead, on the far side of the room by the window, there appeared to be a clearing. As they reached the end of the path, Hopkins let out a wretched noise. He jumped backwards a good six inches, almost colliding with Blake.

"Holy mother of God." he rushed forward again.

As Hopkins cleared the path, Blake got a view of what had caused Hopkins' reaction.

There, on the floor in front of the window, was the old woman's dead body. And not even her whole body. It was only her head and torso. No arms, no legs.

Blake crouched down and looked at her face. It was Cathy, for sure. The same woman who had shot him dirty looks from that very window almost every day since they got there. It seemed they were one day too late.

Close up, she was nothing but skin and bones. Her hair looked as though it were a solid mass that hadn't been washed in years.

Behind her was a rocking chair, positioned in front of the window. The chair from which she would have sat and taken in her view of the outside world. It was caked with feces, just as the floor was below it.

How did she get in this condition? Lucas said he was taking care of her. He said he was feeding her. But he wasn't. He had neglected her. Murdered her. And desecrated her body by hacking her into pieces. He *was* a true monster.

Hopkins crouched down next to Blake and leaned in close to the body. He pointed his gloved finger toward the edge of her short shirt sleeve.

"Check this out. If you look from this angle, you can see the stump, it's healed over."

Blake shifted to get a better view.

"Wait," Blake said, "Did you see that? Is her chest moving slightly? Is she breathing?"

"Not possib—"

Her eyes snapped open.

What the—

Both men sprung backward as Hopkins let out a startled yell. Blake stopped himself before he crashed into the tower of trash behind him. Likely preventing an avalanche that would have buried them all in filth.

"She's alive," Hopkins hollered.

Blake could see that. He took a breath as his heart rate declined toward a normal level.

"Cathy," Hopkins said. "Can you hear me?"

She opened her mouth to speak, but nothing came out but an awful gurgle. She tried again. Her chest expanded, and she opened her mouth wide.

No. He took her tongue, too.

The empty cavity was the stuff of nightmares. Rotten teeth framed the small slab of mangled meat that remained toward the edge of her throat. And the noise. The horrible noise that could never be unheard.

Hopkins pulled out his phone and dialed. "It's Chief Hopkins. I need an ambulance, right now. Tell them to step it up."

"Shhh. It's okay," Blake said, softly. He touched her hair with his bare hand. "We're going to get you out of here."

41

WEDNESDAY, JUNE 3RD. EVENING

"I KNEW SOMETHING WAS OFF WITH HIM," CHIEF SAID. "I MEAN, BESIDES THE obvious."

"Not me," Blake said. "He had me hook, line, and sinker. I actually liked the guy."

"Me, too." Gwyn added. "He seemed sweet. How could we have ever known?"

"We couldn't have," Blake said.

"No one had a problem thinkin' *I* was somehow involved in this," Chief said. "It was bad enough I had to spend two days in Bristol with my daughter's idiot husband and my wife nagging the whole time. Then I get accused of bein' a killer on top of it."

Chief chuckled. His face turned bright red, as it always did when he so much as cracked a smile.

"If it makes you feel any better, I was having a hard time swallowing it myself. But then again, it was your boat slip."

"Yeah, it was my boat slip. But not my boat."

Blake laughed. Not at what he said, but how he said it. Chief's accent amused him.

"I saw that boat on my outhaul a couple days ago, to tell you the truth," Chief said. "I wasn't gonna make a stink about someone using it for a bit. Hell, I haven't used the dang thing in years."

"Don't sweat it," Blake said. "But I've gotta ask you something while I have you. It's very important. Can you say 'wicked smart?' No, 'How do ya like them apples?' Just once."

Gwyn giggled. "Come on, Chief. Say it."

Chief smiled and reddened. "There's somethin' wrong with you two."

Blake let out another hardy laugh, and then a sigh. There was something about that front porch. Sitting there with Gwyn and Chief, it was like living in a time gone by. Where neighbors got together without invitation. Where they were all a part of something, together.

It was good to see that after everything, the sense of community persevered. It was proof that they were all going to be okay.

The creak of the storm door announced Christa's return. She snuck by Chief and sat on the settee, tucking herself in close to Gwyn.

"Lucy's settled in upstairs. I figured I'd give her some space. She said she wanted to watch TV for a bit in her room. I guarantee she'll be out like a light in five minutes."

"She must be exhausted," Gwyn said. "I can't imagine getting any sleep in a place like that. Under those circumstances."

"I can't believe how well she did telling her story to the police. She was so strong. Me? I was trying to hold it together the whole time. All I wanted to do was cry. She did a lot better than I did."

"Me, too," Gwyn said. "Hearing her tell it, she seemed so old. When did she become such a grown-up?"

"That's the saddest part," Christa said. "Whatever innocence she had left was gone the minute he touched her."

Gwyn took Christa's hand. "But we have to remember to keep things in perspective. Lucy was lucky. Compared to the others, her injuries were minor. It's a miracle, really." She turned away from Christa, splitting her attention between Blake and Chief. "Did you know there was another girl in there with them? Besides Misty. A girl named Leigh. Lucy thinks she was also killed."

"That's awful," Chief said. "Two girls dead. One disfigured. And then there's poor Cathy."

"About that," Christa said. "Nobody tell Lucy about what happened to Cathy. She doesn't need to know. It's too disturbing. And she's been exposed to enough horror to last a lifetime."

"Secret's safe with me," Chief pressed his lips together and twisted his hand in front of his mouth as if he were turning a key.

Blake nodded in agreement.

Christa was right. Whatever's Lucy's perception of the danger she was in, she didn't need it compounded. As far as Blake knew, Lucy wasn't aware of Misty's rape, or even the details of her murder. Neither she nor Zoe had been sexually assaulted so, in Blake's opinion, there was no reason for Lucy to know what would have happened to her if she hadn't been found.

"Here he is." Christa motioned toward the road.

Blake looked over his shoulder to see Hopkins pull over in front of the house.

Hopkins had called ahead to say he would be stopping by with information. It was the reason they had gathered there. Not that they wouldn't have been gathered there, regardless.

"Hide the booze," Chief joked, a little too loud for comfort.

Chief was always good for a wisecrack. But what he didn't know was that Hopkins hadn't touched a drop of alcohol since the whole thing began.

Hopkins made his way onto the porch. He carried with him a black padfolio. Blake stood up, offering Hopkins his chair, and joined Christa and Gwyn on the couch.

"Chief, good to see you. Sorry about last night."

"Na," Chief said, "I woulda done the same if I were you. Turns out you're not as much of a bumblehead as I thought."

"I'll take that as a compliment." Hopkins sat. "How's Lucy?"

"Amazing, considering," Christa said.

"Good. Good." Hopkins groaned as he flipped open the padfolio. "Where do I even begin?"

Blake found the transformation amazing. The man sitting before them was so unlike the man Blake had met on that first day in town. His drawn-out features, tired tone, and chippy disposition had been replaced by a sharp, even-tempered professional. The true Tom Hopkins.

Like Blake, Hopkins had been affected in ways he couldn't have predicted. Maybe he had found the strength to let go of his own grief, along with the bottle.

"The fingerprints came back," Hopkins said. "We've identified Lucas as Robert Foster. From Connecticut. We were able to track down a single arrest record out of New Haven. The investigator who handled the incident is retired, but New Haven P.D. was able to put me in touch with him. The cop's name is O'Connor. He had a pretty wild story to tell, so bear with me here."

Hopkins flipped the page.

"Here's what we know, Foster was a first-year medical student at Yale University. By all accounts, he was an extremely bright kid—"

"Wicked smaat," Chief said. He winked at Gwyn, who struggled to hide her amusement.

"Yes, wicked smart kid," Hopkins said. "But all of a sudden he started going downhill. Began flunking his classes, becoming belligerent. Until he was eventually kicked out of school when he was caught impersonating a physician at Yale-New Haven Hospital. Shortly after, he started seeing a shrink and was diagnosed with split personality disorder."

"How long ago was that?" Blake asked.

"About nine or ten years ago, I believe," Hopkins said. "Initially, Foster was living at home and receiving treatment in an outpatient facility. But after he was arrested for attacking a female jogger in front of his house, he was ultimately institutionalized. O'Connor said that from what he could gather during the investigation into the attack, Foster's downfall started around the time he broke up with his high school sweetheart. Apparently, she was a year behind him and still attending high school in Simsbury, Connecticut, while he was at Yale. During O'Connor's interview with Foster, he said that he drove home from school to visit her and caught her cheating on him with some other kid."

"That's what sent him over the edge? A breakup?" Gwyn said.

"Obviously there were underlying mental issues, but it sounds like the event may have exacerbated them. Or brought them to light, anyway. O'Connor said Foster was fixated on the fact that he and his girlfriend had remained celibate, because she insisted they wait until they were married. When he caught her having sex with someone else, he basically lost his mind."

"If he got himself locked up in the looney bin, how did he end up here with his aunt?" Blake asked.

"That's where the story really gets crazy." Hopkins said. "Eight years ago, he escaped from the institution by, you guessed it, posing as one of the doctors. He was never found. In fact, he's still listed as a missing person in the national database."

Christa raised her hand high above her head and waved it back and forth.

Hopkins laughed. "You don't have to... fine, what's your question?"

"Did Cathy know he escaped when she took him in? I mean, was she covering for him?"

"This is the part where you'll need to brace yourself." Hopkins said. "Foster is not related to Cathy in any way."

"No!" Gwyn gasped.

"Lucas wasn't Cathy's nephew?" Chief asked.

"There is no Lucas. Lucas was just another product of Foster's twisted mind. And no, he was not Cathy's nephew. It's been slow-going trying to gather any information from her. She's not in good shape. Mostly it's been a series of yes or no questions. What we think we've determined is that Foster targeted her. He broke in, held her captive, amputated her arms and legs to prevent her from leaving, and kept her barely alive for the past eight years."

"Why?" Christa said.

"Our guess?" Hopkins said. "Foster chose her because she was a recluse. He must have been around for some time. Watching. Planning. It was ingenious, if you think about it. No one would be worried that she hadn't left the house. It was expected. And long as she was alive, Lucas had a life of his own."

"That's why he propped her up in the window." Blake voiced his own revelation. "To make sure people could get a glimpse of her so there was never a question whether or not she was still alive in there."

Blake thought about the old woman's face in the window. How she had looked at him when he was speaking with Lucas. He had assumed she was being nasty. But her scowl wasn't the product of anger. It was the product of pain and desperation. She was pleading for help. With no hands to signal, no way to speak, the most she could do was tap on the glass with her head and hope someone took pity on her. But Blake hadn't. No one had.

"He took control of her finances," Hopkins said. "Drained her savings. The holding company that owns the condo we found in Newport. Guess who's listed as the managing party."

"Cathy," Blake said.

"You got it."

"That's how he was able to buy a boat," Christa said.

"No, the boat was stolen," Hopkins said. "Out of Newport. A week ago."

"I don't understand this split personality thing," Gwyn said. "Foster steals a boat and suddenly he thinks he's a captain."

"I don't think that's exactly how it works. I spoke with our clinician about this after I got off the phone with O'Connor. The original medical records only document the one additional personality. The one who thinks he's a doctor. That makes sense because of the whole med school thing. The others must have come later. When? No one knows. It's possible Lucas and the Captain were created out of need or simply based on environment. She also said each personality is often unaware of the others."

"I don't think that's right," Christa said. "Lucy said that when Lucas— I mean Foster, was acting like the Doctor, he often talked about the Captain. Like the two were at odds with each other."

"That's true," Gwyn said. "But she said that neither ever mentioned Lucas nor acknowledged his existence. Lucy never saw the Lucas she knew. Not until Blake was there."

"For me," Hopkins said, "that's the hardest thing to wrap your head around. That Lucas may have been just another one of the victims, in a way."

"You're saying Lucas didn't know he wasn't Lucas?" Chief said.

"If that's the case," Blake added, "he may have been going to Newport thinking he was going to see his doctor. Maybe he even thought that Cathy was his aunt. Which would also mean that he literally *thought* like he was mentally impaired. It would explain why he brought me the key when I'd asked him to. Because he truly didn't know there was anything wrong with letting us out."

"This is confusing," Gwyn said.

"I know," Hopkins said. "I'm sure things will become a lot clearer as more information is uncovered. But that's all I've got now."

Hopkins stood up. The action prompted everyone else to stand up as well.

"I'd better get back before I get in trouble with the wife," Chief said. "I'll see you later."

Blake understood the subtext. Chief was actually saying he needed to go tell someone what he'd just learned.

"Thank you," Christa said.

"Yes, thank you," Gwyn added.

"Of course," Hopkins said. "Whatever you need, don't hesitate to call. I'll keep you updated if we find out anything new."

Hopkins stepped down on the grass. Christa and Gwyn said goodbye and retreated into the house. Blake joined Hopkins and walked with him to his car.

"How's the processing going?" Blake said.

"I'm letting Charlie handle it. He knows what he's doing."

"Well, good luck tomorrow night, if I don't see you," Blake said.

"Thanks. I don't suppose you want to hang around one more night. An endorsement by a Special Agent of the FBI could go a long way with the council."

"I don't think that's a good idea," Blake said. "There's something I haven't told you. I..."

When Blake decided to use Anja's credentials, he knew it was the only way he was going to get access. Or at least the quickest and easiest way.

What he didn't account for was how bad he'd feel about misleading Hopkins after everything was said and done.

Hopkins slapped Blake on the shoulder. "Relax. I already know you can't. I got a message from the FBI up in Providence. A guy named Harrison. Said he was the agent in charge over there. A little late, but it's the thought that counts, right? I called him back and told him how instrumental you were in this case. Figured there was some kind of commendation they could give you. That's when he told me."

Crap.

Blake was hoping to keep Harrison in the dark on the impersonating an agent thing. For Harrison's sake more than his own.

"What exactly did he tell you?" Blake said.

"Don't worry, nothing specific. Just that you are supposed to be under deep cover in D.C. and that any publicity would negatively impact your assignment."

"Ah, yes, that. Like I said, I'm supposed to be on leave. Lying low."

"Well, I hope you had a nice vacation." Hopkins grinned and extended his hand.

"It had its moments." Blake accepted the handshake.

Hopkins got in the car and started it. "See ya around," he said through the open window. And then he drove away.

Blake hoped the council would recognize the value Tom Hopkins brought to the town. That they would give him the second chance he had earned. Whether they would see it that way was anyone's guess.

He headed inside and found Christa in the dining room, setting the table. Gwyn was digging in the fridge.

"Good guy," Blake said.

"Hopkins?" Christa said. "Yeah, I don't believe a thing about what the paper said."

"Me either," Blake said.

"Are you sure you have to leave tomorrow?" Christa said. "We could take you around. Go out on the kayaks. All four of us."

"Yes, I'm sure," Blake said. "There's someone waiting for me at home. Someone I care about very much."

Christa picked up the bundle of letters from the ledge between the dining room and the kitchen. She held them out toward Blake. "Don't forget to take these."

"You keep them," Blake said. "I already know how it ends."

Christa placed the stack of folded papers back on the ledge, then stepped toward Blake. She put a hand on each of his shoulders, flashed her pearly white smile, and looked him straight in the eye.

"No, you don't."

42

THURSDAY, JUNE 4TH. EVENING

ARLENE WHITMAN TAPPED THE GAVEL AGAINST THE WOODEN BLOCK. THE volume of the chatter far exceeded the clicking noise, due to the sheer amount of people who had crowded into the Town Hall meeting room. She brought the ceremonial mallet down again, this time with enough force to garner attention.

"We're calling this meeting to order. Please take a seat if you can."

The discord settled into a few pockets of chitchat.

"Please, if everyone could stay quiet, we'll begin. Councilman, you have the floor."

Whitman took her seat at the center of the long table along with several other council members, who sat to her left and right based on political affiliation. Across from the panel, Hopkins sat alone at a small table, positioned to face the men and women who would decide his fate.

To Hopkins, the whole thing had a grandiose, self-important quality to it. As if the band of misfits considered themselves something on par with the United States Supreme Court. But he would play the game. Not that there was any other choice.

Councilman Dunkel pulled the tabletop microphone stand closer to himself.

"Thank you, Madam President. I'd like to make a motion to dismiss

Thomas Hopkins from his duties as Chief of Police, effective immediately."

"Do I have a second?" Whitman asked.

"I second," Councilwoman Rutledge said.

"Discussion?" Whitman responded.

Councilwoman Taylor chimed in. "I'd like to say something. To be honest, I was all for this action when it was proposed last week. But I must say that since that time, I've been quite impressed with the way that Chief Hopkins has conducted himself. I've read the letters submitted by some of his subordinates, and I am heartened by the confidence they have in him. I know that many of you on this council have already made up your minds, but I believe we owe it to Chief Hopkins to keep an open mind. We should all remember that there are two sides to every story and as such, we should reserve our judgment until after Chief Hopkins has had an opportunity to explain himself."

"Very well," Whitman said. "Does anyone have anything further before we turn the floor over to Chief Hopkins?"

From the front row, Charlie Fuller raised his hand.

"Yes, Lieutenant Fuller."

"I'd like to say a few words about Chief Hopkins if that's okay?"

Hopkins stood up and faced the group of spectators. "Charlie, that won't be necessary." He raised his voice so that he could be heard over the murmuring and rustling of the agitated group. "I know what many of you have heard about me. That I'm a mess. That I'm a drunk, am I right?"

A few hoots and hollers came from the back of the room.

"Well, I'm here to tell you that everything you've read about me is absolutely true."

A collective gasp seemed to suck all the air out of the room. Hopkins anticipated the reaction. It wasn't often that someone in the public eye spoke honestly.

He continued. "I don't blame you for not having faith in me. For a while there, I didn't have much faith in myself. You see, what many of you don't know is that my beloved wife..."

Hopkins felt the ball forming in his throat. His eyes watering. He paused to collect himself. Then cleared his throat.

"My beloved wife Lindsey was killed in a car accident a few years ago. And like many of you who have ever dealt with the loss of a loved one, I fought through the grief. Forged ahead with exactly what Lindsey and I had planned. Only it was a lie. I hadn't conquered it. I just put it away. Deep inside, where it could fester and feed on me."

The room sank into complete silence.

"Yes, I was a drunk. And yes, I was failing you. I wasn't giving you what I promised. But something happened last week. A wake-up call. A reminder of what matters and how much your safety and well-being mean to me. It rekindled the vigor I have for this profession and the respect I have for it as well. I'm not going to make excuses for my behavior. I just thought you all deserved to know the truth."

Hopkins took a deep breath. The exhale was audible throughout the room.

"And that's why I'm stepping down."

The room erupted. Some celebrated the announcement, but many others, to Hopkins' surprise, seemed to protest the decision.

"Order. Order," Whitman yelled. "Hold on a moment, Tom. Let's not be hasty. This has been a very trying time for everyone in this community. In light of everything you've told us and the demonstration of your commitment that you've displayed over the past week, I don't think there is a need to resign just yet. Let us deliberate."

"Thank you, Madam President," Hopkins said, "but it's the right thing. For me and for this town. But I would be most honored if you would consider my recommendation for my replacement. Lieutenant Charlie Fuller. Stand up, Charlie."

Fuller reluctantly stood.

"There is no one who knows this job better than this man. No one who has more passion and talent and compassion. The job he did managing this horrific case was nothing short of amazing. At this point, I think everyone in this room knows I don't bullshit, right?"

A wave of laughter moved through the crowd.

"Then trust me when I tell you that Lieutenant Charles Fuller is ready to lead."

Whitman stood. "I believe your recommendation carries a lot of weight. And I wholeheartedly agree with your assessment of Lieutenant Fuller. I respect your decision, Tom, and if it's your wish, I accept your resignation. Which, as of this moment, leaves us without a Chief of Police. According to the charter, in the case of a vacancy it is my duty to appoint an interim Chief until the proper formalities can be observed. Therefore, effective immediately, I hereby appoint Lieutenant Charles Fuller to the position of Interim Chief."

A round of applause prompted Fuller to acknowledge the promotion by waving and mouthing the words 'thank you.' As uncomfortable as his body language looked, his giant grin gave away his true feelings on the matter.

Hopkins walked to Fuller, saluted him, and shook his hand. Then he turned to the panel.

"I want to thank this council," Hopkins said, "Arlene, I appreciate everything. So, that's it. I'll leave you to it."

In anticlimactic fashion, Hopkins turned and walked away. He cut through the aisle and headed outside.

As he emerged into the warm night air, he noticed John Perrington standing at the base of the stairs that led to the sidewalk. The man everyone called Chief.

He had earned the nickname because, once upon a time, he did the job. Now, Hopkins had joined his ranks. He was officially a 'Former.' And, if he was being honest, it felt good.

"Chief," Hopkins said.

"Chief," Perrington responded. "I guess you won't need me as a character witness."

"Doesn't look like it."

"Ya know," Perrington said. "A few of the retired guys get together for coffee on Saturday mornings at Slice of Heaven. I was thinking, maybe you'd like to join us. Tell a couple of war stories, you know."

"Yeah," Hopkins said. "I'd like that."

43

THURSDAY, JUNE 4TH. EVENING

THE KIA SEDONA CAME TO A STOP. BLAKE COULD SEE THE DRIVER EYEING him in the rearview mirror. With the phone still pressed to his ear, he lifted his finger to buy himself a few more seconds.

"Thanks again for understanding. I owe you, again. But I've gotta run. We just pulled up."

"Don't be a stranger," Harrison said. "Talk to ya later."

The phone disconnected.

Blake tipped the driver and stepped out onto the street.

His street.

He looked around at the row of townhouses. The homes of the neighbors he never knew.

As nice a place as Alexandria was, there was a sharp contrast between life there and a place like Jamestown. It was evident in the speed at which people moved. They walked fast, drove fast, always heading somewhere.

Everyone was sequestered to the piece of the world they had carved out for themselves. Even the trees and shrubs were contained to boxes cut into the sidewalks or in small patches delineated by miniature iron fences. It was a sharp contrast to the lush landscape of the little island. With all of its plant life sprouting up wherever it pleased.

But maybe it wasn't as it seemed. Blake knew that much of his own seclusion had been of his own doing. Secrecy and privacy had been a priority for much of his life. A necessity, really. Sure, he had a community, the Intelligence Community. But it no longer seemed to be enough.

After his early afternoon flight turned into a late afternoon flight, due to mechanical issues, Blake had occupied his time by reading about Jamestown and the area around the Narragansett Bay. Its history as a military stronghold dated back to the Revolutionary War.

Originally inhabited by the mighty Narragansett tribe, the land that would become the colony of Rhode Island was gifted to Roger Williams by the tribe's Chief Sachem, Canonicus. A fierce and cunning warrior in his own right, Canonicus was highly respected by all, natives and colonists alike.

It seemed that Jamestown had a longer history of outstanding chiefs than Blake had realized.

Before reaching his townhouse, Blake stopped to collect the parking ticket from the windshield of his Challenger. He stuffed it in his pocket and continued on.

At the top of the steps, he punched in his code. The solenoid deadbolt drew back with a clunk. He swung the door open and stepped over the threshold.

No matter how many times he did it, there was always something satisfying about that first step into his home after being away for a period of time. But now, it was different. It wasn't just his home anymore. It was *their* home. He and Haeli together. The idea of it made it all the warmer. All the more inviting.

"Haeli," Blake called out as he dropped his bag and kicked off his shoes.

There was no answer.

"Haeli?"

Blake looked at his phone. It was late for her to still be at the gym.

He had texted that the flight was delayed. She hadn't responded, which meant she was probably swimming laps at that time. But that was hours ago. Maybe she got sick of waiting and went out to grab a bite to eat.

Blake walked into the kitchen and flicked on the lights.

There, on the granite island, was a single sheet of lined paper. A handwritten note.

Blake picked it up and read it.

"Mick," it said, "Thank you for asking me to move in with you. I know it was a big step, and I really appreciate it. Over the past few days, I've had time to think, and I realized it wasn't fair for me to push you. You and I both have things we need to work through, and I'm not sure either of us are ready to play house. This isn't about Anja, but it is about being realistic. I can't move in with you. I'm sorry, Mick. I need to go away for a while. There are some things I need to do. Please don't do your hacker voodoo to try to find me. I do love you. Please know that. -Haeli."

Blake flipped the paper over. There was nothing written on the back.

The pit in his stomach travelled into his throat. It wasn't right. He was ready. His mind was clear, and he knew exactly what he wanted. He wanted her, more than anything in the world.

If only he could tell her. Make her see that the past no longer held sway over the future. He could change her mind.

She had asked him not to look for her. But had she really meant it. Was it a test? Haeli was not normally one for emotional games.

He read the note again, methodically picking apart each word.

There are some things I need to do, it said. Did it have to do with her father? Or Levi Farr, God forbid? Or had she just realized she didn't want to be with him?

He dropped the note onto the counter and walked to the top of the steps that led down to the thick vault door. Behind it, the state-of-the-art computer lab would have all of the tools he would need to track her down. To give him one last opportunity to explain. To make it right.

I am a fool.

The truth was, he had gotten caught up. First, by the shock of seeing Christa, then by the task of finding Lucy, then by the overwhelming drive to put an end to the murderous psychopath. Even to Haeli, it would have been understandable, if not considered unavoidable. But he had shut her out of all of it. Led her to believe she didn't matter to him.

But she did matter. And it was for that reason that he felt compelled to respect her wishes.

Blake stood, perched on the precipice of that top step. The crumbling edge of the proverbial rabbit hole. He closed his eyes and took a slow, deep breath.

Then he descended.

***

Blake Brier returns in *DRAWPOINT*, available for pre-order now!

https://www.amazon.com/dp/B091MKG7QF

Or turn the page to read a sample of *DRAWPOINT*.

DRAWPOINT

BLAKE BRIER BOOK FOUR

by L.T. Ryan & Gregory Scott

DRAWPOINT CHAPTER 1

By the time Blake reached the bottom step his resolve had hardened.

His fingers punched in the code with focused accuracy. The familiar thunk of the steel bolts preceded the equally familiar whir of the cooling fans.

The positive pressure, created by the hefty air conditioning units sitting behind the townhouse, sent a puff of icy air through the stairwell. It was enough to rustle a lock of fiery red hair across his right eye. He swept it back and pushed his way inside.

Déjà vu.

After everything that Blake had been through over the past week alone, one would think there would be nothing left in the world that could surprise him. Then, there was the note.

A few minutes earlier, he had returned home with a head full of vivid images. A romanticized version of a life that would begin the moment he crossed the threshold of the Alexandria townhouse. He and Haeli. The way it should have been from the beginning.

But with a simple paragraph, written in Haeli's own hand, he would again have to come to terms with the disaster he often facetiously referred to as his 'charmed life.'

Although he had left the piece of lined notebook paper on the kitchen counter, he could still see the words as clearly as if they were hanging by a thread in front of him.

One passage, in particular, pulsed in his mind.

I need to go away for a while. There are some things I need to do.

The sentence he should have been fixated on was the one where she explicitly asked him to not try to find her. Or, if not fixated, at least mindful of. But that specific sediment had been deleted from his recollection the moment he had decided to disregard the request.

What things do you have to do, Haeli? What is it that we can't do together?

The thought had occurred to him that there wasn't actually a *thing* at all. That the fictitious task had been invented in order to spare his feelings. The truth was, a week ago, Blake wasn't sure he possessed such a thing as feelings. Not the way he imagined normal people did. But his experience with Christa, Gwyn and Lucy had caused him to reevaluate that notion. Allowing himself to be vulnerable was no easy transition. Still, the result was good even if the timing had turned out to be less than optimal.

Blake circled the perimeter of the subterranean room. He ran his fingers along the racks of processors mounted to the wall. He could feel the heat radiating from behind the blinking red and blue LED indicator lights.

In a way, the state-of-the-art computer equipment seemed a pathetic character. Built to churn complex code-breaking algorithms, the system was not unlike a greyhound being kept in a cupboard. It's powerful legs atrophying with lack of use.

It had been some time since Blake had utilized the full capability of the system he had so meticulously built— if he had ever used its full capability at all.

Before his dust-up with the Cryptocurrency Evangelist Army, he had spent many hours a day in this room. Locating, exploiting and cataloging vulnerabilities in supposed secure networks. Maintaining classified software that he had built for the Central Intelligence Agency while he was still under their employ. Building software for clients as a freelance developer after retirement. But, since then, he had done little of any of it.

This day would be no different. Except, while he had no intention of using the system to thwart a nefarious foreign government or to infiltrate a global communications network, he would be using it to find something much simpler and far more elusive. The truth.

Blake moved to the center of the room. He lowered himself into the seat of the Herman Miller chair with a sigh and spun himself toward the desk. With the press of a switch, the terminal came to life.

It was deceiving, really. The single station, situated in the center of the room, looked no different than one might find in any office. A few screens, a keyboard, a mouse. But it was merely an interface. An abstraction. Just as the buttons and levers of a fighter jet's cockpit enabled the pilot to unleash the beast's fury with the twitch of a muscle, it connected Blake's fingers to the awesome power of the system.

I need to go away for a while. There are some things I need to do.

At first glance, the note seemed a mystery. But, in Blake's experience, there was no such thing as a mystery. Only an unsolved equation. Haeli had left Blake's home and his life, that much was a given. But where was she going? Where was her trajectory taking her? If he were going to solve for x, he would first need to define y.

Of the list of traits he would have used to describe himself, the one he most recently embraced was pragmatism. It was a peculiar approach in his circles. Most preferred to skip the shovel and go straight to the dynamite. But, while the dynamite might be effective, it also drew a lot of attention.

Blake withdrew his hands from the keyboard and pulled his phone from his pocket. He tapped the icon for the text messaging app and again on the thread entitled 'Haeli.' He brought up the 'info' tab. An image of a map flashed on the screen, then faded to gray. 'Location not found.'

It was worth a shot.

The callous message meant Haeli had either turned her phone off or switched off the ability for Blake to see her location. It also meant he would need to employ less conventional methods after all.

Back on the keyboard, Blake entered the command to list the tools and scripts he had installed. The green text scrolled over a black screen. The command was on the tip of his tongue but, for the sake of time, he welcomed a quick reminder. Three quarters of the way down, he found what he was looking for.

He typed.

CTST.

Talk about Déjà vu?

During his time with the Agency, Blake had used this command line interface, or CLI, on a daily basis. With the forced cooperation of all United States based communication providers, federal agencies such as the CIA, NSA, and, to a limited extent, the FBI, were provided access to real-time cell tower data. Blake had built the CLI to simplify the process of downloading and interpreting it.

The CTST tool, short for Cell Tower Signal Triangulation, takes two parameters: The provider and the cellular phone number. The software gathers the raw data from any tower with which the cellular device is communicating and uses it to derive a location. By measuring the time delay between the device and each tower, and the direction from which the signal is originating, or azimuth, the position of the device is triangulated using a basic mathematical formula. While its level of accuracy often fluctuated based on signal strength and other environmental factors, it would be accurate enough for his purposes.

Blake input Haeli's number. The blinking cursor froze for a moment, then spit out the result. Instead of a set of coordinates, as he had hoped, the software balked.

No signal detected.

The phone was off. And, if she was serious about not wanting to be found, she had probably already discarded it in the Potomac. The words she wrote weren't just idle talk. No, she was taking steps to disappear.

Blake could have easily pulled her data from iCloud and obtained full backups of her device, but it wouldn't have done any good. She knew enough to turn the phone off before she ever left the house. What he needed was a totally different vector.

There was one other option. A script that Blake had not used since becoming a civilian. But if the previous options had been the shovel and the excavator, he would be reaching for the dynamite.

Although the public was probably not aware that their cellular

provider was streaming their usage data to the federal government —
unless they made it a habit of reading the thirty-seven pages of fine print
— it was legally given and readily available. Its use was so commonplace
that it carried little oversight. Access to the Transportation Security
Administration database, on the other hand, was highly scrutinized.

Before committing to his new plan of attack, Blake ran a traceroute to
be sure the proxies and tunnels were sufficiently obfuscating his Internet
Protocol Address. Satisfied, he typed the name of the script and hit enter.

An 'Authorized Use,' warning popped onto the screen. Below it, a
prompt. He had half-expected the old script to have been obsolete in its
method of gaining entry. But, just like that, he was in.

Fingers flying across the keys, Blake entered names and dates of birth
for each of the aliases Griff had set up for Haeli when she arrived in
Virginia.

Haeli Becher.

As expected, there was nothing.

Jessica Ruben.

Nada.

Cynthia Brook.

Nope.

Allison Gaudet.

Bingo!

There it was. As plain as day.

British Airways. IAD (Dulles-Washington) to TLV (Ben Gurion - Tel Aviv).
She had gone home.

It hit him in the gut. He told himself he understood. That he didn't
blame her. Haeli had left behind everything and everyone she had ever
known and traded it for him. It was too much to ask. Too much to expect.

As the pit in his stomach dissolved, it was replaced with a sense of
relief. Not because she was gone, but because, for once, he wasn't an
impediment. She knew what she needed and she acted.

With the kind of sincerity one can only have within the confines of
their own thoughts, he wished her well. He wished her happiness. Still,
he couldn't help but worry about her safety. She was supposed to be
dead. And Blake had no doubt Levi Farr continued to harbor a burning

desire to get a second crack at her. By returning to Israel, she was flying dangerously close to the flame.

He reminded himself that she was capable of taking care of herself. More than anyone else that he had ever met. She would make her way. A new life, loosely modeled after the old. A reimagining of an early version of herself, perhaps. It was what he had risked his life to make possible. And, as selfish as it felt, he hoped she remembered it that way.

Such regression wasn't an option for Blake. There was but one path for him. Forward. He was on the starting blocks, again. Pointed in an arbitrary direction.

He pressed the glowing button. The monitors went dormant.

Ready. Set...

Sigh.

DRAWPOINT CHAPTER 2

One Week Ago. Pavel Nikitin tightened his core, shifted his weight and drove his fist deep into Adam Goldmann's liver.

Goldmann wheezed and hunched over as far as his restraints would allow. By now the pain was numbing. Despite the fact that Nikitin's fist carried a disturbing amount of force, as if it were a concrete pendulum being dropped from the highest rafter of the old warehouse building, Goldmann was content to receive the blows. It was what would come next that frightened him. He had no delusions that it was going to get worse. Much worse.

Pavel Nikitin was an artist. A master of administering pain. Goldmann had seen his work in the past. At the time, he felt pity for the poor soul in the chair. He remembered praying that he would never find himself on the receiving end. But he knew his time would come. No one can run forever.

Nikitin had honed his skills over a lifetime. Anyone who set eyes on him could see that his education came from personal experience. The scars on his face, arms and hands were a roadmap through a brutal past. His large stature, square jaw and piercing eyes may have been a prerequisite for someone in his profession, but there was one feature that set him apart — a mound of scar tissue where his left ear had once been.

It was his calling card. A main tenant of his folklore.

There were many stories about how Pavel Nikitin lost his ear. Passed around the seedy corners of the underworld, each iteration morphed into something further from the truth.

It was generally believed that Nikitin was born in the gulag. A product of rape, he was delivered in secret and kept hidden in sewage tunnels under the camp. It was there that the rats gnawed off his ear.

As he grew, he would emerge under the cover of darkness to prey on unsuspecting prisoners. Legend had it that he would drag his victims underground and feed on their blood to acquire their strength.

Through the early nineteen-eighties in the Soviet Union, many families lost loved ones to the prison camps. Dozens of men and women disappeared, never to be heard from again. There was no explanation. No recourse. The Kremlin routinely denied that the Stalin era camps still existed, never mind acknowledging maleficence within them. For many, the idea of a soul-sucking demon child was as good an explanation as any.

While Nikitin reveled in the absurdity of his reputation, there was some truth to it. He was, in fact, born in the gulag. His mother, the wife of a mid-level mafia boss named Stan Nikitin, was imprisoned after her husband was killed for violating one of the postulates of the organization's code. Forbidden from marrying or having a family, the couple married in secret. The priest promptly turned them in.

The assassination of Nikitin's father fell to an ambitious young KGB officer named Olezka Sokolov, who himself was rising through the ranks of the crime syndicate. After Nikitin was born, it was Sokolov who took him in.

Separating from the KGB under less than amiable circumstances, Sokolov was forced underground. He devoted himself to the acquisition of power. And it didn't take long.

Through extreme brutality, Sokolov rose to the head of the organization. But he didn't stop there. To send a message to all that might oppose him, Sokolov murdered the heads of the ten most powerful criminal organizations. Not only in the USSR, but throughout the world. China.

Columbia. The United States. It was a bold move that would make him one of the most feared men on the planet.

Sokolov had a knack for sending messages that were never dared forgotten. Nikitin knew this better than anyone.

As Nikitin matured, he became invaluable to Sokolov. An exceptional student driven by an insatiable bloodlust, Nikitin's own brutally surpassed even that of his guardian. It was the reason Sokolov took his ear. A lesson in humility, he called it, but Nikitin knew it was a warning.

The truth was, Sokolov's fear of challenge was unfounded. Nikitin was as loyal as they came. He lived by the thieves' code. He believed in it. Especially when it came to Sokolov.

But he didn't begrudge Sokolov his assertion of dominance. Just the opposite. Nikitin relished it. It was what spawned his own habit of collecting the ears of his victims. And the collection was extensive.

The practice wasn't rooted in some emotional hang-up. It was just fun. Sure, maybe the first time was motivated by a subliminal need to even the score. But it became a deliberate tactic to strike fear into those who would consider crossing them. Each time a body washed onto shore or was pulled from a shallow grave, the missing left ear would tell the world all they needed to know. Pavel was here. After all, every artist must sign his work.

Goldmann knew all of this. It was what fueled his fear. Death, he thought, was inevitable. Whether by hand of Nikitin, Sokolov, or old age. But the thought of being mutilated, before or after, didn't sit well with him.

He didn't have a chance to dwell on it. As the plastic bag slipped over his head, Goldmann gasped, sucking the thin plastic film toward the back of his throat. His body convulsed and his vision began to blur.

He envisioned his death and the desecration of his body. It was different than he thought it would be. More welcoming.

Then Nikitin yanked the bag from his head.

Thick, delicious air filled Goldmann's lungs. The sensation consumed him and he wondered if that was what it felt like to be born.

"What are you waiting for?" Goldmann panted. "Do it already."

Nikitin said nothing.

Since Goldmann had been removed from the trunk and carried into the abandoned industrial building, Nikitin had not uttered a single word. There would be questions, but not by him.

Goldmann wasn't stupid. Far from it. His intellect was the reason he was able to elude Sokolov and his dog for the past two years. He knew why Nikitin was keeping him alive. Just as he knew who the approaching footsteps belonged to.

Sokolov had arrived.

Nikitin straightened his posture as the footsteps crescendoed and stopped behind Goldmann.

"I trust you've made our guest comfortable," Sokolov said.

"Very comfortable," Nikitin replied.

To Goldmann's ears, their gruff voices and thick Russian accents were almost identical. If Nikitin wasn't standing in Goldmann's line of sight, he would have sworn Nikitin was talking to himself.

Sokolov circled around Goldmann and peered down at him.

Goldmann met his gaze. They even look the same, he thought.

Although older and less grizzled, Sokolov had the same hulking stature, jagged jaw, and piercing gray eyes as his ward.

"I'm hurt," Sokolov said. "You never said goodbye."

Nikitin smiled, displaying a row of chipped teeth.

Sokolov leaned forward. "You should know, your family was very upset with you. Your own wife cursed you as she took her last breath."

"That's a lie," Goldmann said.

"Maybe, maybe not." Sokolov pulled several creased photographs from his pocket and held each to Goldmann's face, in succession. "Look at her face. Even separated from her body, you can see the anger. This anger was for you."

Goldmann swallowed hard and tried to fight the tears. The images of his dismembered wife and children were worse than he imagined. But he forced himself to look.

For two years he tried to prepare himself for the moment when he would come face to face with their deaths. All the while, resisting the urge to blame himself. He knew if he fled, Sokolov would kill them. But he also knew that if he returned, Sokolov would kill them and him.

Sokolov tossed the photos on Goldmann's lap and grabbed his jaw, pressing his cheeks into his bottom teeth. "Now. Where are my diamonds?"

"I don't know," Goldmann said.

Sokolov let go and nodded to Nikitin, who swooped in with a wide hook to Goldmann's nose.

Blood exploded onto his face and lap, spattering the pictures.

"If you want to live, you will give me better answer than this." Sokolov said.

"You think I'm an idiot? I know you're going to kill me no matter what I say."

"Don't get me wrong mister Adam Goldmann, I will cut off your hands and your feet. You must suffer, yes? But I will make sure you live. All you have to do is tell me, where are my diamonds?"

"I told you," Goldmann said. "I don't know."

Sokolov shook his head and motioned to Nikitin once more.

Nikitin made a show of unsheathing a slender fillet knife and slowly walked behind Goldmann. With his left hand, Nikitin grabbed the top of Goldmann's ear and pulled outward.

"Wait, wait," Goldmann pleaded. "It's true, I was going to run off with the stones. Okay, I did run off with the stones. At least, I thought so. But when I opened the case, it was empty."

Sokolov laughed. "This is bullshit story." He shifted his gaze to Nikitin.

"No, no, wait!"

Nikitin brought the knife down with incredible speed. In a flash, Goldmann could feel the searing pain and the warm blood pooling on his shoulder and running down his left arm. Goldmann wailed.

"Sixty million dollars," Sokolov yelled. Droplets of saliva freckled Goldmann's face. "You will tell me where they are. Or you will know pain."

Nikitin reached over Goldmann and handed Sokolov the floppy slice of flesh and cartilage. Sokolov tossed it onto Goldmann's lap.

"I swear it." Goldmann shook his head vigorously in an attempt to avoid passing out. "Someone switched out the case after I left Israel. I'm telling you the truth. I didn't have any contact with anyone except for my security detail. It must have been one of them."

"What are their names?" Sokolov asked.

"I don't know." Goldmann winced as the words came out of his mouth. He had come to learn that Sokolov was not fond of them.

"Take his other ear," Sokolov ordered.

Goldmann twisted in the chair. "Please—"

"And then it will be your eyes and then your balls," Sokolov growled. "We can do this all day, yes?"

"Look," Goldmann said. "I hired the team through Techyon. I don't remember all their names. One of them was a woman. Her name was Haeli. I don't know if that was her real name. That's all I remember. You've gotta believe me. You know I have no reason to lie."

"Shhhh," Sokolov put his finger to Goldmann's lips then patted him on the head. "I know."

Sokolov walked around Goldmann. His even-tempoed footsteps began to recede back the way they had come. Without a break in his stride, Goldmann could hear Sokolov call out from the distance.

"Da, Pavel. You may kill him now."

DRAWPOINT CHAPTER 3

Haeli tossed her knapsack into the backseat of the white Mercedes sedan and climbed in after it.

"Marhaba," the driver said, "where do you like to go?"

Haeli glanced at the taxi license, displayed on the dashboard. *Yusuf ibn Ibrahim.*

"Yigal Alon Street, Tel Aviv," she said. "I don't know the address, but I'll show you where when we get close."

Of course, she did. She knew it well. But that was nobody's business but her own.

Yusuf nodded. "I can give you flat rate. Two hundred twenty. Is this good?"

Haeli did the math in her head. Two hundred and twenty Israeli Shekels would be about sixty-five dollars, maybe a little more.

The main highway, Route 1, was notoriously congested during the daytime hours. The trip could take thirty minutes or it could take an hour.

Two twenty was probably a good deal. Not to mention, there was always room for negotiation. Afterall, only tourists accepted the first offer. But the money was of no concern. What she needed was flexibility.

"Just run the meter," she said.

Yusuf smiled and pressed a button to start the meter running. He jerked the wheel, forcing the front end of the Mercedes between two other cabs that were waiting in line to exit the taxi stand.

Ben Gurion International Airport was as busy as Haeli had ever seen it. And she had seen it a lot. It was the gateway to countless missions and assignments. At the moment, however, there was only one mission on her mind.

"What's your name?" Yusuf asked.

Halei had to think for a second. "Allison."

She had chosen to use that particular alias by using a highly advanced, scientific method— it was the first passport she happened to pull out of her stash. In retrospect, she wished she had chosen a different one. She didn't particularly like the name Allison Gaudet, though she wasn't sure why.

If she could have, she would have brought documentation for several different aliases. But getting caught with passports, licenses, birth certificates and credit cards under multiple names would have been a huge red flag. Haeli was well acquainted with the security apparatus in Israel. It wasn't to be trifled with.

"You are visiting?" Yusuf asked.

"Yep. Just visiting," Haeli kept her answers curt. She didn't want to be rude, but she hoped the short answers would dissuade the man from asking any more questions. She was in no mood for small talk and any conversation, no matter how trivial, would require more brain power than she was willing to devote. The backstory she had devised during the flight was still thin. It was something she would need to rectify before it became critical.

Yusuf merged onto Route 1. The traffic was not as heavy as she expected. But she knew that would change as they got closer to the city.

Haeli settled herself in for the ride and gazed out the window. Past the concrete barriers lining either side of the highway, there was only sky. In this area, none of the homes or structures along the flat landscape rose high enough to be visible over walls.

Ah, the walls.

Israel loved its walls. It was the land of gates and barriers and partitions. Most notably, the enormous one that delineated the border of the West Bank, of course. But that wasn't all. In the city, residential properties often looked like fortresses, with high fences and heavy iron gates. Especially in wealthier sections. Parking lots, driveways, parks. All secured with concrete stanchions or spike strips or high-tech surveillance systems.

It was no wonder. The Tel Aviv district, like many other places in Israel, had been the target of terrorists for decades. Haeli remembered a time when rocket attacks, launched at the city from the Gaza Strip, just forty miles away, were a daily occurrence. Suicide bombers on buses, bars and beaches. Just a normal Tuesday.

But the people of Israel were extraordinarily resilient. For most, the ever-present danger faded into the background of daily life. And it was no different for Haeli.

Since she was a young girl, she had never felt that her home was unsafe. But then again, she wasn't the average child.

Growing up in a paramilitary facility, she was shielded from the outside world for much of her youth. Shielded, but not sheltered. Her experience was more demanding than the outside world could have ever been. All of it had been about control. Controlling her fear. Controlling her body. Controlling her world.

By the time she was a teenager, she was capable of killing a grown man with her bare hands. Not only in theory but in practice. Lots of practice. With rigorous daily training and relentless evaluation, she would be forced to prove it over and over again. It didn't take long before she started to realize that the outside world should be more afraid of her than she was of it.

"There she is," Yusuf said, "Tel Aviv. She's beautiful, no?"

In the distance, skyscrapers of varying heights bristled out of the horizon. The skyline of Tel Aviv and Ramat Gan was a comforting sight.

"She is," Haeli replied.

Since fleeing Israel more than a year ago, she had never felt like she fit in. Especially in the United States. But here, it was different. Here, she didn't feel like an imposter.

As the jagged skyline loomed larger, she found herself wishing that she had spent more time appreciating the place. As an adult, she had been all business, rarely taking a moment to dip her toes into the Mediterranean or explore the rich history of the place.

Raised without religion, the significance of the holy sites never had the same draw they did to the rest of the population, Jews and Palestinians alike. But there was something to be said about the power of such antiquity, even from a secular point of view.

In different circumstances, she might have entertained a bit of soul searching. But not now. It wasn't that kind of homecoming.

"Get off here," Haeli said.

"Here?" Yusuf glanced over his shoulder, then back at the road. "It's better to—"

"I know. Just get off here."

Yusuf took the exit.

Haeli directed him to turn right onto Lehi Road. A green wire fence ran along the median, separating the eastbound and westbound lanes.

Fences and walls.

She directed him to take the next possible left and then rattled off a series of turn by turn directions that would snake them through narrow streets of the residential neighborhood.

Rows of small angular structures passed by her window. Each a variation of the last. A sea of cracked stucco and corrugated metal. It was almost imperceptible where one dwelling ended and the next one began.

Had it always looked like this?

"You are not visiting," Yusuf said. "You are from here, yes?"

The surprise in Yusuf's voice amused her. She knew why he assumed she was a tourist. English had been her first and primary language. Her tutors had always been American and her accent reflected it. Not that she couldn't blend in if she needed to. As part of her schooling, she was required to achieve fluency in several other languages, including Hebrew and Arabic.

"Let's just say I'm familiar with the area." She left it at that.

They were close now. Two blocks from her intended destination. She took a deep breath.

Along the right side of the road was a pair of multi-story apartment buildings. In the courtyard between them, something that stood out in Haeli's memory.

"Stop here."

Yusuf stopped the car as abruptly as she had blurted the command.

"This is good. How much do I owe you?"

"Two hundred thirty-two." Yusuf twisted his body to look at her. "See, flat rate is much better."

Haeli handed over two hundred forty shekels, grabbed her bag, and stepped out without responding. Her attention remained fixed on the courtyard. Yusuf pulled away.

Behind a wrought iron fence, the faded colors of the plastic slide and swings stood out against the sand. A flood of memories washed over her and tears welled in her eyes.

Standing there on the sidewalk, staring at the vacant little playground, it was if she were nine years old again.

She remembered how, every weekend, she would beg her father to take her for a walk.

"One last time," he would always say. Then they would walk to the market where he would buy her a sweet treat.

On every trip, they would pass by the playground. On the way there and on the way back. Every time, she would stop and ask if she could go in.

Maybe it was because it was such a foreign concept to her, or maybe it was an innate drive to play that exists in all children, but it called to her from beyond the fence. She could feel its draw, even now.

"This is private property. You don't belong there," he would say, as if reciting from a script. "Come. Let's get you home."

But this routine was not what triggered the emotional response. It was one particular memory, from one remarkable day.

Walking back from the market with a belly full of lemon wafers, Haeli stopped to look in on the playground. "Can I try it today?" she had asked. Her father paused. She knew the answer. Then, the unexpected. He reached down, lifted her up and lowered her on the other side of the fence.

"Come with me," she said. And then, something even more unexpected. Something that had never happened before or since. Her father, the venerable Doctor Benjamin Becher, hopped over the fence, took her hand and jogged to the playground.

For twenty minutes, they played. Swinging. Hanging from the monkey bars. She even got him to go down the slide. And they laughed. Goodness, they laughed! It was the only time she could recall hearing him so much as snicker. Most importantly, it was the only time in her life that she could remember him treating her like a child.

She hadn't realized how impactful that afternoon had been on her. Even now she felt the urge to hop the fence and take a few swings. But there were important matters to attend to.

She pushed the past from her mind and moved along toward the west. A few short minutes later she had reached Yigal Alon Street.

There, directly in front of her was a massive building that sprawled for blocks. From the center of the squat compound was a soaring tower sheathed in tinted glass. At the top, six foot tall letters read: Techyon.

PRE-ORDER YOUR COPY OF DRAWPOINT NOW!

https://www.amazon.com/dp/B091MKG7QF

ALSO BY L.T. RYAN

Visit https://ltryan.com/pb for paperback purchasing information.

The Jack Noble Series

The Recruit (Short Story)

The First Deception (Prequel 1)

Noble Beginnings (Jack Noble #1)

A Deadly Distance (Jack Noble #2)

Thin Line (Jack Noble #3)

Noble Intentions (Jack Noble #4)

When Dead in Greece (Jack Noble #5)

Noble Retribution (Jack Noble #6)

Noble Betrayal (Jack Noble #7)

Never Go Home (Jack Noble #8)

Beyond Betrayal (Clarissa Abbot)

Noble Judgment (Jack Noble #9)

Never Cry Mercy (Jack Noble #10)

Deadline (Jack Noble #11)

End Game (Jack Noble #12)

Noble Ultimatum (Jack Noble #13) - Spring 2021

Bear Logan Series

Ripple Effect

Blowback

Take Down

Deep State

Rachel Hatch Series

Drift

Downburst

Fever Burn

Smoke Signal

Firewalk - December 2020

Whitewater - March 2021

Mitch Tanner Series

The Depth of Darkness

Into The Darkness

Deliver Us From Darkness - coming Summer 2021

Cassie Quinn Series

Path of Bones

Untitled - February, 2021

Blake Brier Series

Unmasked

Unleashed

Uncharted - April, 2021

Affliction Z Series

Affliction Z: Patient Zero

Affliction Z: Abandoned Hope

Affliction Z: Descended in Blood

ABOUT THE AUTHOR

L.T. Ryan is a *USA Today* and international bestselling author. The new age of publishing offered L.T. the opportunity to blend his passions for creating, marketing, and technology to reach audiences with his popular Jack Noble series.

Living in central Virginia with his wife, the youngest of his three daughters, and their three dogs, L.T. enjoys staring out his window at the trees and mountains while he should be writing, as well as reading, hiking, running, and playing with gadgets. See what he's up to at http://ltryan.com.

Social Medial Links:

- Facebook (L.T. Ryan): https://www.facebook.com/LTRyanAuthor

- Facebook (Jack Noble Page): https://www.facebook.com/JackNobleBooks/

- Twitter: https://twitter.com/LTRyanWrites

- Goodreads: http://www.goodreads.com/author/show/6151659.L_T_Ryan

Printed in Great Britain
by Amazon